SAMANTHA STEPPED BACK, ELUDING HIS HANDS.

She stepped back again. It was her last retreat. The door was at her back, preventing her from taking another step, while he was in front of her, silently, mockingly inviting her into his arms.

Reid smiled. "Are you afraid of me, Samantha?"

Everything in her railed against the challenge. "No," she snapped instantly. She kept her gaze steady, hoping it gave no hint of the fierce battle that was raging within her. What was there about this man that made her want to slap him . . . and kiss him?

"You've thought about this moment all evening," he said softly, "you and me, alone, just as I have."

Samantha shook her head. "No. I haven't."

He seemed to measure her words, and then he smiled, a deeply curved smile as sensuous as his lowered voice. "Lie to yourself, Samantha, if you have to, but don't lie to me." He reached out and pulled her into his arms. "Your eyes give you away."

BOOK YOUR PLACE ON OUR WEBSITE AND MAKE THE READING CONNECTION!

We've created a customized website just for our very special readers, where you can get the inside scoop on everything that's going on with Zebra, Pinnacle and Kensington books.

When you come online, you'll have the exciting opportunity to:

- View covers of upcoming books
- Read sample chapters
- Learn about our future publishing schedule (listed by publication month *and author*)
- Find out when your favorite authors will be visiting a city near you
- Search for and order backlist books from our online catalog
- Check out author bios and background information
- Send e-mail to your favorite authors
- Meet the Kensington staff online
- Join us in weekly chats with authors, readers and other guests
- Get writing guidelines
- AND MUCH MORE!

**Visit our website at
http://www.zebrabooks.com**

BLACKJACK'S LADY

Cheryl Biggs

Zebra Books
Kensington Publishing Corp.

http://www.zebrabooks.com

ZEBRA BOOKS are published by

Kensington Publishing Corp.
850 Third Avenue
New York, NY 10022

First Printing: April, 1999
10 9 8 7 6 5 4 3 2 1

Printed in the United States of America

Prologue

"You have no choice, *chérie.*"

His catlike eyes bore into hers, sending an icy chill inching its way down her back, a slow, torturous sensation that she knew was only a foreshadowing of the death that would be hers if she did as he demanded. Elyse struggled for breath and jerked free of his hold on her wrist, stumbling as she did, then regaining her footing, drawing back her shoulders, meeting his arrogant, cruel gaze.

"You killed my father," she said, her voice barely a whisper of sound. "How can you even think I'd consider marriage to you?"

A grin pulled at his almost perfectly curved lips, but it was as devoid of warmth as both the gleam in his dark, earth-brown eyes and the offer he'd haughtily proffered, and was now waiting so smugly for her to accept. "Hah. Your father was a fool."

A rush of tears blinded her. "He was a good man. He was—"

"A fool," Valic Gerard snapped again, cutting off her words. "And I am losing patience." He strode across the spacious study her mother had so lovingly refurbished in varying tones of burgundy and ivory only a few months before her death. Eylse shuddered at the very idea of this man being in her home, in this room. Valic flipped open the ornately carved lemonwood box that sat on her father's desk and picked up one of the cheroots from the dozen that lay within it. He played the tightly rolled length of tobacco between thumb and forefinger, assessing its quality, held it briefly under his nose; then obviously satisfied, he slipped it into the pocket of his jacket.

Elyse felt an urge to throw herself at him and rip the cheroot from his pocket. Instead she held herself stiff, silently wishing him to hell.

Sunlight flowing through the window at his back glistened off the waves of Valic's luxurious mane of black hair, but it did nothing to bring any kind of light or warmth to the man himself.

She shuddered, still shaken that one man could harbor so much cruelty and greed within his soul. She'd thought she could do what he wanted, but how could she commit the rest of her life to a man who was nothing more than a murderer—even to save her family? He had killed her father, but not before bankrupting him, leaving him with nothing more to defend than his honor, which had cost him his life. The Beaumonts had nothing left; their land, home, and most of its furnishings now belonged to the man standing before her, and now he was offering her a way out, a way to save herself, her home, her family. A wave of nausea rose into her throat. He was offering her a way out, but it was an unthinkable way ... and she couldn't do it.

She would rather live on the street than do what he was proposing.

He looked up at her, as if having heard her thoughts, and his gaze caught hers. His expression held a note of mockery. "As I said before, Elyse, you really have no choice."

She drew back her shoulders and glared at him. No. She would never give in to him. Not this man. "I believe I do have a choice, Mr. Gerard," she said, surprised at how calm her voice sounded as her insides fluttered with nerves and fear and her pride steered her toward certain ruin. "And it is not to marry you."

Chapter One

Natchez, Mississippi—1858

The challenge had been issued.

The wait was over.

It was nearly time to start.

Samantha looked around the saloon's long, narrow room. It was crowded, but not everyone had come to the Silver Goose for the games that were scheduled to begin in an hour. Many were there merely to watch, maybe make a wager or two on who would make it to the end and eventually win, or be the first to be disqualified.

Her gaze moved over the crowd, and she silently identified several of the gamblers who had answered her challenge: Diamond Dan, Loco Bob, Foxe Brannigan, Jeffers Montayne. Those were only a few. There were others in attendance. Many others. Some she recognized by a trademark hat, suit, stickpin, or overall look; she had no idea of others' identity. But it didn't matter—they'd come. Her challenge had drawn them all, as she'd hoped it would, from the fancy casinos of New Orleans, the stuffy back rooms of Boston, the parlors of New York, the steamers that plied the rivers, and the raunchy saloons west of the Mississippi.

But then the promise of a million dollar pot was strong enticement. Too strong for most professional gamblers to resist.

The lavishly adorned interior of the Silver Goose was virtually a sea of bodies, all male, except for Samantha and the three girls who worked for her.

"Never seen so many pretty men in one room in all my life," Daisy said, moving up to the bar and winking at Samantha. She grabbed a bottle of whiskey along with two shot glasses, and with a toss of her long blond curls, sashayed across the room to deliver them.

Samantha laughed softly. Daisy's comment was true. Everyone who'd crowded their way into the saloon was in their Sunday best it seemed, but the professional gamblers, who were dressed to the nines, outshone everyone. Their suits were expertly tailored, their ruffled shirts made of the finest silks, the buttons on their vests and jackets of solid silver, gold, or diamond studded, as were the many rings on their fingers, the cuff links at their wrists, and the watches slipped into the pockets of their vests.

The three brass and crystal chandeliers that hung from the ceiling of the Silver Goose and their matching wall sconces had been polished to a high sheen, as had the gilt-framed twin mirrors that backed the long mahogany bar.

Samantha heard the *click-click-click* of the wheel of fortune as it turned, its leather strap hitting the brass spokes that spun past. She turned and, through the haze of smoke that hung over the room, watched the wheel begin to slow. It finally stopped and John, one of her faro dealers but now taking his turn at operating the wheel, called out the winning number, eliciting a whoop of excitement from at least one man crowded around the crescent-shaped table.

Samantha turned her attention back to the other men milling about the saloon. The professionals had come to answer her challenge, and she could almost feel the old, familiar spark of daring at the thought of once again handling a deck of cards, of challenging an opponent. With that feeling, memories began to surface, painful memories she didn't want to acknowledge. She fought them back, pushing them into the unexamined depths of recollection that she rarely allowed to surface.

> *"You're cheating."*
> *Samantha looked up, startled by the accusation.*
> *Tom Ryan threw his cards down.*
> *"No, sir," she said calmly. "I am not."*
> *"No woman's that good with a deck of cards," the man sneered. "Especially a whore."*
> *She bolted from her chair at the ugly accusation, her hand lashing out, ready to slap his face.*
> *The man pulled a gun.*
> *Cord, standing at the bar, had already drawn his.*
> *An explosion of gunfire filled the room, and the man who only moments earlier had been sitting across from Samantha, crashed face first onto the table.*

Samantha pushed the memory away. That had been the last time she'd held a deck of cards in her hands—the last time she'd played a game.

But now that would change.

It might appear to Valic Gerard that she was giving in to his blackmail demands, but Samantha knew that somehow in the next few days she would find a way to beat him . . . this time she would see to it that he would be sorry he'd dared to cross swords with Elyse Samantha Beaumont again.

The smell of whiskey, tobacco, and men's cologne, some cheap some expensive, filled the room, all blending with the redolence of the river that seemed to permeate everything Under-the-Hill. The result was an almost overpowering fragrance that was unique to the area. Or maybe it was only unique to her. She didn't know. All she knew was that it was a scent like no other she'd ever experienced, and not one she had acquired a liking for, but merely one she'd been forced to get used to.

Samantha smiled. It was nearing time to start the games. They had come to answer the challenge, each paying her a nonrefundable twenty-five thousand dollar entry fee, and there was no reason to keep them waiting any longer.

She turned and scoured the room for Cord, finally spotting him standing on the opposite side of the saloon talking to Foxe Brannigan. He laughed soundly at something Foxe said. Cord's dark hair was near blue-black beneath the candlelight, and the gray at his temples momentarily resembled wings of silver. Samantha caught his gaze, saw his blue eyes focus on her, and waved again.

He nodded and began to weave his way through the crowd toward her.

Samantha's hand dropped to her skirt, and she absently ran her fingers over the dark blue satin flounce that draped across the front of the pale blue gown she'd chosen to wear that night, one of her most flattering, the gown's deep-colored trim and flounces the same dark color as her eyes.

She turned slightly as Cord approached and felt the garter that encircled her right thigh tighten just a bit, reminding her of the dagger that was tucked snugly within the satin and lace ruffles. Trouble was rare at the Silver Goose, especially since she'd hired Jake to make certain it stayed that way. Her glance darted toward the giant Irish roustabout who stood at the opposite end of the bar, his red hair like a brilliant flame atop a monstrous bulk of body that set him at least a head above everyone else in the room. It also helped that his shoulders were as wide as a mountain and his fists like two sledgehammers.

Samantha sighed. She didn't normally carry a weapon anymore . . . not since that night . . . unless she was leaving the saloon, but things were different now. The grand prize for the final poker game, one million dollars, was in the safe and there were several dozen gamblers in the room who, some might say, would as soon shoot each other as play cards. And even if that wasn't true, and they all conducted themselves like the gentlemen they professed to be, there were others about who were not quite so honorable. One million dollars was a great temptation for any man. Her thoughts momentarily filled with memories of Dante Fournier. He'd swept her off her feet with his sweet words and kisses of passion, and while she'd let her head become filled with a lot of ridiculous dreams, he'd set about stealing every penny she possessed and then promptly disappeared.

That was definitely one mistake she wouldn't make again. She reached up and brushed a stray wisp of red-touched dark brown hair from her cheek.

"Couple more players, Miss Sam, and the tables will be full up."

Samantha turned to the bartender. "I think the best are mostly already here, Curly."

He smiled, his bald pate glistening pink beneath the chandelier light. "Yeah, 'cept for Studs Harriman and Forest McLean. Woulda liked to have seen Rubies Bigelow and you square off over the cards, too, but I guess that ain't never going to happen. Heard he got himself killed down San Antone way a while back."

She nodded and glanced at the tall grandfather clock that stood near the hallway leading to the rear of the building where her office was located. "Well, full up or not, we'll announce the start of the games in forty-five minutes." The million dollar pot was going to be made up of the money lost at the tables during the challenge, but two less players than she'd counted on could mean she'd have to put up fifty thousand dollars of her own money. It would be a risk. If she lost . . . Samantha stopped the thought before it could finish. She wasn't going to lose. She never had before—that's why they'd come in answer to her challenge. She'd never lost a game of poker. A hand, yes, a game, no. And each of them wanted to be the one who took that title away from her. The million dollar pot was important, staggering even, but she knew that beating her was the real reason most of them had come. Samantha felt the threat of that challenge fuel the spark of daring in her and cause it to flame brighter, stronger. She had never lost, and she wasn't going to lose this time. She couldn't. There was too much at stake.

Most present didn't know it, but this would be the most important game of her life.

Her gaze roamed the room until she spotted the man who had forced her to risk everything and issue the challenge in the first place. She knew sparks of loathing danced in her eyes, just as it filled her heart, and she found herself able to maintain her self-control only by forcing her gaze to move on, hoping no one else had seen. If it was the last thing she ever did, she would destroy Valic Gerard.

She took a step away from the bar, intent on meeting Cord at the stairs as they'd agreed upon earlier, so that they could announce that the games were about to begin.

Just then the swinging entry doors pushed open, their red paint catching the light of a chandelier and glimmering a brilliant, fleeting reflection. But it wasn't only the movement of the doors or the momentary flash of color that caught Samantha's attention, it was the man who stepped past the doors and into the room. She knew almost every gambler who traveled the Mississippi, if not by name, then by face and reputation. But this man, she was certain, was a stranger to her.

He exuded an air of confidence without appearing arrogant.

Her gaze raked over him as he stood in the entryway and casually surveyed the room, the pale moonlight at his back. He wore a Western-style hat, the wide brim pulled low over his face so that his eyes were left in shadow.

Samantha wished the hat were gone so that she could see his face.

Suddenly, as if hearing her thoughts, he reached up and swept the hat from his head.

His hair shone dark and golden beneath the soft light of the chandeliers.

There was something about him that instantly intrigued Samantha, a suggestion of strength and forcefulness in his stance, an air of purpose in his belyingly lazy and casual manner.

His shoulders were broad beneath a black cutaway coat that tapered inward to a slender waist that gave way to long, lean legs, snugly encased within trousers held taut by a sous pied beneath each booted foot.

Her gaze returned to his face as he moved toward her, and Samantha felt a flush of unreasonable and unexpected warmth sweep through her as their eyes met.

She tried to look away and found she could not. Brown eyes—a rich, warm combination of darkness and cinnamon slashed with sparks of gold—held hers.

His face was a contrast of character, hard lines melding with aristocratic curves, rough edges fusing with sculptured valleys, savage ruggedness fighting for control against chis-

eled perfection. The dark eyes were deep set beneath a
wide forehead and gracefully curved golden brows. High
cheekbones were like majestic cliffs, dipping to incredible
hollows, and his jaw was a line of granite, hard and unyield-
ing. A hint of a smile suddenly pulled at one corner of
sensuously rather than perfectly shaped lips drawing her
attention to the thin, almost indiscernible scar that sliced
through the left side of both.

She wondered if it had been a knife, a rapier, or merely
a childhood accident that had marred that strong, handsome face.

The smile momentarily softened the lines that framed
his mouth, while the scar shattered the illusion that the
almost patrician face was a sculptor's masterpiece rather
than merely human.

Samantha shook herself and forced her gaze away from
his.

"The more handsome the man, the more dangerous the man."

The phrase, one she'd heard her mother use often
enough when she'd been growing up, echoed through her
mind. If only she had paid heed to those words several
years ago, Samantha knew now she could have avoided
inviting disaster into her life. As it was, she had learned
the hard way just how true her mother's warning had been.
Both Valic Gerard and Dante Fournier were devastatingly
handsome men, and both, in their own way, had left her
destitute, thoroughly devastated, and wanting nothing
more than to kill them.

Her gaze moved to Valic Gerard, standing at the bar. It
had been eight years since she'd seen him last, and she'd
hoped never to see him again, but obviously fate wasn't
on her side. She had learned one thing in that time though:
killing Valic would have been too easy a punishment for
what he'd done to her, and who knew how many others.
And now he was back for more. A flame of hatred seared

through her. Ruining Valic Gerard, leaving him with nothing—that was what would hurt Valic the most, and somehow that was what she had to do. Turn the tables on him. Let him think he was winning, and then find a way to destroy him.

As for Dante, the last she'd heard he had gone out west in search of new prospects several years ago. For months afterward she'd prayed every night that his *prospects* had been found at the end of an Indian's arrow or a hangman's rope. Not exactly the forgiving way her mother had taught her to think, but her mother was gone now, and Samantha's life was a far cry from the one she and Sarah Jane Beaumont had once envisioned it would be.

She pushed the unpleasant thoughts from her mind. Her problems with Dante had been a long time ago, and she preferred not to think about them anymore. Anyway, that crisis had brought Cord into her life, so even if she could go back and change the way things had happened, she wouldn't. Unless there was some way she could prevent Staunton Beaumont from having been so senselessly killed, arrange it so that she never met Dante Fournier or Valic Gerard at all, and still have Cord Rydelle in her life.

As if summoned by her thoughts, Cord moved to stand beside her. "Where the hell did *he* come from?" he murmured under his breath.

Samantha started at the savage edge she heard in his tone. It was uncharacteristic of him. She looked up sharply and noticed that his dark blue eyes were riveted on the stranger moving toward them. "I don't know." She looked at the man approaching, then back at Cord and frowned. "Why? Do you know him?"

He surprised her again with an ascenting nod. Steely hardness drew Cord's features, while something she couldn't quite define seemed to darken his eyes until the blue nearly disappeared, taken over by an intense black that was neither warm nor cold, but more disturbing than anything she'd ever seen. "I knew him," Cord said. "A long time ago."

A blend of curiosity and fear skipped through her, touching her blood, her heart, her mind, and sending a little shiver of apprehension racing over her skin. "Who . . . who is he?"

"Blackjack Reid Sinclaire."

She had guessed the man was a gambler, not that there were any specific telltale signs. Gamblers usually wore suits of black broadcloth, but then so did many other men. The more flamboyant gamblers also wore ruffled silk shirts, diamond rings, and vests adorned with silver threads or made of elaborate tapestried fabric. Some even wore huge silver rings around their necks that held the chain of their watches, rather than a fob. Blackjack Reid Sinclaire wore a suit of black. Other than that, and his name, there was nothing about him that said gambler, unless it was an aura only another gambler could detect. His shirt was unruffled, his cuff links and buttons were plain silver, and he wore no jewelry, unless one counted the watch that lay in the pocket of his vest, attested to by a simple chain that looped across his midriff and disappeared within the opposite pocket. Even the cut of his clothes was plain, seemingly purposely so, but nevertheless spoke of quality and expense, and an eye for detail.

He could well pass for monied gentry to all but the most trained of eyes, and Samantha guessed that if he wanted, he could also fool most of them.

She turned her back to him and spoke to Cord, keeping her voice low so that no one else could hear. "Do you want me to have Jake make him leave?"

"No. I'll . . ." Cord looked past her and swore softly.

Samantha's shoulders instantly stiffened. She turned, believing it always better to face a foe than retreat or be surprised. Though why she instantly assumed he was an enemy she had no idea, unless it was merely because Cord obviously didn't relish the idea of his presence. She wondered why. Cord was usually affable to everyone, even some Samantha would have rather seen sent promptly on their way. But judging from his attitude now and the gleam of displeasure she'd seen sparking in his eyes, she knew he wasn't feeling affable toward Blackjack Reid Sinclaire.

Behind her, she felt Cord move closer to her. His hand suddenly pressed against her back in a subtle but unusually possessive and protective gesture. It intensified her uneasiness and brought her a tinge of fear. Who was this man from Cord's past?

"Be careful," Cord whispered softly. "He's dangerous."

Startled, Samantha glanced up at him, but there was no time to question his words, or their meaning.

"Cord."

Samantha's gaze whipped back to the man who had just paused before them. Though he had only spoken the one word, Cord's name, she instantly sensed a strain of animosity emanating from him. His deep brown eyes seemed chilled with contempt.

"Reid," Cord responded quietly, more reserved than she'd ever heard him.

"I heard you were here," Reid said.

"I heard you were in England."

"I was." Reid smiled, though the seemingly warm gesture did nothing to soften the hardness that held his handsome features rigid.

"I also heard you had some trouble there."

"Nothing I couldn't handle."

"As always," Cord said.

Reid tipped his head, insolence pulling at his features. "Almost always. As we both know."

"So, to what do we owe the pleasure?"

The truculent smile widened and Samantha shivered at the artifice she saw momentarily flash across his handsome face.

But rather than answer Cord, Reid turned his gaze to her. The smile suddenly seemed genuine, and she watched in bewildered surprise as the frosty harshness in his eyes instantly warmed to a heat that could rival the most sultry of summer days. There was also invitation there in the smoldering depths of those dark eyes, but it was an invitation she did not welcome.

He drew one of her hands into his, the warmth of his fingers, the strength she felt there, wrapping about her own like velvet ensconced talons of steel. *Dangerous.* Cord's warning repeated over and over in her mind, but even if he had never offered it, she would have known Blackjack Reid Sinclaire was a man to beware of.

The blood in her veins turned from warm to hot and her pulse raced as his hands continued to hold hers, and his eyes held hers, as if delving into her thoughts. Her heart thudded resoundingly.

"You must be Samantha." The deep drawl of his voice slid over her quietly, slowly, quickly, tauntingly, much as the provocative stroke of a feather to sensitized flesh. He smiled as his thumb stroked softly over the back of her hand. "And much more beautiful than all the rumors I've heard while traveling downriver."

She stared at him, half mesmerized and silent, wanting to dislike him, both for her own sake and for Cord.

He raised her hand and, turning it over, pressed his lips to the soft, center of her palm. "Reid Sinclaire, at your service."

"Blackjack Reid Sinclaire," Cord corrected curtly.

Tiny fingers of prickling heat rushed up Samantha's arm at Reid's touch. Startled, she tore her hand from his grasp, remembering once before having experienced that sudden physical sense of excitement, that instant and unreasonable attraction. She had been young and innocent then, and had unwittingly allowed herself the indulgence of those feelings. But following her heart had wrought dire consequences . . . and they had been ones she was not willing to suffer again, especially for a gambler with nothing more than a charming line and a devastating smile.

"She knows who you are, Reid," Cord said, his tone ruthlessly hard now. "And what."

A glint of mischief or malice, Samantha couldn't tell which, lit Reid's eyes as he straightened and looked at Cord.

Though she kept her expression cool and remote, Samantha was surprised by the unistabkle challenge she'd recognized in Cord's words.

"Then I guess there are no secrets left, are there, *old friend?*" Reid said softly.

Samantha nearly shuddered at the flash of hatred she saw spark from the brown depths of Blackjack Reid Sinclaire's eyes as he looked at Cord. She had to do something, stop this, before words became insufficient and they were literally at each other's throats. She flipped open the bejeweled fan that hung from her wrist by a soft, silk loop of rope, and fluttered it before her. "Have you come to answer the challenge, Mr. Sinclaire?" she asked, her tone as cool as the soft breeze that wafted up from the river and through the saloon's swinging doors.

His gaze returned to hers. "A game of poker with the legendary Samantha," he mused, his voice velvet edged. "And a million dollar pot. That is definitely a challenge no man"—he paused, and the smile that had begun to pull at his lips became a caressing promise, a suggestion, a hope—"could refuse."

"To play against me," Samantha said, lifting her chin

defiantly, "you must beat the others. I will be playing only four of you . . . the best."

One dark, golden brow rose slightly in amusement at her words, then Reid tipped his head toward her. Daring shone from his dark eyes and arrogance, or perhaps it was merely confidence, Samantha wasn't certain, settled smugly upon his shoulders.

"Then I'd best get started," he said softly, "on being the best." He reached into the inside pocket of his jacket and retrieved a billfold. Opening it, he took out a handfull of greenbacks, which he handed to her. "Twenty-five thousand dollars," he said. "My entry fee." He handed her another stack. "And twenty thousand more for playing."

Samantha handed the money to the bartender, who handed her back a tray of betting chips she'd had made just for these games.

"Thanks, Curly," Samantha said. "As soon as you deposit that, we'll announce the start of the games."

He nodded, and with a Navy Colt held tight in one hand, and Reid's money in the other, the bartender made for her office at the rear of the building to place Reid's entry fee in the safe with the money already collected from the other players. Samantha handed the tray of chips to Reid. "You'll play with these," she said. "They represent your twenty thousand."

A movement at the entry doors of the saloon caught her attention and Samantha glanced toward them, seeing Studs Harriman and Forest McLean pausing to look around the room. Evidently they would be full up after all.

Reid glanced at Cord. "Until later?"

Cord gave a curt nod of his head. "Until later."

Reid looked back at Samantha. "I'll look forward to playing against you, Samantha, and perhaps buying you a drink." With a slight bow of his head, he turned and took a seat at one of the tables.

"Pretty confident he's going to make it to the end, isn't he?" Samantha said, looking up at Cord.

"He has every right to be." Cord turned to the bartender and motioned for the man to bring him a drink. "He's one of the best there is."

"I've never heard of him."

Curly placed a shot glass before Cord and, reaching to a concealed shelf under the bar, retrieved a bottle of high-grade whiskey, private stock. He filled the glass, and started to return the bottle to its shelf.

"Leave it," Cord growled.

Samantha and Curly exchanged a quick glance. Cord's self-imposed limit was one drink a night.

"He's been in England the past few years," Cord said, drawing Samantha's gaze back to him. He held the shot glass up and stared appreciatively at the amber liquor that reflected golden beneath the light of the chandeliers. He downed the whiskey in one gulp, set the shot glass down on the bar with a resounding crack, and turned to look at Samantha. "Stay away from Sinclaire, Sam."

She frowned. Cord had never even tried to tell her what to do before. Even though she'd had no intention of getting anywhere near Blackjack Reid Sinclaire except for a game of poker, if he made it to the final round, Cord's words, and his dark tone aroused her curiosity now, along with a little defiance. "Why?" she asked simply.

His blue eyes hardened as they settled on Reid Sinclaire, who'd taken a seat at a table across the room. "Because he's married," Cord said, turning back to her. "Because he's ruthless. And because he's wanted for murder."

Chapter Two

Reid set his chips on the table and threw a casual glance at the men already seated there, his opponents for the evening. He didn't know any of them. But it didn't matter. It wasn't really them who had his interest at the moment, or his attention. Samantha was nothing like the other women he'd met who made their livings in saloons or at gambling tables. No matter how beautiful they were, there was always something jaded about them, a feeling of having been used by life. He didn't sense that with Samantha. She was more beautiful than all the descriptions he'd heard, than he'd imagined, and there seemed a sense of vulnerability and innocence about her that had surprised him, had taken him aback for a moment, but her beauty and whatever other rare qualities she possessed would only make what he intended to do that much more pleasureable. Reid nodded to the other men at the table and then smiled to himself as he caught another glimpse of Samantha out of the corner of his eye.

It wasn't hard to spot her. She was like a delectable spot of brilliance in an otherwise colorless sea of humanity, the others crowded into the long, narrow room, seeming to almost disappear into a blur of grayness as she moved among them, colorful and alluring. Reid turned to look fully at her. The plunging décolletage of her blue gown with its trim of dripping, darker Valenciennes lace accentuated a subtle yet amply tempting bosom and gently sloped shoulders of creamy ivory that his hands fairly ached to caress. His gaze dropped lower. Her waist was narrow, and even with the velvet sash that encircled it, Reid felt certain he could easily span its circumference with a stretch of his hands. Her legs would be long and exquisitely formed. He instinctively knew that, even though they were hidden from his view within a voluminous mound of satin folds and petticoats.

He wondered just how good it was going to feel to slip his hands within the lustrous waves of that dark red hair, to hold her body tightly against his and watch passion fill her blue eyes.

"You going to bet, Sinclaire?" one of the other players said brusquely, interrupting Reid's appreciative, though assessing, scrutiny of Samantha.

He forced his attention back to the game, giving the man who'd spoken a hard glare before pushing several fifty dollar chips toward the center of the table. Reid frowned. "You in a hurry to lose, friend?"

"No, to win, *friend,*" the man retorted, putting a sneering emphasis on his last word.

His face wasn't familiar to Reid, but his name was. He'd been around the casinos and riverboats for a long time, long before Reid had left the states for England, long before he'd even started gambling himself. But gambler was only one of the words Reid had heard used to describe Valic Gerrard. Cheat, swindler, charlatan, thief, and murderer were some of the others. Reid placed his cards on the table and stared at the man. His face, like his body, was lean and rigid, his nose long and straight, his dark eyes holding a gleam of cunning, the line of his lips even when curved in a smile bespeaking a penchant for cruelty.

But maybe he only saw those things in Gerard's face because he expected to see them there. "I call," Reid said. He glanced swiftly at each man as they looked at their cards; then Reid turned his gaze back to Samantha. She was still standing at the bar, this time talking to a burly giant of a man whose wild mane of hair was as orange as a bushel of carrots, and whose wide, muscle-rippling shoulders looked like a miniature mountain range.

Reid dismissed the man and concentrated on Samantha, feeling a knot of warmth begin to develop within his groin. Taking his revenge against Cord was definitely going to prove more pleasurable than he'd anticipated. Sweet revenge, he thought to himself. Sweet, delicious revenge.

As if she felt his gaze on her, Samantha turned. Her gaze met his, hard, direct, and challenging, but Reid did not look away. Embarrassment and even subtlty were two things he knew little about. Instead, he studied her, slowly and thoroughly, noting the way her auburn brows arched gracefully over eyes that slanted slightly upward at the outer corners, the pert upturn of her nose that gave her a look that could be either innocent sass or haughty and purposeful arrogance. Her hair flowed about and over her shoulders in rich, cascading waves of deep brown that seemed laced with threads of silky redness, shimmering and lustrous. But it was her eyes that drew his gaze time and again, china blue depths surrounded by a deep shadow of black and flecked with slivers of silver that resembled tiny, jagged bolts of lightning. They reminded him of a summer storm—a quiet afternoon sky devoid of clouds suddenly rolled upon by the blackness of thunder and rain, sliced into pieces by brilliant shards of lightning.

He saw her gaze move away from his finally and settle briefly upon Valic Gerard. Surprise gripped him as a look of loathing sparked within her eyes, igniting the silver slivers and turning them to fiery darts of icy flame that seemed suddenly able to reach out and burn the object of their interest.

The hatred he saw flash over Samantha's face as she stared at Gerard was so intense it startled Reid and left him wondering. Yet as swiftly as the emotion swept over her features, it was gone, and he was left uncertain he'd actually seen it at all.

"Take the damned pot, Sinclaire," Gerard said, breaking into his thoughts, "and shuffle the cards."

He forced his attention back to the game. A smile pulled at his lips. Yes, he was definitely going to enjoy his revenge against Cord Rydelle, but if he didn't start putting his mind to the game instead of Samantha, he wasn't going to be around long enough to do more than speculate about his plans. Reid looked at Foxe Brannigan, who sat to his right, and forced his smile to widen. "I hear you're one of the best around these parts now, Brannigan."

Foxe grinned, his lips turning upward beneath a dark, well-trimmed mustache, brown eyes alight with amusement. "Depends on what you're referring to, Sinclaire." He glanced toward Samantha.

"Cards, my friend," Reid said. "Cards." He accepted the deck the dealer handed him and shuffled it, spread the cards across the table, then gathered them back up into his hand and shuffled them again.

Foxe laughed. "Then I guess you've heard right."

Reid smiled knowingly. "We'll see." He set the cards in front of Dancing Jack Dillon, who sat to his left; the scar that cut across Jack's left cheek was like a white snake upon his otherwise tanned flesh, highlighted grostesquely beneath the flickering light of the wall sconce.

Reid wondered if the man got his name because he loved to dance, as one rumor he'd heard claimed, but had jilted the wrong woman, or because the Texan had done a little dance around a few bullets in an effort to stay alive and hadn't noticed that one of his taunters had a knife rather than a gun—another rumor Reid had heard. He glanced at the man and decided not to ask. Dancing Jack Dillon looked like he was better with the gun holstered to his thigh than he was with a deck of cards, and Reid didn't figure it was a good day to die.

Jack cut the cards and thrust them back toward Reid, who pushed them on to the house dealer and watched as he quickly reshuffled, then dealt five cards to each man.

Reid picked up his cards, holding them in the palm of one hand and spreading them slightly with a movement of his thumb across their faces. The top card was the queen of hearts. Before he had a chance to look further, a flash of dark blue caught his eye. He looked up to see Samantha moving past the table. Queen of hearts. He smiled without moving his lips. *But not my heart, darlin'*. The cynical thought tugged at a long ago memory he refused to let surface. *No. Never my heart.*

The games progressed for another four hours.

"Last round, gentlemen," Curly called out.

Those who had been watching the games moved to the bar or grabbed one of the chairs vacated by the gamblers who'd gathered at one end of the bar. Glasses slammed onto tables and bartop and bottles clinked as drinks were hurriedly poured and downed.

Cord climbed halfway up the staircase that was set to the rear of the room and called for everyone's attention. "The first night's games are over," he announced loudly, "with two players being disqualified: Loco Bob Tompkins and Seth Fitzroy."

A round of cheers filled the room, accompanied by a few curses from the two men just mentioned.

Cord held up his hand in a bid for silence again.

Reid saw Samantha move to stand beside the newel post at the foot of the stairs. A surge of desire coiled tight within the nether regions of his groin and sent a flash of burning heat searing through his veins. He smiled as the thought of just how he planned to enact his revenge against Cord filled his mind and intensified the ache of desire knotting within him. Damn, but he'd never met a woman he'd wanted so instantly, and so thoroughly.

"That's it for tonight, gentlemen," Cord called out. His deep baritone boomed across the room. "The games will resume tomorrow night, same time, same place."

A series of grumbles immediately followed as Curly refused to pour more drinks. Bottles were hastily emptied and the three women who worked for Samantha began to gather discarded glasses. The men good-heartedly started for the door, already talking among themselves as to who they thought would lose the next night's game.

"Hey, Cord, how come you ain't playing?" one of the men yelled over his shoulder as he pushed open the door.

Cord just shook his head and waved the man off, then went back to talking to one of Samantha's girls.

Reid stood at the end of the bar nearest the door to the street. He stepped back against the wall and into the shadows created by a tall, elegantly carved armoire that served as a liquor storage cabinet. He was visible to anyone looking in from the street or moving from the room toward the door, but not to anyone remaining in the saloon.

He leaned against the wall and sipped at the glass of bourbon he held in his hand, giving any who happened to look the impression that he was merely finishing his final drink of the night.

A reflection of the room in the tall windows that faced the street gave him a clear view of most of what was happening in the saloon.

Within minutes the last patron had departed. A short while later, Reid heard Samantha say good night to the bartender, who left by a back door. Reid frowned. The saloon was quiet, yet he hadn't seen Cord leave, or that red-haired mammoth he'd heard Samantha call Jake. Maybe they were having one last drink. Reid leaned forward and peered around the corner of the armoire.

The giant suddenly rose from behind the bar.

Reid's heart nearly jumped into his throat, and he pushed back out of sight. A few seconds later, having caught his breath, he peeked out again.

Jake was walking down the hallway that led to the rear of the building. He entered one of the rooms and shut the door behind him, calling out a grumbled good night.

Cord was ascending the staircase. Halfway up he paused and turned to look down at Samantha, who was standing near the bar.

Reid pushed back into the shadows again.

"Jake turn in?" Cord asked.

"Yes, just now. He worked down at the docks for a while this afternoon; they needed an extra hand at one of the boats. I think he's exhausted."

"The safe locked, honey?"

"All tight and secure."

"What about the doors?"

"I'll get them. Go on to bed. I'll finish up here and be up shortly."

Reid heard the sound of heavy footsteps on the stairs. A moment later, he chanced a look around the corner of the armoire again and saw Cord disappear through one of the doorways to an upstairs room.

He watched Samantha raise a long stave to one of the chandeliers and begin to douse its candles. When it was completely extinguished, she moved to the second of the three chandeliers that hung from the ceiling. Within minutes she was done, and the room was lit by only the weak light of two wall sconces and the pale moonlight that streamed in through the two street front windows.

Shadows hung everywhere, turning innocent corners into eerie caverns of blackness, tables into crouching monsters waiting to pounce on an unsuspecting victim, the huge mirror behind the bar into a silver landscape of mystical shapes and mysterious reflections.

It was a scene he knew well, having spent most of his adult life in casinos, saloons, and betting parlors. Some were opulent, some little more than ramshackle dumps, but in the end they were all the same.

Samantha moved past Reid to the entry, giving no indication that she saw him. She closed a pair of tall, double-paneled cypress doors over the red batwing swinging doors and threw the large, black wrought iron bolt lock that secured them.

Reid set his glass down on the bar and quietly stepped from the shadows.

Suddenly sensing someone behind her, Samantha whirled around.

Reid smiled. They were finally alone.

Chapter Three

Samantha's hands flew to her mouth and she gasped as the dark silhouette of a man suddenly blocked her path. He was going to rob her. She felt her heart slam against her breast as fear caught in her throat and robbed her of the ability to cry out for help. She remembered the gun hidden within the folds of her gown. Her hand shot down toward the flounce-concealed pocket.

"I didn't mean to frighten you."

She recognized his voice instantly, yet didn't know why or how. He was a stranger, a lothario, a murderer and wanted man. She wanted nothing to do with him, yet even as she told herself this, she knew it was a lie. There was something about him that intrigued her, something that drew her. She'd felt it the moment he walked into the Goose. It was the same kind of instant attraction she'd felt when she had first seen Dante Fournier, which was why she'd been desperately fighting the sensation ever since it had assailed her that evening, even before Cord had warned her of who and what Blackjack Reid Sinclaire was.

The fear that his surprise appearance caused her subsided as quickly as it had filled her, but rather than calm, it was replaced with a hot, burning anger that she found almost overpowering. "What . . ." She cleared her throat as the word came out more a hoarse screech than the hard, cold-edged challenge she'd meant it to be. "What are you doing here?" she demanded, indignation straightening her shoulders and holding her back stiff.

"I wanted to see you, to talk to you," Reid said, his voice a deep roiling drawl that seemed to reach out and caress her still trembling nerves. "Alone."

He smiled, and Samantha felt her anger unreasonably subsiding. She rubbed a clammy palm against her skirt and felt flushed with warmth, the heavily laced gown suddenly suffocatingly tight in the airless room. There was nothing about her neck, and yet she felt as if she couldn't breath, as if someone or something was pressing down on her throat, robbing her of the ability to draw in air. "We've closed for the night, Mr. Sinclaire," she said, calling her anger back, pulling it around her like a shroud and holding it to her as a shield. If nothing else, it gave her strength and kept a much needed distance between them. "I'm sure you heard the announcement."

Suddenly he was standing close to her, damned close, ignoring her anger, his warm breath fanning the wayward strands of hair that curled at her temples. "I heard."

"The games will resume tomorrow night," she said icily, and tried to pay no heed to the racing beat of her heart. "If you want to talk to me, I will be here then."

"Tomorrow night's a long while away, and as I said, I wanted to see you alone."

He'd seen the spark of anger in her eyes and heard it in her tone, yet he sensed there was something else there, too, something hidden beneath Samantha's cool, sophisticated exterior that he hadn't expected; but whether it was fear or merely uncertainty, he wasn't sure. He only knew that it was there, it intrigued him, and it was the last thing he had expected to encounter from her.

But it didn't change his plans. She could scream, he knew, which would bring Cord Rydelle running. And perhaps that giant redheaded neanderthal, too, but somehow he knew she wouldn't do that. He saw it in her eyes, in the way she held her shoulders, the stiffness of her spine. She was proud. Maybe too proud. She would try to defend herself if necessary, and call for help only as a last resort. He reached out for her.

Samantha stepped back, eluding his hands.

Reid smiled and stepped toward her, effectly slicing the distance between them to even less than it had been before she'd moved.

The black and white cat he'd seen earlier, the dark green leaf of a magnolia, even a greenback . . . all were larger, wider than the narrow space left between his body and hers now.

The scent of jasmine touched his nostrils. He inhaled deeply, savoring the fragrance and knowing without consciously calculating the thought that whenever he encountered it in the future, he would think of her.

She stepped back again. It was her last retreat. The door was at her back, preventing her from taking another step, while he was in front of her, silently, mockingly inviting her into his arms.

He smiled. "Are you afraid of me, Samantha?"

Everything in her railed against the challenge. "No," she snapped instantly. She kept her gaze steady, hoping it gave no hint of the fierce battle that was raging within her. What was there about this man that made her want to slap him . . . and kiss him?

"You've thought about this moment all evening," he said softly, "you and me, alone, just as I have."

Samantha shook her head. "No. I haven't."

He seemed to measure her words, and then he smiled, a deeply curved smile as sensuous as his lowered voice. "Lie to yourself, Samantha, if you have to, but don't lie to me." He reached out and pulled her into his arms. "Your eyes give you away."

Much like the instinctive panic of a bird who suddenly realizes it has become prey to a hunter, Samantha knew she should push him away and run, should flee his presence as swiftly as she could, and not look back. He was as dangerous as Cord as warned, and more.

But instead of twisting away from him, she remained still, her eyes pinioned by his, held his prisoner as surely as if he had bound her gaze to him with invisible shackles. A torrid rain of shivers washed over her flesh as the warmth of his invaded hers, firing her blood and turning the steady pace of her pulse to an erratic, mad dash that left her senses spinning.

She heard the beat of her heart echo like crashing thunder in her ears. Her mind fought for control, struggling for calm against a storm-swept sea of tumultuous, suddenly out of control emotions. Her reaction to him was exactly the opposite of what it should be. She didn't know him, and should have no desire to know him. Yet she had been painfully aware of him all evening, watching her as blatantly as she'd been furtively watching him. The world was full of handsome men, and many visited the Goose and were her friends. So what was it about Blackjack Reid Sinclaire that was different, that drew her and stoked the fires of her desire even as she fought to extinguish them?

Samantha looked into his eyes and knew immediately that the move had been a mistake. She felt suddenly as if she were drowning in a sea of rich, fathomless darkness, her senses aware of nothing but him, tuning out the rest of the world with its cares and concerns as if it had ceased to exist. Her heart hammered in her breast and her pulses raced madly, causing her to feel faint.

Run! the faint voice of self-preservation yelled from somewhere deep within her mind. *Run!*

Samantha pressed her hands to the door at her back, part of her mind frantically seeking a means of escape, while the other part taunted her with the question of what it would be like to be kissed by Blackjack Reid Sinclaire.

He smiled, as if able to read her thoughts, and his head began to lower toward hers.

"No." The word had been meant as a command, but slipped from her throat as little more than a soft plea. Her hands curled into fists, her fingers squeezing in on each other.

The pale golden light still emanating from the wall sconces at his back cloaked him in a facade of light and shadow. It weaved through the dark blond locks of his hair to transform them to shimmering threads of gold, while turning his eyes to a midnight amber that held hers mercilessly, refusing to allow her either escape or retreat, but it also left his face haunted by ridges of darkness.

Angel of Darkness. Samantha shuddered at the thought. That was the description that had eluded her all evening, that was what he reminded her of. A golden figure surrounded by an aura of darkness. Lucifer—a golden angel, fallen from his heavenly perch because of the hidden darkness within his soul. So beautiful, but so lethally sinful. She tried to draw away from Reid, placing her hands to his chest and pushing against him.

"Don't deny what you know you want, Samantha," Reid whispered. He brushed his lips across hers, a touch so faint, so light, it was almost not a touch at all. "What we both want."

She felt the gentle kiss sweep to the core of her being, like wings of light lifting her from a darkness she hadn't even been aware of.

His tongue traced the outline of her lips, slowly, sensuously, teasing her senses and silently beckoning them to respond, to answer his seductive call. He was forbidden fruit. He was everything she had vowed to stay away from. Everything she knew she should avoid.

Samantha's hands pressed against the lapels of his jacket. A small part of her, almost infinitesimal now, still cried for her to resist him, to flee him, to push him away. But its entreaty was too weak against the onslaught of emotion his embrace, the mere touch of his lips to hers, was stirring within her body. She was on fire, her senses reeling.

He cocked his head to one side, and his lips slid down the side of her throat.

Samantha trembled. "No," she whispered, but whether it was an appeal for him to stop, or an order to herself to deny the feelings he was causing to surface within her, she wasn't certain.

"Yes," he answered softly. His mouth claimed hers then, his kiss no longer soft and cajoling, but hard and demanding, commanding her to respond in kind, the fires of his passion reaching out to ignite hers.

As if with a will all their own, her hands slid up and over his shoulders, her fingers plunged into the thick locks of his hair, slipped within the silken blond tresses and held his head to hers.

She felt the invading plunge of his tongue into her mouth, the probing, exploring twist of it, and tasted the faint tang of the bourbon that still clung to his mouth.

For a few brief seconds, as emotion overrode intellect and reason, she reveled in the feel of him, of the desire he was awakening in her. The faint redolence of his cologne, a blend of spices that lent her images of exotic, faraway places, teased her nostrils, while his strength wrapped about her like a mantle of security, promising to protect her from the world, to keep harm at bay, and to make everything all right again.

The thought jolted Samantha from her reverie and jerked her from her deepening stupor of rising passion to the hard, cold world of reality. Protect her? What in heaven's name was she doing? He was exactly what and who she needed protection from.

She yanked her hands from his hair, tore her lips from his, and pushed at his chest. "No. Stop. Let me go," she said, gasping as much for breath as for control.

Reid remained still, holding her to him.

"Let me go, dammit, or I swear I'll scream for Cord and Jake."

Reid let his arms drop from around her and took a step back. He wasn't afraid of Cord Rydelle. Nor was he frightened of the redheaded giant she called Jake. Though maybe he should be. He did not, however, want to confront them just yet. It would spoil everything, and he'd waited too long for things to be ruined now just because he'd let a little thing like passion get in the way. He smiled down at Samantha with what he hoped was a look of contrition. "I'm sorry," he said. "I shouldn't have done that."

She stiffened, her hands balled into fists at her sides, and glared at him. "That's right, Mr. Sinclaire, you shouldn't have."

"Forgive me, please?"

"The games begin promptly at eight o'clock tomorrow night." She turned and drew back the bolt that held the entry doors closed, then stepped aside and drew one open. "Do not be late, or you'll forfeit your seat . . . and your money."

* * *

Samantha moved to one of the windows in her bedchamber and drew back the lace panel. Moonlight slipped into the room, surrounding her, but she paid no attention. Her mind and thoughts were elsewhere.

She stared out at the night-shrouded landscape of Natchez Under-the-Hill. The soft glow of the night's light sprinkled the landscape, turning the shabby riverside buildings to quaint structures of earlier times, the nearby river to a wide, glistening sheet of rippling silver, and the ridge of trees that lined the opposite bank to a ragged, black silhouette that was neither threatening nor inviting, but merely there, as always.

A dozen packets sat docked at the wharf. Their tall black smokestacks glistened against the rivaling blackness of the night, white wooden decks gleamed in the reflection of the moonlight, and the boats' huge red paddle wheels waited with majestic patience to once again be put into action and churn through the muddy waters of the wide river.

A sigh, as soft and silent as the gentle fluttering of a butterfly's wings, slipped from her lips. Sometimes she wished for nothing more than to board one of those riverboats and ride into oblivion, to a place where no one knew her, past or present. Not as Samantha or Elyse Beaumont. A place where she could just start all over and be herself, whoever that was. Part of her was still Elyse, another part was Samantha, but there was another part of her now that wanted to be neither of those women, that longed to be someone else entirely. It was nights like this that she yearned the most for a place where there were no secrets to keep, responsibilities to be met, old debts to pay, or revenge to be sought.

A place where there was only peace, and quiet, and maybe a little happiness.

It had been eight years since she'd come to Under-the-Hill. Eight years since Valic Gerrard had murdered Staunton Beaumont . . . since Riversrun had been taken away from her because of Staunton's huge gambling debts; since she had become Samantha, leaving her life as Elyse Beaumont behind forever; and since she had learned how to hate, and wait for the day she could seek her revenge.

She had been only seventeen then, a fairly innocent young woman with a promising future, a handsome and wealthy beau, and supposedly a healthy sized dowry. But it had all begun to fall apart when her mother died. She should have seen what was coming, but she'd been up north at school and too engrossed in her own life. A year later the world she'd been born into, the only world she'd ever known, ended abruptly with one lunge of Gerard's rapier into her stepfather's heart.

She could still remember the hurt she'd felt, the utter and intense despair, but most of all the anger. That was the one emotion that still lingered in her heart about what happened—anger.

After they'd lost the plantation, it had been up to her to find a way for the family to survive, for her nine-year-old sister Clarissa and their spinster aunt Dellie to go on. And all they'd had left was the town house and her aunt Dellie's savings. Samantha sighed. Who would have ever thought that Elyse Beaumont, of the once wealthy and prestigious Natchez Beaumonts, would end up living Under-the-Hill and running a saloon?

Dellie had been outraged when Samantha had first broached the subject with her, but in the end, there had been no other way.

She remembered the night she'd left the town house as if it were only mere hours ago. It had been raining. Jeremiah, who had been their gardner at Riversrun for as long as she could remember, had escorted her to the delapidated old hotel she'd bought with part of Dellie's savings. He'd helped her get settled in that night, but Samantha had refused to let him stay and help her refurbish and convert the place into a saloon. People from Top-the-Hill were always traveling through the Under-the-Hill district on their way to or from the landing docks, whether from a trip or merely to check on shipments of cargo, and one of them might recognize Jeremiah. Then their plan would be ruined.

She sent him back to Dellie, ignoring her own fear and the desolation that came over her as she stood in the door of the ramshackle building and watched him trudge up the hill. Within only a few months, however, he'd disappeared.

Those first few months after opening the Goose she'd been terrified someone would recognize her, in spite of the fact that she'd changed her name, donned a wig, and covered her features with face paint. But no one had. Slowly over the years she'd used less and less face paint, her figure had changed and blossomed, even her voice had changed a bit, becoming deeper and softer. And she'd finally discarded the wig. Now she was Samantha. Elyse Beaumont no longer existed, except in the memories of just a few people, and the lies her aunt circulated about her niece's dazzling life in Europe with her French husband.

A movement in the shadows, beneath the overhanging roof of the general store directly across the street from the Silver Goose, caught Samantha's attention. She stared hard into the darkness, trying to discern who or what stood there, but could see nothing.

"Forget it, Samantha," she mumbled to herself. "You're seeing things." It was most likely only a stray dog or cat, or a roustabout too drunk to make it back to his cot. Or perhaps it had merely been her imagination, or a flicker of moonlight against a glass window.

But no sooner had she spoken the self-chastising words, than she saw a faint glow of light emanate from the same spot where she'd seen the movement. She squinted and leaned closer to the glass, as if by doing so her eyes could better pierce the blackness of the night. The glow appeared again, tiny and round, and as it did, she saw the faint image of a man's face behind it.

Samantha dropped the lace panel but continued to look through it to the street below, and the man standing directly across the street from the Silver Goose.

As if beckoned by her gaze, he stepped forward and looked up at her window.

Samantha started and backed away as moonlight settled upon the brim of his hat, then touched the golden sweep of his hair that brushed the collar of his shirt.

Reid drew a long drag off his cigar as he looked up at Samantha's window, fully aware that she had been watching him, that she was mostly likely still watching him from behind that thin panel of lace.

He had come here to kill Cord Rydelle, but seeing his mistress had caused Reid to change his plans. He was going to destroy his old friend, finally and completely, and what better way than the same way Cord had destroyed him all those years ago? But Reid would do a much more thorough job of it than Cord had done.

Thoughts of Bethany filled his mind, but her image didn't come as clear to him anymore as it had years ago. Too much time had passed, and he'd tried hard to block the memories out for too long now. But the anger was still there. And the hate. They hadn't gone away, hadn't dulled with the passing of years.

Reid threw his cheroot down and stepped back on the

boardwalk, his dark clothes blending with the shadows and allowing him to all but disappear within them.

Long minutes later he saw the curtains at Samantha's window move and Reid smiled.

She looked down at the boardwalk, where he had stood, but he knew she couldn't see him now. She pressed closer to the glass and turned to look up the street. Moonlight flowed through the sheer threads of the batiste nightgown she wore, outlining the subtle curves of her body. It caressed each lithe line like the soft touch of a gentle lover's hand . . . just as his would do before long.

Chapter Four

The sultry heat of late afternoon hung heavy in the dark room.

A sharp knock on Samantha's door broke through her dreams, but she shrugged acknowledgment of the intrusive sound away, and burrowed deeper beneath the covers.

A tall man with golden hair, penetrating brown eyes and a devilish smile held her in his arms, the heat of his body seeming to surround her and invade her own blood. "I wanted to be alone with you," he whispered. A delicious shiver of longing raced through her as he brushed his lips tenderly across hers.

"Sam? You awake?"

Samantha groaned at the sound of her maid's voice. She denied its existence and tried to recapture the dream. *"I wanted to be alone with you."*

"Sam!"

The image of Blackjack Reid Sinclaire instantly disappeared and Samantha's eyelids fluttered open. Light, seeping into the room around the edges of the drawn draperies, assaulted her eyes. It couldn't be morning already, she protested. She'd just fallen asleep. She rolled over and burrowed herself deeper beneath the covers. The large poster bed had belonged to her mother, handed down through several generations, and was one of the few possessions Samantha and her aunt Dellie had managed to get out of Riversrun when they'd left.

Molly entered without waiting for Samantha to answer. She moved about like a small whirlwind, her dark hair, a mass of light brown curls held behind her ears by combs, bounced atop her shoulders. She set a serving tray on the night table next to Samantha.

The clatter of silverware against china seemed to echo within Sam's brain, causing her to groan.

Molly scurried across the room toward the windows. "Lord and geholdzafat, Samantha," she scolded, "this room is like an oven. It's a miracle you didn't roast yourself to well done in here."

"How can anyone be so perky in the morning?" Sam muttered into her pillow. All she wanted to do was go back to sleep and . . . dream about Blackjack Reid Sinclaire? Her eyes shot open and her whole body went stif as she remembered her dream. *"I wanted to be alone with you."* Lord, was she that lonely for a man in her life that she'd actually dream about a scoundrel like *him?*

"Well, for one thing, it's not morning," Molly said, pulling Sam from her reverie as she poured her a cup of coffee from the silver carafe on the serving tray. "And for another thing"—she handed Sam the coffee as she pushed herself to a sitting position on the bed—"like my pop always used to say, greet the day with a cheery smile, and it'll smile back at you."

"Right," Samanatha said, sarcasm heavy in the lone word. She closed her eyes and took a sip of the strong, hot coffee, then waited for it to wake her up.

"Well, maybe if you'd try it sometime," Molly said, "you'd see."

Samantha wiped a hand over her eyes, trying to shrug away the last, druglike feelings of sleepiness. She drank some more coffee, set the cup down, yawned, and stretched her body, flinging her arms out wide. Lord that felt good. She glanced at Molly. "So, what time is it, two minutes after noon?" she teased.

"Too late for you to be lollygagging about in bed, that's what time it is, and there's still lotsa things to do before tonight." A smile curved her heart-shaped lips, while the sun shining through the windows highlighted the blanket of freckles that sprinkled across her nose and cheeks. "Now, you get yourself moving, and I'll bring up your bathwater and lay your gown out for tonight's party."

"Party?" Samantha shot upright, nearly spilling the second cup of coffee she'd just poured for herself. "Oh, no, Cord's birthday. There's so much to do. Molly, exactly what time is it?"

"A littler after two."

"What? You let me sleep half the day away? With all the things I have left to do before Cord's party tonight?" She threw the covers aside and scrambled from the bed. "Oh, Molly, how could you?"

Indignant, Molly's small hands clenched into tight fists, rammed onto her hips, and she threw an exaggerated glare at Samantha. "You were up late last night, missy, and you looked a mite peaked, too, so I figured you needed your rest. Anyway, I didn't just 'let' you sleep, I banged on that door twice this morning already. Even came in once, but you wouldn't wake up, so I went on about my chores. I

figured if you didn't wake up this time, I'd have to send
for the doctor to see if you were even still alive.''

"I'm never going to get everything I have left to do for
the party done in time," Samantha fretted, looking about
for her robe.

"Now don't go worrying yourself half to death. Me and
Suzette already took care of everything. Isn't anything left
for you to do but get yourself ready and make a last minute
check of things.''

"But the decorations . . . the gift . . . the food . . .''

Molly tossed her a satisfied smile. "It's all taken care of,
just like I said."

"Where's Cord? Did you get him out of here like we
planned? He hasn't seen anyth—''

"Sam." Molly's smile turned back into a glare. "Will
you calm down? Jake took Cord upriver with some excuse
of looking at a horse he wants to buy. Cord didn't really
want to go, but you know Jake: he can be a real pain when
he's decided he ain't gonna take no for an answer. And
he knew he better not take no for an answer this time."
She laughed softly as she pulled Sam's underthings for the
day out of the armoire. " 'Course, I don't know what the
fool's going to do with the horse if he actually buys it.
Everybody knows if it ain't a draft horse, it sure as heck
can't carry Jake without dragging its poor belly on the
ground."

Not quite two hours later, Samantha lifted the voluminous folds of her white gown and descended the stairs that
led down to the barroom. At the bottom of the steps, she
had to pause and marvel at the room's transition. White
and red streams of satin ribbon had been looped about
the chandeliers, bar, mirrors, windows, and doorways. A
huge linen banner had been tacked to the wall above the

wheel of fortune, and painted across it in huge, bright red letters was HAPPY FIFTIETH BIRTHDAY, CORD.

"He's not going to be too happy about that," Samantha said, chuckling at the banner that declared Cord's age to one and all, and knowing how sensitive he was about growing older. "Not that I have to ask, but I will." She gave Molly a knowing wink. "Whose idea was it?"

"Suzette's," Molly said, smiling wryly. "Said she figured maybe if she reminded him that he was getting to be an old man, he might be a little more likely to think of settling down a bit."

"Could work just the opposite," Samantha said, and shook her head. "Might make him feel he has to go out and sow a few more wild oats before it's too late."

"Can't hide from the truth forever," Molly quipped.

Samantha looked at her quickly, the words stinging. Hiding from the truth was exactly what she'd been doing for the past eight years, though no one Under-the-Hill knew that her entire life, as they knew it, was a lie except Cord. In the beginning, it was meant to be temporary—the saloon, her masquerade—just something to help her, Dellie, and Clarissa survive for a while, but . . . She sighed quietly. Her life could have turned out a lot worse. And more than once it almost had. She shrugged the thought away. This was supposed to be a happy day.

Suzette appeared from behind the bar and tacked a last ribbon to the door, then looked up at Samantha and Molly. "Well, think he'll like it?" She lifted a hand to pat her dark curls in place and Samantha wasn't sure if Suzette was referring to the room decorations or the bright red gown she'd donned for the occasion, its daring neckline and skirt, tacked to her waist on the side to reveal a long length of leg, leaving little to the imagination.

"Well, I'm not too sure how he's going to take the sign,

but . . ." Samantha smiled. "I'm sure he'll be wild about the gown."

Suzette laughed and did a quick pirouette. "I've been saving it for tonight."

"So, it's almost seven," Samantha said, and turned to Molly. "When did Jake say he'd have Cord back here?"

Just then the front door opened and several men entered. "Looks like we're the first to arrive," one said, smiling at the three women and sidling up to the bar.

Curly placed shot glasses before each man, and they immediately delved into a conversation between themselves as they watched Curly tip the bottle of house whiskey over each glass, then leave it in front of them.

Within an hour, the Goose was packed with more than a hundred people. Though the saloon was not officially closed, all those present, most of the gamblers who'd come for the challenge, as well as many of Cord's friends from Under-the-Hill, were invited guests. Several tables had been pushed up against one wall and were laden with food, including a big chocolate cake.

Samantha hoped none of the contestants for the games minded that they would be skipping them tonight, but there had been no way to warn them and keep the party for Cord a surprise. She'd just been lucky that Suzette had managed to hand each an invitation last night without Cord seeing her.

For a gambler, Cord was a very private man, and Samantha had never been able to find out his birthday until just three days ago, and then it had been quite by accident. It had been too late to change the announced date for starting the games, so she'd just decided a little intermission wouldn't kill anyone, and Cord would never, ever suspect.

"Where's Jake and Cord?" she asked Molly for the umpteenth time since coming downstairs. She glanced at the large grandfather clock that stood against the wall near her office door. "They're late."

"They'll be here, Miss Worrywart."

Suzette suddenly frowned. "Unless they got waylaid along the Trace somewhere by those awful Delaney brothers. I swear, why can't somebody just shoot those dreadful people and be done with it?"

Just then the entry door opened and Cord walked in, then stopped short.

Jake, directly behind him, nearly barreled over him. Then he looked over Cord's shoulder and a smirk of satisfaction curved his lips.

"What the . . . ?" Cord muttered.

"Cord!" Suzette called loudly, to alert everyone in the room of the guest of honor's arrival.

All eyes turned toward the door and a gale of shouted "surprise" and "Happy Birthday" filled the air. Men raised their glasses in salute, laughed, stomped the floor, and clapped hands down on the bar and tables.

Cord stared in shock at the crowd, his gaze darting from one person to another. The deep hollows of his cheeks did a slow turn to pink.

Jake, unabashedly sniffing the air now and catching a whiff of the tantalzing aroma of the food, pushed past him and quickly made for the tables.

Samantha wove her way through the crowd and took Cord's left arm, while Suzette took his right.

"You two . . ." he sputtered, shaking his head and trying to look angry. "I ought to . . ."

"Enjoy yourself," Samantha finished for him. "You only have one birthday a year."

"And you only turn fifty once," Suzette chimed in, a mischievous glint of amusement in her eyes.

He caught sight of the sign and growled softly. "No need

to ask who did that," he said, throwing Suzette a mocking glare.

"An elf." She laughed and rose on tiptoe to press a quick kiss to his cheek. Her voice dropped to a husky whisper. "Happy birthday, handsome." He turned toward her, and Samantha suddenly felt like a third wheel on a cart that only needed two.

The trio of musicians she'd hired for the evening played merrily, the mountain of food steadily dwindled, the drinks flowed, and everyone seemed to be having a good time. Everyone except Samantha. It was only eleven o'clock and she felt too restless to even stand still. Her gaze wandered the room continuously, paused to stare at each occupant, smiled when they smiled, and then moved on to rest momentarily on the next person.

Only one person had complained about her temporary postponment of the games.

"I have been looking forward to sitting across a table from you, Samantha, and as you know, I'm not a very patient man. I don't appreciate the delay."

He had put special emphasis on her name as his catlike eyes raked over her.

A shudder she was unable to control had ripped through her and Valic smiled, as if pleased by the effect his words, and gaze, had on her.

She'd wanted to tell him she didn't care what he did or didn't appreciate, and the last thing she was looking forward to was sitting across a table from him, for any reason, but she'd held her tongue. It would give her satisfaction for the moment, but in the long run would only make matters worse.

Thoughts of Valic Gerad turned the taste of the sarsaparilla she'd been sipping as bitter as she imagined the watered-down, rat-aged whiskey they served down the street at Jubilee's must taste. She had hated Valic eight years ago,

and if it was possible, she hated him even more now. But
then, he'd given her more reason for her hatred to intensify in the last few days.

She glanced at the clock. Almost eleven-thirty now. Her
eyes moved back over the crowded room. Suzette was happily attending to Cord's every whim, the other girls were
seeing to the rest of the guests, and Jake and Molly were
dancing. Samantha watched them for a moment. At six
foot five and three hundred pounds, Jake was like a giant,
while diminutive Molly didn't even reach five feet in height,
and Samantha doubted she weighed a hundred pounds.
But she knew Jake was as sweet on Molly as any man could
be for a woman, and Molly was more in love with Jake than
she'd admit.

The party was a success. Tables were abuzz with activity,
and laughter filled the room. So what was the matter with
her? Why did she feel there was still something missing?
She inhaled deeply, about to sigh, and stale air combined
with a gray haze of smoke filled her lungs. She coughed
and made her way through the crowd toward the front
door. Maybe what she needed was merely a lot of fresh
air, and a little solitude and quiet.

She slipped outside and onto the wide gallery that
fronted the Silver Goose; then she moved to stand beside
one of its thin supporting pillars. In spite of the late hour,
the air hung heavy with the sultry heat of the day and the
thick humidity of the quickly approaching summer. She
looked out at the night, tuning out the sounds coming
from inside of the saloon behind her. High above a thousand stars glistened against a black sky like the shining
eyes of heaven looking down upon the earth, while a thin
sliver of moon struggled to light the night-entombed earth.
From where she stood, she had a clear view down Earhart's
Alley to the now silent Robitaille and Earhart landing
docks, both crowded with moored steamboats that gently

swayed upon the ever-lapping waves of the wide, murky river. Across that dark expanse, the low bluffs of the Louisiana shoreline created a barely discernible horizon as its trees blended with the darkness of the night to become merely dim shadows.

Samantha leaned against the post and let her head drop back, her eyes closed. The smell of jasmine filled the air, drifting to her from the tangle of vines that clung to the side of the old clapboard walls of the saloon. She planted it the day after she'd come to Under-the-Hill. It was a scent she loved, because it took her mind back in time, back to better days, to Riversrun, around whose majestic white pillars just such a plant had wrapped itself, back to when everything had been good, when her family had all lived happily, with never a worry toward tomorrow.

And maybe that had been their mistake.

The tinkling sounds of the piano drifted out to her as the musicians, who'd taken a short break, picked up their instruments and began to play again.

Samantha opened her eyes and looked up at the sky, then sighed wearily. It was time to go back in.

He stood in the shadows, watching her.

She shook her head slightly, as if attempting to ease a stiffness from the back of her neck, or an unwelcome thought from her mind. A cloud of auburn curls fanned out across her shoulders at the movement.

A long, soft sigh, barely audible to him, slipped from her lips.

He watched as she straightened the puffed sleeves that hugged her arms, just below her bare shoulders, lifted a fold of her skirt in each hand and turned to go back into the saloon.

The light of the moon shone on the Caledonian silk of

her gown, causing the tiny squares of green silk that were woven beneath the overlaying threads of white to catch the faint rays of the night's light and shimmer richly, giving the fabric an irridescent quality.

She took a step toward the entry door.

If he was going to stop her, now was the time. "I thought you'd never come out," he said.

Samantha stiffened and whirled around, recognizing his voice instantly, and wondering just as instantly how she had. She peered into the darkness, into the shadows, not seeing him at first. Her eyes narrowed. Her pulses began to race erratically. Then he moved, only slightly, but enough so that she caught it, and saw him. She took a step back, away from him. "What are you doing here?"

In the dark shadows of the overhang, Reid leaned casually against the wall of the saloon, the spill of pale moonlight that lit the street not quite reaching him. He straightened to his full height at her words, and stepped up onto the boardwalk. "Waiting for you," he answered simply, his tone a seductive drawl.

His eyes traveled her form, dropping to linger for several long seconds upon the daring cut of her gown's neckline. It revealed just enough to tease a man's senses and spark his imagination.

Samantha felt the thick ruche of white Valencienne lace that trimmed the neckline brush against her breasts as her breathing accelerated under his gaze.

She knew she should go in. Instead, she turned toward the street, presenting him with her back, and looked out at the river. "I'm afraid your wait was for naught, Mr. Sinclaire. We have nothing to discuss."

Reid closed the distance between them and his hands clasped her shoulders. He forced her to turn back and face him.

She gasped in surprise, then damned herself for doing

so, knowing it showed a touch of vulnerability, maybe even a touch of fear.

"I don't agree." He lifted one hand to cup her chin and tilted it upward, forcing her gaze to meet his.

"Then you're a fool." She made to jerk away.

Reid's other hand had slipped to her waist, and he held her still. "Don't pull away from me, Samantha," he whispered softly, his lips so close she could feel the warmth of his breath on her temples. His fingers gently brushed the curve of her jaw, slid down the line of her neck, then slipped around to her nape and held her firmly, burying themselves in her hair.

She tried to hold herself away from him, her body rigid in spite of the fact that every molecule within her was on fire. She was fighting a battle, her body portraying treacherous mutiny, while her senses struggled to cling to some sense of reason.

He pressed his lips to her cheek. "You know you want this as much as I do."

She pushed forcefully against his chest then. "No, I don't."

But he had been prepared. His arms tightened around her, dragging her up against him as his hands pressed to her back. Her breasts were crushed against his chest, her hands and arms pinioned between their melded bodies. Her heart pounded, maddeningly fast, a blend of excitement and fear rushing through her.

"Yes, you do, Samantha. You can't deny that you feel what's between us." The underlying sensuality of his words, his tone, touched her. "I can see it in your eyes. I can feel it in the rapid beat of your heart, pounding against my chest."

"No, you—"

Her protest was cut off as his lips captured hers in a kiss that was at once gentle in its seduction of her senses and ravaging in its demand of her acceptance and acquiescence. Never had she been kissed so thoroughly, so deeply. The flames of a thousand fires burst to life within her body, and though her mind knew she should resist, should strike out at him, her emotions held her body in mutiny, traitorous to rational thought and intention, prisoner to her fledging and suddenly fiery desires.

His lips caressed hers as his tongue slipped into her mouth, flicking fire everywhere it touched, stoking the emotional upheaval that had erupted within her, fanning the sparks of the passion she'd kept in such tight control for such a very, very long time.

His mouth left hers and moved across the hollow of her cheek.

She leaned into him, her body too weak to do anything else.

He kissed the column of her neck, and pressed his lips to the curve of her shoulder. "I want you, Samantha, and you want me," he said, his voice ragged with emotion. "What sense does it make to deny it?"

Her hands moved to his shoulders.

Lord help her, she did want him. He was a stranger, a man she didn't know, but knew enough about to know she should stay away from him. He was no better than Dante. But it didn't matter. Whatever he was, whoever he was, she wanted him, had since the moment he'd walked into the Goose, and she didn't even know why. It made no sense.

His head lowered, and his lips touched the soft mound of flesh revealed above the plunging neckline of the luxurious white-green gown. His tongue slid between her breasts, hot, wet, and seeking, and Samantha, unable to help herself, moaned softly.

"I can give you more pleasure than Cord Rydelle,"

Samantha," Reid said. His hand cupped her breast. "You deserve better than an old man."

The words were like a bucket of ice water being thrown on her burning body, splashing against her senses, chilling her heart.

Heat instantly turned to cold, passion to shock, desire to disgust.

I can give you more pleasure than Cord Rydelle. The words screamed through her mind. A frost-edged shiver snaked its way down her back. Realization struck. He thought Cord was her lover!

The wherewithall to resist him that had deserted her earlier suddenly returned to her with volcanic force. Her hands slipped to his chest and pushed. At the same time she twisted around and tried to jerk herself free of his embrace. "Let me go."

He held her firmly.

"Let me go, or I'll scream," she threatened, and ripped away from him, stumbling as his hands released her.

Samantha's breasts rose and fell rapidly with her outrage, and she gasped for breath. She turned to push past him and return to the saloon.

Reid grabbed her arm, forcing her to pause. She looked over her shoulder at him, too furious to say anything else. Many men on the river assumed Cord was her lover, and she'd never cared. But this time . . . this time it was different. She didn't know why, she just knew it was, and that angered her all the more.

"It's not done between us, Samantha," he said, the softly spoken words edged with a hint of steel.

Whether his words were meant as a threat or a promise she wasn't sure; she only knew that she had to get away from him.

* * *

The next morning, after an almost sleepless night of tossing and turning, Samantha trudged out of bed, no more happy to see Molly's smiling face than she had been the previous morning. Maybe less. At least yesterday she had been in a fairly good mood because of Cord's party. Today she felt like the black clouds of hell were hanging over her head and threatening to remain forever.

Thoughts of Blackjack Reid Sinclaire wouldn't leave her alone, and yet even as she was forced to acknowledge to herself that she was attracted to him, she was also afraid. And she didn't know why. Cord had told her the man was a murderer, but she'd met murderers before. Cord had also told her Reid was married, but since she didn't have any designs on him that way, it shouldn't have mattered.

Yet there was something about him that made her uneasy, something more than the fact that she was attracted to him. She remembered how Cord and Sinclaire had looked at each other that first night, the cold, hard tone of the words they'd exchanged.

She sighed and tried to push the thoughts aside. What did it matter? So they didn't like one another. And she was attracted to him. In a few days the games would be over, and he'd be gone. She could avoid him for that long. Samantha dressed in a plain blue and black checked cambric day gown, minus the cumbersome crinolines and hoop cage. Instead, she wore a muslin underskirt. The saloon would need a thorough cleaning after last night's party, and she didn't need to look pretty to do that. After running a brush through her hair and tying it at her nape, she left her room and moved across the wide landing that fronted the doors of the upstairs rooms. At the top of the staircase she paused. A small shriek of surprise escaped her lips at the sight that met her eyes. Then, stifling a chuckle, she smiled.

Never had she seen such chaos in the Goose. Ribbons and streamers lay everywhere, empty bottles and glasses littered the bar, roulette, faro, poker, and wheel of fortune tables, and prone bodies draped over gaming tables, chairs, bar, and floor. Near the far end of the room Cord lay stretched out atop one of the buffet tables, fast asleep. His hat was propped over his face, and the garish multicolored silk neck scarf Suzette had given him was spread across his chest, as if to act as a blanket.

Suzette herself sat slumped in a chair beside the table, her dark head propped on top of Cord's thigh, her arms wrapped securely around his legs.

At the base of the staircase, Jake was curled into a huge ball, the bottom step acting as a pillow for his head. His loud snores reverberated through the otherwise silent room, and Samantha marveled at how any of the others could sleep, even if in a drunken stupor, in the midst of what sounded like a rumbling train straining at its bindings and about ready to explode.

A ball of black and white fur lay curled within the small space created between Jake's muscled wall of a chest and his pulled up legs, the cat's soft purring sounds no match for Jake's vociferous raling.

"Blossom," Samantha whispered, alarmed. "You're going to get yourself killed sleeping beside Jake like that. Come on, let's get you out of there." She stepped carefully over several other sleeping bodies that lay on the staircase. One man grunted loudly, turned, and nearly tripped her as he threw out his arm. She grabbed the railing and a moment later stopped beside Jake and bent down to lift Blossom into her arms.

Suddenly Jake released a thunderous gurgling snort, shuddered briefly and grumbling to himself, began to roll over. Samantha saw what was about to happen but couldn't move quick enough to stop it.

Blossom's tail was suddenly caught beneath the huge Irishman's stomach.

The cat woke instantly, eyes wide, claws extended, ears flattened in alarm. Panic turned to immediate frenzy. Blossom screeched loudly, frantically twisting and jerking her body about in an attempt to escape the avalanche of weight that had imprisoned her tail.

Samantha jumped back and yanked her hands away as claws flailed the air. Blossom's hair stood on end as her tail remained trapped and her panic turned to hysteria.

Jake came awake with a start as the sound of Blossom's high-pitched screams met his ears and one of her claws raked his muscular chest, leaving behind broken skin and a trickle of blood.

"Jumpin' catfish, what's the matter with that thing?" he yelled, wide eyes staring at Blossom as he scrambled away from the small cat as if she was a mountain lion on the attack. "Sam, get that crazy animal away from me. Geez and all amighty!"

The moment Jake jumped up, flattening himself against the wall and releasing Blossom's tail from beneath his weight, she quieted. With a look of cold indignation in her large green eyes, the cat assumed a regal pose and began to fastidiously lick at her tail, ignoring both Jake's mumbled curses and Samantha's efforts to keep from laughing.

A few snorts and rustles sounded in other parts of the room. Samantha straightened and looked around. The small but noisy riot of battling man and cat had managed to wake most of the half dozen or so others who'd also fallen asleep in the saloon.

Cord groaned deeply and pushed himself to a sitting position on the table he'd used as a bed. His foot hit an empty metal sandwich tray and it fell to the floor with a loud crash.

Suzette nearly jumped a foot off her chair, startled into wakefulness.

Another groan escaped Cord's lips and he dropped his head into his hands.

Suzette rose, and without a word to anyone, stumbled sluggishly toward the staircase.

Samantha approached Cord as everyone else began to shuffle toward the front door.

"Overdo it a bit last night, did we?" She handed him a cup of coffee from the tray Molly had just brought into the bar.

"Somebody drugged me." He winced as he lifted his head to bring the cup to his lips. "Or gave me rotgut." A second later he finally opened his eyes and looked around. "What the hell"—he winced, and when he spoke again it was in a whisper—"happened?"

Samantha smiled. "You had a birthday party, remember? But I'm beginning to think maybe you're getting a bit long in the tooth for such late nights and raucous celebrations," she teased, biting her lip to keep from chuckling aloud.

"That's not funny, Samantha," he moaned, closing his eyes again.

She frowned and her voice took on a serious note. "Maybe it's time you gave some thought to settling down. You know, you and Suzette could get married, move to a house Top-the-Hill, and . . ."

"Samantha." Cord's tone held a warning edge.

"I could throw you two the best wedding Under-the-Hill has ever seen, and . . ."

"Sam!"

"Cord, what happened before wasn't your fault," she said, ignoring the glare in his eyes. "None of it was. You shouldn't . . ."

"That's enough, Sam."

"But you can't let that stop you from . . ."

He slammed a fist down on the table, then grimaced as the sound reverberated through his head like a cacophony of tom-toms. "From what? Making the same damned mistakes all over again?"

"From trying again."

"I think I've had enough disasters in my life, thank you very much."

"But . . ."

"Look, I've messed up the lives of three women, Sam, not counting you. That'd make four. I think that's enough, don't you?"

"I'm fine, and none of it was your fault."

He set the coffee cup down and slid from the table, towering over her now at his full height. "I offered you a chance to try again, Samantha," he said softly. "I offered you a chance to go back to what you were before you opened the Silver Goose, and you refused. Remember?"

"That's different. People would find out. They wouldn't accept me. And I have to consider Clarissa." She shook her head. "It would never work. I can't go back."

"Fine. And neither can I."

"But . . ."

"Leave it alone, Sam."

She sighed. He was right. He had respected her decision, so she must respect his, even if it was wrong.

Cord leaned down and pressed his lips to her cheek. "I'm going to bed, honey. Wake me when the drums stop beating."

She watched him climb the stairs.

Molly stepped from the kitchen and approached Samantha. "You really shouldn't push him, Sam," she said quietly, watching Cord disappear past the door to his room. "He still blames himself."

The door closed with a soft click.

Samantha thought of the tintype of the woman and little girl that was attached to the inside lid of Cord's pocket watch. She'd only seen it once, but she had known instantly that it was a picture of the wife and daughter he'd lost years before. "But he shouldn't," she said softly. "Especially about Mary Lynn and Julie. He didn't know he'd contracted the fever."

"Doesn't matter," Molly said. "He brought it home to them, and they died." She shook her head. "That's a powerful guilt for any man to be carrying around."

Chapter Five

Reid paused on the corner and stared across the street at the ornate doors of the Bank of Natchez. Cord's mistress was conducting a poker game with a pot worth a million dollars, which meant she needed money. She'd charged each of the players, and he'd counted forty-eight, a twenty-five thousand dollar entry fee. That accounted for the million dollar pot, but it was obvious she intended to win it herself. The question was, why did she need that much money? And what would happen if she didn't win it?

He shook the last question away. It didn't concern him. He had his own plan to follow, and it would work without an answer to either of those questions, though his revenge might taste just a bit sweeter if he knew why she, and maybe Cord, was so desperate for money. He mulled the situation over in his mind. Something was wrong, he finally decided, and he was going to find out what. Then he would turn it to his own useful purposes.

He crossed the street, then held one of the bank's doors

open for a little old lady who looked like the perfect grand-mother.

Dellie nodded her thanks to the courteous young man. He was a handsome one, she thought. Too bad about the scar. Then again, it gave him a sort of rakish bent, just like Virgil had had. She felt a tug of emotion at the memory of her late beau as she moved to stand in line for the teller. Funny how she could still get all choked up thinking of Virgil when he'd been gone for over forty years. She patted a wisp of silver hair back into place and looked into the big mirror that hung on one of the bank's walls. The man who'd held the door open for her was standing several feet away from her, looking at a piece of paper he held in his hand. She looked him over closely. He would be perfect for Elyse. Dellie could just see them together. Elyse with her dark brown red hair, and this man with his golden good looks. What a handsome couple they'd make.

A sigh slipped from her lips. Well, it didn't really matter if he was perfect for Elyse or not, because Dellie knew her eldest niece wouldn't hear tell of meeting any man from Top-the-Hill. No respectable man, Elyse was constantly tell-ing Dellie, was ever going to accept what she did for a living. And anyway, hadn't they circulated that story years ago about Elyse having married and moved to France? How would they explain that away?

Dellie absently screwed her lips into a curve of disdain. Elyse was right, of course, but she was never going to meet a respectable young man while she was parading about Under-the-Hill as Samantha. As soon as Clarissa was mar-ried, she'd broach the subject of Elyse leaving that dreadful place and coming home to the town house. Then they could start working to really get her a husband.

The person in front of her concluded his business and left.

Dellie opened her reticule and stepped up to the teller's

window, but her attention was momentarily drawn from her business as a deep, gruff voice yelled out at someone across the room.

"Reid?"

He turned at hearing his name, somewhat surprised that there would be anyone in the bank who would recognize him.

"Rubies?" Reid said, half startled out of his wits to find Rubies Bigelow standing in a respectable bank. In fact, since he'd heard that Rubies had been killed a while back, he was shocked to see the man at all. "Hey, I thought I heard you were . . ."

Rubies waved away the comment and shushed him. "Yeah, I know. Six feet under, right? And the name's Rowland now," he said hurriedly before Reid could answer. Clapping a beefy arm around Reid's shoulders, Rubies urged him toward one side of the bank's lobby.

Reid frowned. "Rowland?"

"That's my name now," Rubies said. "Rowland T. Bigelow, and as you can see for yourself, old friend, I haven't played my last hand yet."

"But . . ."

"Yeah, I know. Pretty good story, huh? And necessary. I'm respectable now. Got myself a good wife and a plantation just outside of town. No need for the past to come tromping dirt on my door, if you know what I mean." He puffed out his well-endowed chest and, clasping his lapels, smiled from behind a bushy gray mustache that was seriously threatening to overtake his mouth. "You ought to try it, Sinclaire," Rubies said, smiling now. "Respectability, I mean, not tromping dirt to my door."

Both men laughed.

"Yeah, well, maybe someday," Reid said. "But I don't understand. Why'd you . . . I mean how . . . ?"

"Met Eugenia on one of the boats. Pretty little thing,

all blond curls and big blue eyes. She just stole my heart away, Sinclaire. Like a little thief. One minute I was just plain ol' me, gambling, drinking, having a good time, and looking for my next rube. Next thing I knew, all I could think about was taking care of Eugenia. She lost her first husband about five years ago." He shook his head. "Tragic. Got thrown off his horse and broke his neck. Died just like that." He snapped his fingers. "Anyway, they'd both come from good families, had some money"—he smiled broadly—"and damned if she didn't fall in love with me." He shook his head, grinning. "Can you believe it? A lady? A first-class lady falling in love with me." He chuckled softly and his generous girth shook. "Beats all, don't it?"

"Congratulations Rub . . . Rowland. That's great," Reid said, thinking of his own past foray into the realm of love and respectability and wondering if Rubies' would turn out any better.

"Listen, I got an idea. My Eugenia's having a little soiree at our place tomorrow afternoon. Just a few good friends. Why don't you come? Meet some of the 'nice' people of Natchez?"

"Well . . ."

"C'mon. Never know. You might want to settle down around these parts. Life's good here, Sinclaire. Real good. You could change your name, like I did, and no one would be the wiser," Rubies said, laughing again.

Reid made up his mind quickly. He didn't have anything to lose by taking Rubies up on his offer to attend his wife's soiree, but he could have a hell of a lot to gain—if things went well. And changing his name just might get Lillian off his tail.

If nothing else, he might be able to help Rhonda. If she could land one of these Natchez genteels for a husband, Reid knew he'd never have to worry about his little sister again. Not that he minded worrying over her, but he

wanted the best for her, and following him around from
saloon to saloon, riverboat to riverboat, wasn't exactly what
he had in mind as "the best."

"Add Jonathan Reid to your guest list," Reid said, using
the name he'd dropped years ago. "What time does this
little party of your wife's start?"

Samantha tried not to look at Reid. She busied herself
behind the bar for a while, went to her office and attempted
to work on the accounts, stepped outside for a breath of
air, and once back in the saloon, pretended to listen to
more than one person's opinion of why the South should
secede from the Union. But none of her attempts to divert
her thoughts worked; she remained plagued by him.

She stood at the corner of the bar and surveyed the
crowded room. Foxe Brannigan looked like he was going
to be the high winner at his table tonight. Brett Tanner,
however, wasn't doing so well. Nathan Forest didn't seem
to be pulling any winning cards his way either. The way
things were going, she figured that by the end of the night
they'd be down another two or three players. Things were
proceeding quicker than she'd anticipated.

Her gaze wandered to where Reid was seated: the third
table in from the front door. He sat with his back to the
bar, one booted foot hooked over the bottom rung of the
chair of the person sitting next to him. She felt a slight
tightening within her breast as her gaze moved over him.
Annoyance, she told herself. He was too arrogant. Too
forward. And that annoyed her. She preferred a man to
be a gentleman. To treat a lady with respect and manners.

Samantha closed her fan, then dropped it, letting it
dangle from the silk cord that encircled her wrist. She had
things to do. But instead of turning away, she continued
to watch Reid.

He played his cards close to the vest, or flat on the table, taking no chance of anyone nearby spotting his hand over his shoulder. Some of his movements—the way he held his cards, the setting of his hat on one knee, the brand of cheroot he smoked, and the way he absently flicked the corner of one card with his thumb while waiting for the other players to make their moves—they all reminded her of Cord.

She studied his face unhurriedly, her eyes moving over every line of his profile, appreciating the symmetry and aquiline definition.

Reid turned then, as if feeling her gaze on him, and looked back at her, satisfaction and maybe a hint of wry amusement in his eyes as they met hers.

Samantha felt a flush of warmth sweep through her and quickly turned away. *He's no good,* she told herself sternly. *No better, really, than Valic Gerard or Dante Fourneir. Worse maybe.*

He hadn't gotten much sleep, his mind refusing to cooperate and stop conjuring up images of Samantha to torture his libido. Then this morning, that woman checking into one of the other rooms on his floor sounded like a banty hen whose tail feathers were being plucked as she screeched orders and demands to the porter. Reid drew a hand over his eyes in another effort to rub away the sting of a nearly sleepless night. He reined his horse in before a set of tall pillars that framed a curving drive, and stared in surprise. This couldn't be Rubies's house. He'd followed the man's directions, but this just couldn't be right. Reid glanced at the pillar. Upon a small brass plaque attached to it was engraved the name Bigelow. He laughed to himself, and looked back at the house. Actually it was a mansion, and sat at the end of a curving drive like a white jewel. Six Doric pillars graced the front gallery, dark green shutters adorned every tall window, and a half dozen dormer windows peeked out from a sloping slate roof. Tall live oaks, their spreading, gnarled limbs heavily draped with Spanish moss, framed it on either side, while a profusion of blooming flowers cast a rainbow of color to each side of the shallow, brick entry stairs.

If not for the music wafting to him on the still afternoon air, and the sight of at least sixty or seventy people milling about the side of the house and within the shade of a tall oak, Reid would have been sure he had the wrong place.

He urged his horse up the drive.

Had some money. Reid felt like laughing at Rubies's words. His wife obviously had more than "some" money. Either that or Rubies had staked himself to one hell of a poker game before his untimely "demise."

"Reid," Rubies said, as Reid handed the reins of his mount over to a footman minutes later.

Rubies walked toward him, hand outstretched. Rubies the gambler had been left far behind, in another part of the world, another lifetime. Now he looked as if he'd been born to royalty.

Reid laughed. "You know Rubies . . . Rowland," he corrected himself hurriedly, not wanting to give the big man away to any of his guests, "I never would have pictured you in something like this." He swept his hand toward the house. "You always seemed to like being on the move."

"C'mon," Rubies said, draping an arm around Reid's shoulders and dropping his voice low. "As one old riverboat gambler to another, I think there's a few people here you should definitely meet."

Reid looked at him skeptically. "I've never known you to do anything out of the goodness of that stone you have for a heart, *Rowland,*" he said, chuckling as he put an emphasis on Rubies new name, "so tell me, what do you get out of it if anything comes of these 'introductions'?"

"Oh, just a little finder's fee." Rubies grinned. "Just a little finder's fee, and maybe a bit of a real challenge at the poker games these gents hold up here Top-the-Hill if we can entice you to stay. I'll tell you, I love to win as much as the next man, but I like a little derring-do, you know what I mean? And not a one of these gents could bluff their way out of a teacup. But of course, it's a different life up here. Slow and easy. Quiet. Sometimes too damned quiet." He raised his hand toward a tall man who looked old enough to have fought in the Revolutionary War, and thin enough to be blown away by a faint breeze. "Benjamin."

The man turned toward them.

"Eugenia would have my hide though," Rubies continued in a whisper, as they walked toward the old man, "if I raised any kind of ruckus up here. It can get downright boring sometimes, but I gotta admit, the security of a home, a wife, and"—he winked slyly—"a nice little nest egg, is a real satisfying feeling to a man my age."

Reid's eyebrows soared. He'd known Rubies for about twelve plus years, and the man looked exactly the same as the first day Reid had met him.

"Benjamin Moreleigh," Rubies said, as they stopped before the old man, "I want you to meet an old friend, Jonathan Reid. He's from up north, been dabbling in the shipping business for a while," Rubies said, chuckling at his own pun. "Transport, export, import, that kind of thing." He grinned at Reid. "Did pretty good for himself, and now he's looking to invest in our little valley here."

An hour later Reid had been introduced to just about every man Rubies had business dealings with, and then some, and had been offered several very tempting investment opportunities of his own.

"Aren't you interested in making the acquaintance of any of the ladies here this afternoon, Mr. Reid?"

He turned at the sound of the sultry voice that held just a touch of poutiness to it.

Her blue eyes flashed up at him, and she smiled coyly.

"I'm sorry," Reid said, and tilted his head in acknowledgment.

She held out her hand. "Then prove it, sir." The invitation in her eyes was as far from hidden as her challenging words.

Reid took her hand, bemused by her impudence, a quality not possessed or appreciated by too many women of refinement. She looked slightly familiar, but he couldn't figure why, since he was sure they'd never met. Her eyes were as blue as the sky, her hair dark, and her skin the creamy hue of a freshly blossoming magnolia. A very beautiful woman, and obviously not afraid to speak her mind. "My pleasure," Reid said, his gaze slipping over her quickly, and confirming the first impression he'd had, that she was a very enticing woman. "Jonathan Reid." He pressed his lips to her offered hand.

She smiled. "Clarissa Beaumont."

"Well, Miss Beaumont, may I make up for my lack of manners, and have this dance?" He urged her toward the makeshift dance floor that had been set up in the adjacent gardens. "And then," he said, his tone deep, drawling, and suggestive, "maybe we can become better acquainted."

She slipped gracefully into his arms. "A dance is nice, Mr. Reid," Clarissa said, a sultry, coy look in her eyes. "But wouldn't you rather get better acquainted by taking me for a ride through the countryside tomorrow?" Clarissa asked as they waltzed. "Alone?"

Reid laughed. "Are you always so bold, Miss Beaumont?"

Clarissa's smile was wicked. "Are you always so evasive, Mr. Reid?"

He saw the challenge in her eyes. Perhaps there was more life Top-the-Hill than Rubies realized. Especially if it concerned Clarissa Beaumont. "Sorry, you just caught me by surprise, that's all."

"Good. Does my being bold bother you?"

"No." He caught sight of a man watching them, the scowl on his face looking nothing if not murderous. "But I have a feeling it bothers that gentleman over there, who I believe, has been watching us ever since we took to the dance floor." He nodded toward the man standing near one of the serving tables.

Clarissa glanced in the direction Reid indicated. "Oh, him." She tossed her head and smiled back at Reid. "That's just my fiancé, Phillip."

Reid nearly choked on a laugh of surprise. "Then I guess he has good reason to object," he said. "To both your invitation into the country, and about our dancing together."

"He has no reason at all," Clarissa snapped, "and no right."

"But if you're engaged to be . . ."

"Phillip knows I haven't really made up my mind about . . . things, but he insists we not break our engagement, so . . ." She shrugged. "He insists on considering himself still my fiancé and . . ." She laughed softly. "Maybe he is, and maybe he's not. I haven't decided."

"I think you're an interesting woman, Clarissa Beaumont," Reid mused.

"Does that mean we're going on that ride?"

Could he so easily, without much effort on his part, actually accomplish the same thing as Rubies Bigelow? The real question was, however, did he want to? He looked down at Clarissa. Finding out the answer to that question might just be quite pleasureable. "It would be my pleasure, Miss Beaumont."

She smiled. "Call me Clarissa. After all, we are going on that ride tomorrow. Alone."

Brett Tanner was disqualified. So were Jeffers Montayne and four other men.

Samantha smiled at Jake. "If things keep going at this rate, I just might be playing winner take all before week's end."

"Just hope the winner's you," Jake grumbled, staring at Reid. "Ain't seen him lose more than a hundred dollars all night."

"He's not the only good poker player in the room," Samantha said. "Foxe Brannigan isn't doing so badly." She refused to let her gaze wander to where Reid was sitting.

Her gaze fell on Valic Gerard, who smiled as his eyes caught hers. She might have to let anyone who had the money play in the competition, but she didn't have to like them. Or be friendly with them.

Samantha shuddered as a hot flood of loathing rushed through her veins. If there was ever a man who reminded her of a snake, a very ugly, very poisonous, very deadly snake, it was Valic. She knew some women considered him devastatingly handsome, but she wasn't one of them. Oh, she could see his good looks, even admit to them, but she also knew what lay behind them, who the real Valic Gerard was . . . and it wasn't the polished, oh-so-charming rake he pretended to be.

His brown eyes were so dark they bordered on being black, and the slight upward turn at their corners gave an almost exotic slant to his features. Extremely high cheekbones, a straight nose that flared just slightly, and dramatically at the tip, and black hair, slicked straight back, accentuated the impression of good looks.

The women who didn't see him for what he really was were fools. He had murdered Samantha's stepfather, though because Staunton had been foolish enough to accept Valic's challenge to a duel, there was nothing the law could do about his death. But it had been murder as surely as if he'd shot Staunton in the back. But killing Staunton hadn't been enough. Valic had proceeded, all quite legally of course, to take almost every worldly possession the Beaumonts had owned, and called it payment on a gambling debt. She'd learned that his arrogance and audacity had no bounds, however, when he'd come to her and explained that she could save her family, and her precious Riversrun, by marrying him.

She would have rather been thrown into a pit of water moccasins.

A shudder swept up her back, but whether from the thought of being in a hole with a pile of squirming, deadly snakes or being married to Valic she wasn't sure. Both thoughts were equally repulsive.

Samantha had discovered something else that day as well, but it was something about herself: she'd found out just how deeply she could hate another human being.

And now, as if all her past disasters weren't enough to teach her a lesson, she was attracted to a man who was not only a gambler, but a lothario and a murderer. It was becoming quite evident that she didn't learn a thing from her past mistakes. Or at least, her heart didn't.

The stale air of the crowded room combined with the gray haze of smoke created by the mens cigars, cigarillos, and cheroots filled her lungs and seemed to permeate and press in on her. The room seemed suddenly too small, too closed, too devoid of air. She couldn't breathe. Her temples began to ache. Her stomach roiled. Samantha glanced at Jake. "I need to get some fresh air."

After weaving her way past the patrons crowding the

bar, she stepped past the swinging entry doors and out onto the covered gallery. It was late, well past one in the morning, and the games would be over any minute anyway, so no one would miss her now.

The smell of the river met her nostrils the moment she stepped onto the boardwalk, and the sultry air of the night wrapped around her and caressed her bare arms. The storefronts and warehouses along the river's docks were closed tight for the night. Samantha walked slowly toward Falconer's Landing, where huge, tightly bound bales of cotton were stacked everywhere, along with wooden crates full of any variety of things, farm equipment, and even a mule or two waited for the roustabouts who would show up at dawn and load them onto the boats.

Several riverboats, their tall black smokestacks and giant paddle wheels glistening in the pale moonlight, were docked at the landing as well as several more to her right at Forsythe and Michie Landings. To her left Spark's Landing held only a few keelboats and cargo barges, unusually light traffic for the time of year.

The music blaring from the saloons on Silver Street became fainter the further she walked.

The gently lapping waves of the murky river sloshed against the docks' pilings, and tiny diamond points of light drifted upon the moving water in reflection of the bright stars that dotted the night sky overhead. The air was cooler here by the water, though no less humid, the sounds of Under-the-Hill softer, and a slight breeze rustled through the trees along the shoreline, whistling softly in and out of the cabinways of the elegantly built riverboats that gently rocked and swayed upon the water.

The melancholy whine of a screech owl suddenly pierced the air and Samantha jumped, then smiled at her own foolishness. An old superstition she'd once heard the slaves at Riversrun talk about flitted through her mind. They'd believed the doleful cries of the "shivering owl," as they'd called them, were of death or dire trouble, and their remedy had been a quick handful of salt thrown into the fire to nullify the evil forebodings.

The owl's whine stopped abruptly and feathered wings suddenly flapped against the night air, causing a soft swishing sound. Samantha turned toward a nearby stack of crates just in time to catch sight of a small owl swoop down, catch its prey, and fly back into a cluster of trees.

The shivering owl's cry had indeed been one of foreboding, she thought, for whatever small creature had just found itself the owl's prey.

Samantha paused at the edge of the wharf and stared out across the dark river, but the scenery before her was no longer what she was seeing. Instead, her mind was fixated upon the image of a tall man with dark blond hair and mesmerizing eyes the color of cinnamon and amber.

She nearly groaned aloud at realizing where her thoughts had wandered. Blackjack Reid Sinclaire. A gambler. She was attracted to a blasted gambler. She had sworn it would never happen again. Every instinct in her railed against the very thought . . . but she couldn't deny that there was something about him that brought out feelings in her she didn't welcome.

A string of curses she wouldn't dare mutter in front of anyone slipped softly from her lips. She didn't even dare to think what Cord would do if he found out she was attracted to Reid Sinclaire. And if he knew Sinclaire had kissed her . . . The thought sent her speculations whirling. She really didn't want to even contemplate what could happen.

Samantha watched a small mouse run across the dock.

The games wouldn't last much longer, she told herself. The way things were progressing, it would only be a few more days, then it would be time for the final round. Maybe Reid would be gone by then.

The thought should have lightened her mood, but it didn't. Sighing, Samantha turned to walk back to the Goose. Wandering about the docks in the middle of the night feeling sorry for herself wasn't going to solve or change anything. She'd just have to exert a little caution, and a whole lot of self-restraint.

Suddenly, three men stepped out from behind a stack of cotton pales, blocking her path. Moonlight glinted off of a knife one of them held, while another swung a length of rope back and forth before him, its ragged end brushing across his badly scuffed boots.

She tried to see their faces, but their hats were pulled low, and the night was too dark. *Don't panic,* she told herself, and drew her shoulders back stiffly. She knew most of the men who regularly traveled the river. Once they recognized her, they would leave her be.

"Well, whaddywe got here, Argus?" the man on the left sniggered, spitting a mouthful of dark liquid onto the rough planking near Samantha's feet.

She jumped back from the disgusting pool of black saliva that had just missed hitting the hem of her skirt, realizing at the same time, with a sinking feeling, that she'd never seen these men before.

"Looks like a real purty one, Smithy," Argus said, and took a step toward Samantha.

She stiffened, but made no move to retreat. "I'm Samantha," she said coolly, hoping just her name would get them to back off. A lot of men had a reputation on this river, but she had one, too, and it was well respected.

"Samantha," one of the men echoed. "Well, Samantha," he said, dragging out her name sarcastically, "whadya say we have us a little party, huh? Jus' you and me and

Argus and Paddy." He jerked a thumb toward the other men.

The breath caught in her throat at his words and a surge of panic enveloped her.

The quietness of the night suddenly beat down on her.

Samantha fought to keep her senses, knowing she was lost if she didn't. The last thing she could allow them to see was that they'd frightened her.

The men moved closer, out of the shadow of the stacked bales of cotton.

Moonlight fell on them, and Samantha saw their faces. The sinking feeling knotted in the pit of her stomach intensified. She'd been right: they were strangers. A shiver raced up her spine as her mind spun, trying to decide what to do, how she was going to get away from them.

"Yeah, you look like you'd enjoy a party, missy. And we're just the ones to show you a good time."

The man called Smithy took another step toward her, and pushed his hat back off his forehead. His face was unshaven, huge jowls drooped from either side of his face, framing fleshy lips and a fight flattened nose. Samantha watched in disgust as the spittle of tobacco juice ran down his chin and his mouth reased into a leering grin.

"I was just leaving, gentlemen," she said, trying to sound commanding. "So, if you'll excuse me?" She started forward, as if to brush past them.

"Nah, I don't think so, missy," Argus said, stepping in front of her. His skeletal frame seemed almost frail, but the boney, callus-covered fingers that suddenly reached out and wrapped around her arm were as strong as an eagle's talons.

Samantha tried to jerk away.

"C'mon darlin'," the man the other had called Paddy said, "don't ya wanna have a little fun tonight?" He reached out a huge hand and slid his fingers across her cheek. "Be a shame to let such a good night go to waste."

Samantha shrank from his touch and whipped her head away. Fear lodged in her throat as her heart hammered wildly against her breast. She could scream at the top of her lungs, and no one was likely to hear. Then she remembered the derringer tucked deeply within her pocket. If she could get her hand into the skirt, she could reach the small gun.

"I don't think she likes you any, Paddy," Argus said.

"Well, Arg, maybe she'll change her mind after we show her how lovin' Kentucks can be."

"Yeah." Argus sneered and jerked her toward a nearby keelboat that was tied to the dock.

"Let me go," Samantha screamed, trying to jerk free. He was holding her right arm, and the gun was on her right thigh. She twisted around, flailing against Argus with her free hand, ramming her fist into his chest. She tried to kick at his legs, but he was hauling her across the landing so fast she needed her feet beneath her just to keep her balance and keep from falling.

"Dang it, Argus," Paddy growled, "keep that she-cat quiet. We don't want no constable after us just 'cause we're out to have a little free fun with a whore."

"Whore?" Samantha screeched, indignation overriding her fear. She lunged toward him, reaching out to claw his face with her fingernails.

Smithy laughed as Paddy hurriedly jumped back to avoid her hand.

"Sure got a mouth on her," Paddy said.

Argus jerked violently on Samantha's arm. "Yeah, and she's gonna quiet it, right now." His hand swung out and struck her squrely across the side of the face. She staggered backward, dizzy, but he maintained his grip on her arm and yanked her toward him. "You ain't going nowhere but where I say."

Samantha blinked rapidly. She had to stay calm, had to get away from them. She reached across herself, as if holding a stomach suddenly queasy with fear, and plunged her free hand into the folds of her skirt. Her fingers found the handle of the derringer and wrapped around it. She dug her heels into the planks beneath her feet.

Argus felt her resistance and with an angry scowl, turned his hand raising in the air again.

"Don't," she said, whipping the gun out and ramming it into his stomach. "Unless you want to die."

Surprise raised his brows, and his arm slowly lowered.

"Now, let go of me, or I swear, I'll kill you," she said softly, fear and anger causing a quake in her voice.

Argus instantly released his grip on her arm, but before she could do more than step away from him, strong hands flashed down on either side of her from behind and smashed against her fore arms. Samantha screamed and the gun flew from her grasp and skittered across the rough planking of the dock.

"Tar and blazes, Argus," Smithy said, grabbing her. "Can't you even keep hold of a bitty thing like her?" He bent and scooped up the derringer, then dropped it into his shirt pocket and straightened. He grabbed Samantha's breast, his short, grimy fingers digging into her flesh. She cringed against the pain and tried to jerk away from him, but the man called Paddy stepped up and stood directly at her back, grabbing her by the upper arm and holding her in place.

Smithy's fingers squeezed harder, his dark, beady little eyes bore into hers, and a wide, ugly grin pulled at his lips.

She twisted frantically. Paddy's hold on her arms tightened, while Smithy's fingers dug deeper into her flesh.

Pain filled her now, and her eyes burned with unshed tears.

Smithy abruptly released her and laughed. "See, guys, now that's how you keep 'em in line. Show 'em who's the boss." He grabbed Samantha's arm again and yanked her away from Paddy and toward one of the keelboats. "C'mon, girlie, we got a party to start."

Samantha drew on what little strength she had left. "Let me go!" She tried to twist away, knowing it might be her last chance.

"I don't think the lady wishes to accept your hospitality, gentlemen."

Startled by the interruption, the three men whirled around, looking for whoever had spoken.

Argus roughly jerked Samantha to him, forcing her to stand in front of him as if a shield. "Who's there?" he demanded, his free hand inching toward the gun tucked into the waistband of his baggy trousers.

"I wouldn't touch that gun if I were you, friend," Reid drawled easily, stepping from the shadows. Pale moonlight washed over him, settling upon the black rim of his hat, pulled low onto his forehead and leaving his face in shadow, and his broad shoulders, the black broadcloth of his jacket catching the light and devouring it. If anyone looked the epitome of menace, he did, and Samantha had never been so glad to seen anyone in her entire life.

Silence hung heavy in the air as the men stared at Reid, silently sizing him up, and assessing their situation.

Argus's fingers tightened their hold on Samantha, digging into her soft flesh under her arm, and she winced, biting down on her lower lip to keep from crying out.

Paddy snickered, and shuffled a foot. "Hell, he ain't nothing, Argus."

Samantha tried to hold herself stiffly away from her captor, and kept her eyes on Reid, praying he wasn't here

alone, that he had someone nearby to back him up. Otherwise they were probably both goners.

"Whaddya want, dandy?" Argus growled. His whiskey
and tobacco tainted breath wafted past Samantha and
nearly made her gag. She gritted her teeth and swallowed
the bile that tried to rise into her throat.

"I want you to let the lady go," Reid said simply, choos-
ing to ignore the man's insult. "Otherwise"—he shrugged
nonchalantly—"I might have to kill you, and I'm sure
you'd all find that a real shame."

Harsh, guttural guffaws filled the air as the three men
exchanged quick and overly confident glances.

"You're gonna kill us over this here *lady*?" Argus said,
sneering. "Well, first off, mister, she ain't no lady."

The men laughed again.

"And you're a might outnumbered to be talking so big,
ain't you, slick?"

Reid smiled. "Two against three? Not bad odds, really.
If they don't bother you, they suit me just fine." He turned
his gaze to Argus's cohorts. "What about you, gentlemen?
Those odds meet with your approval?"

The three men looked confused and their gazes jumped
around hastily, puzzled at Reid's reference to another party
and looking for someone hiding nearby.

"Whaddya mean two against three?" Argus said. "I don't
see nobody but you, and I might not be no slick like you,
but I can still figure that makes it three against one."

"Oh, sorry," Reid said, sounding slightly chagrined.
"Did I forget to introduce you boys to my friend?"

Samantha stared past him, expecting Jake or Cord to
step from the shadows.

No one appeared.

"Ain't nobody here but you," Paddy growled, taking a
threatening step toward Reid, the large, silver blade of the

knife gripped tightly in one hand glistening in reflection of the moon's glow.

With lightning speed, Reid's hand disappeared inside his coat and reappeared holding a gun. "Boys, this is Colt, one of my best friends."

He'd moved slightly, so that his face was now visible to them and they saw the deadly smile that drew at Reid's lips.

"Want to hear how he says hello?" Reid asked. His thumb pulled back the hammer.

"Dagnabit!" Smithy swore. "C'mon, Argus, I ain't about to get killed over a roll in the sack with no whore. Give her back before he goes crazy or something."

"Shut up, you whiny no good," Argus growled, still sneering at Reid as he kicked a foot at his friend. "I could crush this little lady's ribs in a flat second, you know." A vicious, self-satisfied grin split his face, and the arm he'd wrapped around Samantha's waist tightened until she gasped and struggled against him.

"Go ahead," Reid said, "and when the lady goes all limp on you and falls to the ground"—he shrugged nonchalantly—"I'll kill you, and maybe your friends, too." He looked at the other two men. "I figure that would just about even the score up, don't you, fellas?"

Samantha could sense Argus's indecision and feel his heart hammering in rapid thumps against her back. His breathing was ragged with apprehension now. She thought about trying to jab an elbow into his ribs or stomp on one of his feet, but fear that an abrupt action like that could result in his trigger finger flexing, which would send a bullet through her body, kept her still and indecisive.

"Aw, hell," Argus suddenly spat.

Instant relief filled Samantha at the resignation she heard in the keelboatman's tone.

He pushed her roughly away from him. "We were only

gonna have us a little fun, slick. Can't blame a man for that, now can ya?''

"Only when the lady's unwilling," Reid said, his finger remaining steady on the trigger of his gun. "And I'd say this lady is definitely unwilling."

Samantha turned to glare at the three men.

"Now, good night, gentlemen," Reid said.

"My gun," Samantha demanded, holding a hand out toward Smithy.

He slapped it onto her palm, then turned away.

The three men turned, and ambled down the landing.

"Didn't mean no real harm," Argus grumbled.

"Nothing but a whore anyway," Paddy said. "So what?"

"Yeah," Smith said, spitting out a wad of tobacco, so what?"

Samantha watched them until they were out of sight, thankful they were gone, but still spitting mad at what they'd intended to do.

Reid slid his gun back into its holster and looked at her. "Guess it was a lucky thing for you I came along, gorgeous. You all right?"

She had been about to say that exact thing, and thank him for risking his life for her, but he'd spoken first and, unreasonable as it might be, his arrogant tone swept all feeling of gratitude from her mind and prodded her temper. Her chin shot up defiantly and she glared at him. "I could have handled them," she said coldly.

"Oh, really? And just what were you waiting for . . . the appropriate moment?"

"I thought . . ."

"No, you didn't," he said, cutting her off. Anger that he knew was unreasonable and unwelcome overwhelmed him. "If you had, you wouldn't have come out here alone. What the hell were you thinking anyway?"

"It's none of your business what I was thinking." She

wanted to slap him, push him into the river, pick up one of the nearby crates and bash him over the head with it. He'd most likely just saved her life, or at the very least her virtue, but his insolence was more than she could stand.

Fury seemed to emanate from her like a live flame, and as far as Reid was concerned, it was totally unwarranted. He'd just saved her pretty hide, and she was mad at him. Some thanks.

"Now, if you'll excuse me, Mr. Sinclaire, I need to get back to the Goose and help close up." Grabbing up her skirts she started to rush past him.

"Yeah, well, you're welcome."

"Fine. Thank you," Samantha said, the words curt, her tone sharp. "You saved my honor, my person"—she threw up her arms dramatically—"maybe even my life. Now"— she glared at him—"feel better?"

An avalanche of emotion assaulted him. He wanted to slap some sense into her, and he wanted to kiss her until she had no defiance left in her. She was every man's nightmare and every man's fantasy all rolled into one. Without thought to his actions, he grabbed her arm. "No, I think I feel like hell, and as far as I'm concerned, it's all your fault. But this will help." He pulled her up against him, his arms going around her waist, crushing her to him and momentarily robbing her of breath.

Her gaze caught his in the split second that existed between them before his mouth descended upon hers, swift, hard, and deadly, a hunter rushing in for the kill.

A gasp struggled into her throat, but it was too late for release.

His lips were hard and hot as they descended on hers, branding her with a kiss that was more a hard, fiery demand than a caressing touch, its force meant to conquer her hesitations, command her surrender, and stoke her simmering desires.

She grabbed his arms, but instead of pushing him away as she should have, as she'd intended, she merely held on as wave after wave of hungry, pleasurable sensations rolled over her, like a trembling force of heat moving through her veins, rushing over her skin, consuming her.

She had felt desire before. It had stirred in her when Dante had kissed her. His embrace had chased away her loneliness and let her dream again—before his treachery had shown her what he was really like. But those long-ago kisses . . . that passion was nothing like this. Reid's kiss was a mastery of seduction, a hungry brush of flesh upon flesh that was igniting yearnings in her she'd never felt before, never imagined she would ever feel. They commandeered every cell in her body, pervading and spreading, vanquishing all thought or consideration from her mind but that of Blackjack Reid Sinclaire. A gnawing need she couldn't control moved rapidly through her body, invading her limbs, turning her languid in his arms, and threatening to banish reality from every crevice of her mind.

At the same time that the rest of the world, and all of its beautiful and ugly realities, seemed a thousand miles away, Samantha was overwhelmingly aware of everything about Reid: from the strength of his body wrapping about hers to the rapid pounding of his heart beneath the hand she had moved to rest upon his chest to the scent of his cologne, a fragrance that reminded her of exotic islands, blue skies, and pristine clouds. A sense of timelessness touched her, and for the first time in a very, very long time, Samantha felt as if she were right where she belonged, right where she had always wanted to be.

A scuffling noise sounded from another part of the wharf, loud against the otherwise silent night.

A woman's high-pitched voice suddenly sliced through the night. "You silly old coot, get your dirty hands off me now, you hear?"

Samantha jerked away from Reid and spun around.

A woman stumbled off one of the keelboats docked nearby. Her long, white-blond hair was a disheveled tangle about her face, and one sleeve of her red satin dress hung off her shoulder.

The boat's owner staggered after her. "Ah, c'mon, Prissy, me love, just give us one little bounce in the hay for ol' times' sake, huh, girlie?"

"Go bounce yourself a mule, old man," Prissy spat, and stomped her way down the wharf, not even glancing toward Samantha and Reid.

Samantha watched the woman leave, but she wasn't really paying any attention. Her mind was elsewhere, lost in a befuddled maze of confusion and fear. How could she have kissed him like that? It wasn't right. She hadn't meant to. He'd made her feel things she didn't want to feel . . . not with him.

She felt the cool air of the night against the burning surface of her skin, still hot from his touch. She felt as if she were on fire, as if she couldn't breathe.

Her heart beat frantically, and a little voice in the back of her mind yelled at her to run, while another urged her to turn around and throw herself back into his arms.

She turned and looked up at him.

Chapter Six

Clarissa twirled about in front of the full-length mirrors that were set into the doors of her armoire. "Perfect," she said, smiling at her reflection. "Absolutely perfect." The white day dress, with its dark blue velvet trim and matching bolero-style jacket accentuated her eyes as well as her petite figure. Sometimes she wished she was a little more voluptuous, like her sister, but men seemed to like her just the way she was. She pinched her cheeks to give them a little color, then propped her hands on either side of her waist and turned this way and that for a last assessing look. Maybe voluptuous belonged Under-the-Hill. She adjusted the little hat and veil that sat jauntily on her head.

If Dellie or Elyse knew what she was doing they'd both have hissy fits, but she didn't care. Why should she marry Phillip Letrothe? He was rich and handsome, but so was Valic, and she was certain Jonathan was rich, too, or Mr. Bigelow wouldn't have had him at the soiree and been introducing him to all of his friends. Anyway, Dellie and

Elyse just didn't understand. It was much more fun having several different beaus than being tied down to just one man.

Clarissa wrinkled her nose and sniffed at the thought. There would be plenty of time later during which she'd have to satisfy herself with only one man because she was married, but she was fairly certain she just wasn't quite ready to make that sacrifice just yet.

Anyway, if Samantha could have more than one man in her life, and she certainly had, how could she deny Clarissa the same delight?

And as far as Aunt Dellie was concerned . . . Clarissa chuckled smugly. Her spinster aunt probably had never even been kissed by a man, let alone felt even a stirring of excitement in her blood at being held and desired, so how could she possibly understand?

The sound of carriage wheels rolling over the crushed oyster shells that lined the narrow road in front of the Beaumont town house caught Clarissa's attention, and she ran to the window.

He was here.

Turning, she grabbed her reticule and dashed from the room. The last thing she wanted or needed was for Jonathan to come up to the door. Then she'd have to introduce him to Aunt Dellie, and Aunt Dellie would probably question the dickens out of him, and have another fit, just like she'd had when Clarissa told her the engagement to Phillip was off because Phillip was being a boor about things.

But of course that reaction had been mild compared to the one Dellie had exhibited when she'd learned that the "someone else" Clarissa was interested in then was Valic Gerard. Dellie's eyes had almost popped out of her head and she'd started throwing her hands about wildly, pacing the room, and screaming at Clarissa.

"Don't you realize that man murdered your father?"

"It was a fair duel," Clarissa insisted stubbornly. "Everyone says so."

"Your father had never fought a duel before in his life. He hadn't even held a rapier in years," Dellie said, angry now. "It was murder, plain and simple, and after that no-good scoundrel got rid of your father, he took everything away from us. Everything, Clarissa! He's the reason we were forced to leave Riversrun, the reason almost everything was auctioned off, the reason your sister had to . . ."

"My sister is doing exactly what she wants to do," Clarissa said, stamping her foot, "and that's what I intend to do, too. Exactly what I want. Anyway," she said haughtily, "Mr. Dutton told me that Daddy was so drunk every night that he could have played cards with a complete fool and lost. Valic didn't steal Riversrun, Aunt Dellie. Daddy just gambled it away."

Dellie stared at her. "Your father is probably rolling over in his grave right this minute, hearing you talk like this, young lady." She waved her hands about in frustration and disgust. "Just the thought of you being with that murdering no good thief gives me the shivers."

"Oh, Auntie, he's very nice. Really. He's a bit old, I know," Clarissa mused, "but he's charming, and handsome, and rich."

"He's a murderer," Dellie shrieked, fanning herself rapidly with a hand as if she were about to swoon. "Saints be with you, girl, I don't understand how you can't be ashamed to even be in the same room with that devil."

"Well, I'm not!"

Clarissa nearly cringed just remembering. That was a scene she didn't need to repeat. Clarissa practically flew down the staircase. "I'm leaving, Aunt Dellie. I'll see you later."

Dellie looked up from her needlepoint. "Leaving?" she echoed, frowning. "Where are . . . ?"

The front door closed and Clarissa hurried down the walkway, meeting Jonathan on his way to the door. She slipped her arm around his as he turned back toward the carriage. "Oh, isn't it a beautiful day for a carriage ride, Jonathan?" she said, smiling coyly and batting her eyes at him. "We should have asked Mary Twileigh and her beau to go with us and have a picnic."

For the next hour, Reid listened to Clarissa talk about this person and that person of Natchez. He hadn't made up his mind if he was going to try going the same route as Rubies. Marriage, a stable home, respectability. It was tempting, and obviously profitable, but he'd also tried that road already. The first time he hadn't quite made it to the altar, but the whole thing turned into a disaster just the same. The second had been even worse, it had left him almost penniless and wanted for murder.

Memory of that last day, when he'd gotten home early and walked in on Lillian and her lover, played swiftly through Reid's mind. He'd killed the man, but none of it had happened the way Lillian had claimed to the authorities, and it sure as hell hadn't been murder. More like an instinctive dive toward self-defense.

He threw his hat down on the table in the foyer. The night had been a total waste. He'd felt lucky, too, and what good had that done him. Bellivard, the sap, was going to get himself killed tomorrow in a duel, and all because he was moon-eyed over Waithe's daughter and had taken a few liberties with her. Their little ruckus had certainly ended any prospect of continuing their

*poker game, especially after Hunt and Beckwith had decided to
leave before Waithe took exception to them, too.*

*Reid poured himself a drink from the liquor cart in the parlor,
then trudged up the stairs. The last thing he wanted to do was
see Lillian, so if he was lucky, she was out. At the threater, or
someplace.*

*He opened the door to the bedchamber and stopped dead in his
tracks after taking only two steps into the room.*

*Lillian whipped around on the bed. "Reid!" she screamed,
grabbing for the sheet to cover her nakedness.*

The man beside her scrambled from the bed.

*Reid watched as he dived toward his trousers, but instead
straightened with a sword in his hand.*

"Reid, it isn't what you think," Lillian said hurriedly.

*He glanced at her. How could it not be what he thought? She
was naked, the man was naked, and they'd been in bed together.
In the bed Reid and Lillian shared. Unless they were playing strip
poker, there was only one other logical conclusion to come to. And
knowing Lillian, Reid felt certain that a game of strip poker was
the last thing she'd be doing in bed.*

*A smile tugged at the corners of his mouth as he looked back
at the man he recognized as Sir Percival Brownley. He had been
humping Reid's wife, and Reid felt like laughing. Not only did
he find he didn't care, but he was having difficulty not bursting
out in laughter at the sight of Brownley, buck naked, his private
parts dangling freely as he jittered about the room now, bran-
dishing his military dress sword.*

*"You are a swine, sir," Sir Percivil suddenly bellowed, and
slicing at the air like some medieval swordsman, he rushed at
Reid.*

*Startled, Reid reacted instinctively. He stepped back, drew the
gun that lay sheathed in its holster nestled against his ribs, and
fired.*

Lillian screamed.

Sir Percival stopped, looked down at the hole in his chest as it suddenly started spurting blood, then keeled over face first onto the floor.

"Murderer!" Lillian shrieked. "Murderer!" Grabbing her robe, she ran past him and down the stairs, screeching at the top of her lungs.

Minutes later the house was filled with police, Lillian was accusing Reid of murdering poor, poor Sir Percival in cold blood, and the authorities were talking like they were going to arrest him.

Knowing when his hand was played out, and another player had just bested him, Reid slipped quietly from the house when no one was looking.

Three days later, with wanted posters with a sketch of his face on them plastered all over London, he managed to disguise himself and take passage on a ship headed for St. George, Bermuda.

Rhonda had met him at the docks with her satchels. As their ship left dock, she'd filled him in on what had been happening. Lillian had claimed Sir Percival was merely a houseguest, and had done nothing wrong, but Reid, who'd been out playing cards and drinking, had come home, stumbled his way into the wrong room, and just up and killed poor Percival for no reason.

Shrugging those memories away, Reid turned his thoughts back to the situation at hand. He had to admit there would be advantages to staying in Natchez and following in Rubies's footsteps. Blackjack Reid Sinclaire was wanted for murder in England, and he had no doubt that sooner or later bounty hunters would be on his trail, if they weren't already. Possibly even Lillian herself. On the other hand, Jonathan Reid was nothing more than an honest businessman from up north, and he had the very respectable Mr. and Mrs. Rowland Bigelow to vouch for him.

And now maybe he even had the beautiful, if talkative and brash, Clarissa Beaumont.

"Oh, naturally Valic was jealous when he saw me with you at the soiree," Clarissa said and laughed, "and Phillip was furious, but I am not married to either one of them . . . yet . . . so"—she turned a beguiling smile on Reid—"I am free to see whomever I want. Even fall in love."

Reid glanced at her. She was smiling at him flirtatiously, her eyes full of daring.

There was obviously a lot more to Clarissa Beaumont than he'd at first thought. Rather than a simple but beautiful and outspoken Southern belle, he realized now she was a very conniving young woman, and one he might just have to exert a little caution toward.

"Anyway"—she slipped an arm around his and pressed against him—"it's not like Valic could believe I would actually be interested in him in that way." She laughed softly, as if to emphasize her comment.

"Really?" Reid mused. "Why not?"

Her delicately arched brows soared upward. "Well, he's a gambler, for heaven's sake. Oh, I mean, I know he's gotten into more respectable things now, business and such, but still. And anyway"—she dropped her voice to a whisper—"my late father had a run-in with him." She dabbed a lace-trimmed kerchief at her eyes. "Some people even called it murder, so you see, I couldn't possible feel anything *serious* for him."

"But you've let him court you," Reid said, surprised. "Isn't that a bit . . ."

"Unseemly?" Clarissa offered. "Some think so, but my father was . . . well, let's just say after the death of my mother he went downhill quite swiftly. Valic and my father fought a duel, Jonathan, over money my father owed him from gambling debts, and my father lost. Some people consider it murder, but I don't. And Valic really is a very nice man."

"Still," Reid said. "I would think you wouldn't want to have anything to do with him."

"Oh." Her smile instantly faded, and a frown pulled at her delicate features. "I hope this doesn't make you think less of me, Jonathan. Don't let the fact that Valic cares for me scare you away from me. I was only trying to look at things fairly when I met Valic. And anyway, I'd much rather be with you than Valic, naturally. I know you could never be like him, or do those kinds of things." She pressed up against him and touched her lips to his cheek.

Reid paused in the doorway of the Silver Goose, his gaze moving over the occupants of the room. Though he tried to tell himself he was merely sizing things up, looking for faces he recognized, he knew exactly who he was looking for. His roaming gaze immediately stopped as he spotted her standing at the far end of the bar.

Beautiful women were plentiful—he knew that. He'd met and bedded enough of them in his lifetime, but there was something about Samantha that made her stand out from all the rest and take his breath away.

If they had met at another time, under different circumstances . . . He shrugged the thought away. He'd come here to do something, and he was going to do it, regardless of any "ifs" that might pop up along the way.

He let himself go back to appreciating her beauty.

Light from the overhead chandeliers played upon the curls of her long hair, dancing within each wave, glistening off of the red strands that laced through the rich brown ones so that it appeared fire shimmered within the dark depths.

He wondered what it would feel like to slip his fingers within those rich tresses.

An image of Clarissa flashed through his mind, and he

realized that her hair was almost the same hue and he'd been unconsciously comparing the two women while staring at Samantha. But they were too different to compare, he told himself, then found himself doing it anyway. Samantha was fire. While his impression of Clarissa was that in spite of her unusual and lusty brashness, she was ice. Samantha's surroundings, her very way of life, put her on a lower stature of society than Clarissa, and she obviously had no blue blood running through her veins, yet she impressed him as a giver, someone who really cared about the welfare of others, especially those close to her. Clarissa, on the other hand, who'd had many of life's better opportunites presented to her on a silver platter, was definitely a taker.

Samantha turned, as if feeling his gaze on her, but as soon as their eyes met, she looked away and then signaled to someone on the other side of the room.

The man operating the wheel of fortune suddenly stopped it and rang a bell.

Silence descended throughout the Goose instantly.

"Gentlemen," the dealer called out, "take your seats please. The challenge is about to begin."

Reid walked to a table and sat down. He looked at the other men who'd already settled at the table, but he didn't know any of them. His gaze moved away in search of Samantha again, but she was gone. He looked around the saloon, expecting to see her standing near one of the tables, the stairs, or the opposite end of the bar. But there was no sign of her anywhere.

He pushed aside the sense of frustration that instantly threatened to overtake him. What did it matter if she was present or not? He had to keep his mind on the game.

Several hours later Reid had managed to win a thousand dollars and lose four thousand. He fanned the cards

cupped within his palm. It was a good hand. Three Jacks.
He discarded the other card.

The dealer tossed him a new one, facedown.

Reid slid it from the table and into his hand.

Damn. He was careful to keep his face expressionless.
Another eight.

One of the other men raised the bet.

Reid tossed two hundred dollars' worth of chips onto
the pile in the middle of the table, seeing the previous bet
and raising it by fifty dollars.

The man sitting to Reid's right slumped in his chair,
the movement so slight most would not notice. But Reid
did. The player to his left began to drum his fingers on
the green baize table as he squinted at his cards. The short
stub of a fat cigar clenched between his teeth wobbled
back and forth as he contemplated his next move.

Reid watched. Most men thought you won the game of
poker because of the hand you were dealt, but Reid knew
better. A good hand helped, obviously, but most times you
won because you read your players better than they read
you.

A squint of the eyes.

A slight settling into one's seat.

A frown, a sigh, a half mumbled curse.

The unconscious drumming of fingers, tapping of a foot,
or biting a lip. They were all telltale signs that relayed to
Reid more than instinct what kind of hand the other players were holding.

The stakes were at eight thousand dollars, the biggest
pot so far.

Reid was down four thousand, but the man with the
cigar was down ten. The man touched his small pile of
chips, hesitated, and rolled the cigar from one side of his
mouth to the other. Desperation was driving him now,
Reid thought, also noticing the slight veil of perspiration

that had begun to form around the man's hairline.
Another telltale sign.

With a final glare at his cards, the man straightened in
his chair, took a long, quick gulp of whiskey, slammed the
glass down and pushed every chip he had left on the table
in front of him to the center of the table. "I raise a thousand, and call," he said gruffly, his gaze meeting each of
the other players before skittering on to the next.

Reid and the four other men still left in the game spread
their cards on the table.

The man with the cigar looked at each hand for several
long, silent seconds, then threw his own cards down with
a mumbled curse. Pushing his chair back, he rose abruptly.

The chair tipped backward, then toppled to the floor
with a loud crash.

Several men at other tables whirled around.

Reid saw Jake, the huge red-haired brute who was Samantha's "bouncer," inch his way behind the man with the
cigar, his fists clenched and at the ready.

Across the room, Cord Rydelle's hand moved to rest on
the gun nestled in a holster beneath his coat.

Reid stiffened and with only a slight movement of his
arm sidled the derringer he kept tucked up his sleeve into
place. With a deft flick of his wrist the tiny double-barreled
gun would be in his palm and pointing directly at the
other man's forehead.

"Knew I shouldn't have come to this damned challenge
thing," the man mumbled, then spun on his heel and
walked out of the saloon.

Samantha looked around. Except for that one incident
with Tom Farrell an hour earlier, the games were progressing smoothly, and without problem. She could leave
for a while and not be missed, and she needed to leave,

because as many times as she fought it, she couldn't quite keep her gaze from straying toward Reid.

She suddenly wished she'd never made the challenge, that she'd thought of some other way to pay off Valic Gerard. At least then she wouldn't have met Blackjack Reid Sinclaire, wouldn't be struggling to fight off these traitorous feelings that welled up within her whenever she looked at him, whenever their eyes met, whenever he touched her.

Samantha felt her cheeks suddenly burn and abruptly turned toward the back hall. She was turning into a swooning ninny, and she didn't like it.

"Sam?" Cord said, as she started to pass him. "Anything wrong?"

She paused and shook her head. "No, I'll be back in a little while." She averted her face and looked back out at the men sitting around the tables, afraid Cord would see her tumultuous emotions displayed there. "I . . ." She didn't want to tell him where she was going. He always worried. He'd insist on escorting her. "I just need to sit down for a while, maybe close my eyes."

He nodded, but there was concern in his eyes. "You sure you're all right?"

"Fine. I'll be back out in a bit." She hurried to her office. Grabbing a flowing back cloak from a hook by the door, she wrapped it around herself, then tucked her hair beneath a wide brimmed black hat and pulled its attached veil netting over her face.

She returned to the door and opened it slowly, then peeked around the doorjamb and toward the saloon. Reid was talking with Curly and Jake. She stepped into the hall and hurried out the back door, hoping no one had spotted her.

Once outside, with her heart slamming against her breasts, as it did every time she sneaked away, she moved around the corner of the building to where she'd left her horse tied earlier. She hadn't intended to go until later, after they'd closed up for the night, but she couldn't wait, couldn't stay in there with *him* there any longer.

And once Cord thought about it when he noticed she wasn't in her office, he'd know where she had gone. He wouldn't like the fact that she'd snuck out on her own, but he'd know where she was.

Rogue whinnied softly upon seeing her.

"Easy boy," Sam said, running a hand caressingly over his neck. She checked the pocket sewn into the skirt of her gown and her fingers closed over the pearl handle of the tiny gun resting there. Cord had given it to her several years ago—after Dante.

Remembering that it hadn't done her much good on the landing, when those three keelboatment had decided she should join their party, didn't exactly bolster her confidence, but she wasn't going to stop going out just because something might happen. She'd lived in Under-the-Hill for eight years now, and that had been the first threat made against her.

She didn't need to check the garter that held secure to her thigh. She could feel the steel of the dagger secured there, and resting against her flesh as she raised her leg toward the stirrup.

Anyway, she'd been right. If those men had forced her onto their boat, she most likely could have defended herself and gotten away once she'd gotten hold of her knife.

Samantha urged Rogue into a swift trot. Within minutes horse and rider had climbed the steep incline of Silver Street that led up to Top-the-Hill. She guided the huge black gelding down the dark streets of Natchez at a brisk pace, Rogue's black coat, and her black cape, allowing them to nearly disappear into the night's darkness. Nevertheless, she made sure to stay close to the side of the roads and out of the ghostly yellow light of the street lamps, as usual. No sense taking needless chances of running into anyone.

No one had ever discovered her secret, or her visits, and she had to make certain no one ever did.

Moving onto Wall Street, the bright lights of Choctaw Mansion shone down on her as she passed. Memories crowded in on her instantly, as they did every time she came Top-the-Hill. It seemed a lifetime ago that this had actually been "her part of town." Years ago, when she had still been Elyse Beaumont, and the world had been her playground, she had attended parties in almost every great house in Natchez. Choctaw, Monmouth, Dunleith, Evergreen, Cherokee, The Briers, Stanton Hall, Arlington, Lynnwood, Richmond. She checked the names off in her head as she rode. Glouchester, The Laurels, Rosalie, Rosewood, Hope Farm, Elmwood, The Elms. Samantha was a bit taken aback to realize she couldn't remember all of them anymore. There were at least another two dozen, and she couldn't recall them to memory.

A hot flash of tears filled her eyes. She couldn't remember them . . . she was moving farther and farther away from that life, a life that had once been hers. And what was she moving toward?

Nothing, a small voice in the back of her mind whispered cruelly. *Nothing.*

A few yards down the road more than a dozen carriages lined the street at the base of a drive that led up a small knoll. Stanton Hall stood upon the crest of the knoll like a glittering white palace. A magnificent jewel shining against the night. She'd attended a garden soiree there one afternoon with Loren.

Memory of her first fiancé brought a rush of anger slicing through her. Everything had seemed so perfect then. She'd been engaged to marry the man she had been in love with since she was a little girl. They were going to build their own house on land his father was going to give them as a wedding present; they were going to fill it with children and spend the rest of their lives together. But the moment it had become known about town that her father had gambled away everything, that the Beaumont fortunes were gone and their plantation had been claimed by Valic Gerard as payment for gambling debts, Loren had broken their engagement.

"I'm sorry, Elyse, but I'm sure you understand my position."

She still remembered the coolness in his voice, the ice in his eyes, the overall contempt that had radiated from him. Yes, she'd understood his position. Her dowry was gone, and without it, Loren D'Aneleuoux was no longer interested in marrying her. And he wasn't sorry at all.

Well, from what Dellie had told her, and as far as Samantha was concerned, Loren had gotten exactly what he'd deserved. He had married Francine Brannene, who'd walked down the aisle accompanied by a huge dowry, but rumor was that Francine was as frigid as the North Pole, as barren as the Mohave desert, and married life had turned her sweet tongue into a serpent's whip.

Dellie had expected that news to thoroughly delight her, and Samantha had, too, but surprisingly it didn't. It was satisfying, she'd admit, but she also felt sorry for Francine. She'd obviously thought Loren had loved her and realized her mistake too late.

Music filled the air around the brightly lit grounds of Stanton Hall and cut through Samantha's memories. Near a cluster of parked carriages a group of lackies knelt in a circle around a pile of money. One man raised his hand and tossed a pair of dice while the others mumbled encouragement and threw down their greenbacks.

Samantha nudged Rogue with her heel, urging him to pick up his pace. She tugged at the dark veil over her face as they passed the men. Through the years luck had been with her and none of her customers, or anyone else she'd come in contact with from Top-the-Hill had ever recognized her, and she didn't want that to happen now when they were so close to Clarissa's making a good marriage.

Even recognition by someone's servant could result in disaster.

Clarissa had been only nine when Staunton had been killed and they'd lost Riversun. Since then, Sam and Dellie had given her the best of everything money could buy so that she would have the life Sam should have had but never would. But it had meant that Sam had been forced to give up her dream of ever getting Riversrun back. There wasn't enough money to keep the saloon going, support Dellie and Clarissa, and save enough to eventually buy back the plantation.

The fact that Valic had just let it sit falling into decay made her hate him all the more, and it was something she didn't understand, unless it was just his way of getting continual revenge on her for refusing to marry him. Whenever she went riding and passed Riversrun, once one of the most beautiful plantations in the area, she looked at the run-down wreck it had become and thought of a hundred ways to murder Valic Gerard.

Dellie called it torturing herself, but Samantha called it remembering.

She pulled Rogue around to the rear of the house Dellie and Clarissa shared. It was nearing midnight, but the parlor glowed with light. Sam tied the gelding beneath the drooping branches of a myrtle tree and quietly slipped onto the rear porch, and then through the back door.

"Elyse!" Dellie cried, setting her teapot back on the stove and rushing across the room to wrap Samantha in her arms. "Oh, I'm so glad you came. I've got just oodles to tell you, and I've missed you terribly, my dear." Dellie's ample figure seemed to quiver with excitement. "It's been what, over a good month since you were up here last? Way too long, my dear, way too long."

"It's only been three weeks, Auntie," Sam said, removing her cape and hat. She bent down and kissed her aunt's cheek. Being called Elyse felt so foreign to her now. "Is everything all right, Auntie?" Dellie's hair looked streaked with much more gray than she remembered. And had those faint dark circles been under her eyes the last time she'd been here? "No problems?"

"I'm fine, honey, fine. Just a bit tired. Oh, but wait until you hear the latest," Dellie said, rolling her eyes and putting a limp wrist to her forehead. "You won't believe the half of what's been happening around the Hill my dear, not a half of it."

Sam groaned inwardly and followed her aunt into the rear parlor. Dellie dearly loved to gossip and seemed to have no end of tidbits she stored up to tell Samantha. "I meant is everything all right with you and Clarissa?" she said, knowing that Dellie would get to that later, after she forced Sam to listen to every other bit of gossip about what was happening with the people who lived Top-the-Hill.

"Come on, child, sit down and let's have some tea. Maribelle just bought a new kind." Dellie settled onto a double settee, and Sam took the chair opposite her. "Well, now, where should I start? Oh, I know," she said, a gleam in her eyes now, "Gaylon Jennings's girl Priscilla." She laughed. "Miss Prim and Proper, remember her, Elyse? Well, prim and proper my foot. Little hussy ran off last week and married Joe Waycross. You remember him, Elyse. He moved here a few years back from Texas."

Sam smiled, having absolutely no idea who Joe Waycross was, and not caring in the least.

"And everybody figures Priscilla is already heavy with child." The gleam in Dellie's eyes turned amusingly wicked as she smiled. "Stomach pooch, you know." She patted her own stomach, then clicked her tongue and shook her head. "Such a shame. Poor Gaylon and Suellen. They had their hearts set on her marrying royalty, you know? What with her being their only child."

Half an hour later Dellie finally ran out of gossip.

"And how are you and Clarissa?" Sam asked again. "Everything all right?"

"I'm fine," Dellie said, "as usual." She shook her head. "But you know Clarissa. If she isn't stirring up trouble, I swear I think that girl isn't happy. Just one thing after another with her."

Sam frowned, and instantly stiffened. "What's happened?"

"Well, you know she broke her engagement to Phillip."

Sam felt her heart sink to her toes. "No, I didn't know. I haven't seen you for several weeks, Auntie, remember? I thought everything was fine between them."

"Well, so did I, then your sister went and started swooning over Valic Gerard."

"Valic Gerard?" Samantha repeated. She'd hoped her aunt hadn't known about Valic and Clarissa.

Dellie waved a hand in front of her face, as if to ward off a fainting spell. "Yes, and I think it's just scandalous. That girl is going to ruin her reputation, Elyse. Just ruin it for sure if she keeps on with this craziness. I don't know what's gotten into her."

Samantha didn't either, but she wished she did.

"I think it's just a little prewedding rebellion thing. At least I hope that's all it is. But I swear, I wish she would have picked someone else, anyone else, to get rebellious with. That man is such a downright snake in the grass it just makes me shudder to even think he's back in town. The nerve of him!"

"I agree."

"But now she's . . ."

Sam saw the deep worry that came into her aunt's eyes. "She's what? What?"

"She's seeing someone else, too, but she won't even tell me this one's name. Can you imagine that? Saints preserve, it makes me wonder if she hasn't found someone worse than Valic Gerard."

Samantha doubted that was possible.

"I heard one of her friends refer to him as John, or something like that, but Clarissa won't say a thing. Tight mouthed as a dog with a bone, I'll tell you. She just keeps saying when she's ready to marry, she'll let me know, and until then she plans on having a good time."

"She'll lose Phillip altogether," Sam said, "if she keeps this up."

"Yes, and he's just about the best catch in town," Dellie said. "Phillip Lethrothe. Oh, I swear, Clari's going to drive me to an early grave, worrying about her. You should talk to her, Elyse."

"Talk to who about what?" Clarissa asked, sashaying into the room.

Dellie looked taken aback. "Oh! I didn't know you were home, Clari."

"I just got here a few minutes ago. I was at Mary's and her brother brought me back. Now, talk to who about what?" she asked again, looking down at Samantha.

"Talk to you about breaking your engagement to Phillip, dating Valic Gerard, and now seeing someone you refuse to identify," Samantha said, figuring it wouldn't do any good to mince words with her little sister. If there was a more headstrong and impulsive person in the entire world, Samantha didn't know who they were and had no desire to meet them. Heaven forbid.

"Oh, that," Clarissa said.

"Yes, that," Samantha echoed, hoping the look on her

face conveyed the fact that she was in no mood to put up with a series of Clarissa's word games.

Suddenly someone's fist banged against the front door. "Clarissa."

"Oh, speak of the devil," Clarissa said, sarcasm dripping from her tongue as she rolled her eyes. "There's my beloved Phillip now." She turned and walked to the door, opening it wide.

Samantha hurriedly grabbed her hat and cloak and stepped into an adjoining room, silently cursing Clarissa for not giving her a few more minutes to get out of sight.

"Why, Phillip, dear, whatever are you doing here at this hour?" Clarissa said innocently.

"You've made a fool of me, Clarissa," he said angrily. "We were supposed to be married next month, and now you're running around town with Valic Gerard and that . . . that . . . Northerner. Everyone's talking about it, and I just won't have it anymore, you hear?"

"Oh, dear," Dellie said, looking stricken. "Not another scandal."

"Oh, piddle," Clarissa said. "Scandal-mandal. Whatever good is trying to be proper all the time if it means you can't have any fun?" She looked back at Phillip. "And you will not tell me what to do."

Samantha's breath caught in her throat as anger burned in her chest. What was Clarissa thinking? Did she want to ruin everything they'd tried to do for her? Sam moved to peek around the corner of the doorway.

Phillip was an extraordinarily handsome man, tall and dark, with a set to his features that hinted at some long past ancestral connection to royalty.

Why didn't Clarissa ever think about what she was saying and doing? Samantha wondered, and sighed. But she'd given up trying to find an answer to that question long ago. Clarissa was what she was. She spoke up, or acted up, on impulse, and damn the consequences.

"Clarissa, I insist you make a choice," Phillip said. "Me, Valic, or that dandy you were with today."

"You were spying on me." Clarissa stamped her foot. "How dare you?"

"I didn't have to spy on you. Everyone in town saw you drive off with him."

"And naturally they all ran to tattle to you."

"Choose, Clarissa," Phillip repeated. "Me, Valic, or him."

"Oh, don't be such a silly goose," Clarissa cooed, reaching out to gently caress his lean cheek. "You know how I'm crazy about you, Phillip."

"Then you won't see them anymore?"

Her bottom lip dropped into a pout. "Oh, no. You want me to be sure how I feel, Phillip, don't you? Before we set a wedding date?"

He stepped away from her, his gray eyes flashing with indignation. "Dammit, I mean it, Clarissa. I won't have my fiancée running around town with another man. No! Two other men!"

"Fine," Clarissa said, stamping her foot. "Then I'm not your fiancée anymore."

Phillip's mouth dropped open. "You . . . you . . . can't mean that," he stammered, shock flashing from his dark eyes. "What about all our plans?"

Samantha had to restrain herself from charging back into the parlor and throttling her little sister.

"Well, you're the one who told me to make a choice, Phillip," Clarissa said. "So now I've made it. I'm not ready to marry you, and if you won't accept that for now, then . . ." She shrugged.

"Clarissa . . ."

She crossed her arms over her breast and glared at him, a stubborn gleam in her eyes.

Resolve suddenly turned Phillip's strong jaw to a slash of granite. "Fine," he snarled, "then goodbye." Spinning on his heel, he stormed from the house, slamming the front door resoundingly behind him as he left.

"Oh, Clarissa," Dellie wailed, "I can't believe you just did that."

"Neither can I," Samantha said coolly, and stepped into the room.

"Whatever is everyone going to say?" Dellie moaned, throwing herself back down on the settee.

"Oh, damn everyone," Clarissa said. "I don't care what they say. It's my life and if I don't want to marry Phillip now, I don't have to."

"Then maybe you'd better explain to us just what you have in mind for your life," Sam said softly.

"I don't know yet." Clarissa raised her chin defiantly. "I just know I'm not ready to marry Phillip."

"Because of Valic Gerard?" Samantha asked, praying he wasn't the reason.

She shrugged. A coquettish movement that annoyed Samantha. "Maybe."

Samantha knew if she tried to order Clarissa not to see any more of Valic Gerard, her rebellious little sister would probably just find the scoundrel that much more appealing. "Who were you with today, Clari?"

"You don't know him," she said haughtily.

"Then maybe Dellie should meet him."

"You can both meet him," Clarissa said, a devilish smile coming to her lips, "at the wedding."

"Wedding?" Dellie practically shrieked, and clutched at her heart.

One of Samantha's dark brows soared. "He's already asked for your hand in marriage?"

"No." Clarissa gave a little shake of her head that sent her dark curls flying about her shoulders. "But he will, and I just might accept, unless I decide to accept Phillip or Valic. Who knows? Maybe it will be none of them, and I'll meet someone else."

Samantha wondered if it was too late to send her little sister to the Ursuline convent in New Orleans.

By evening's end, Reid had not only won back all of his own money, but twenty thousand from the other men seated around the table.

Rising, he handed Samantha's bartender his winnings to hold until the next night, as did all the others in the room. He looked around for Samantha again, but didn't see her. Disappointment swept through him and he pushed it away, angry at himself for feeling it at all. There was plenty of time for Samantha . . . lots of time, in fact, if he decided that Rubies's little suggestion was worth acting on, and Clarissa Beaumont continued to be so willing.

Frustration gnawed at his insides. He had plenty of time.

So why did he feel like staying around until Samantha came back into the saloon?

Because he wanted her. There was no use denying it. He wanted her, and he'd never wanted to bed a woman so badly in his life. It was as if, with just a look, a smile, a word, she had clawed her way under his skin. It was more than just a part of his revenge now. He could have walked away from that if the need arose, but he knew he couldn't walk away from Samantha, not until he had her in his bed, until he felt the heat of her body joined by his, tasted the sweetness of her passion.

If he did walk away, the memory of her, the wanting of her would gnaw at his insides until it drove him crazy, and that was one place he didn't want to be.

One of the other men said something to him he didn't catch, then turned away and walked to the bar.

Reid grabbed his hat from a nearby chair. He'd heard about Samantha even before he'd heard about her challenge. Her name was known from one end of the river to the other and, he was sure, beyond. She had never been beaten at poker and never turned a friend in need away from her door. Some said she was Cord's mistress; others said no man had ever touched her. One thing they all agreed on though: no one knew where she'd come from. She'd just shown up in Under-the-Hill one day, the deed to an old hotel in her reticule, and began refurbishing it. A few months later she opened the Silver Goose for business.

Rubies had added an interesting story to the rest, however. Seems Samantha made the Goose a success on her own for the first couple of years, then she fell for Dante Fournier. That had surprised Reid. He remembered Dante: a real ladies' man, with a store of sweet talking lines a mile long. He was also one of the best cardsharps Reid had ever encountered. The man could cheat you blind with a smile on his face and walk away leaving you thinking you'd just had nothing more than a real bad stroke of luck.

She'd almost lost the Goose after Dante took off with all her money, then Cord had shown up and become her partner in the saloon and, most assumed, in her personal life as well.

Cord stepped up to the bar just then and, leaning across it, quietly said something to the bartender.

Reid slammed his hat onto his head. Dammit, he was thinking too much again. He wanted to see Samantha because he wanted his revenge against Rydelle, and that was the best way to get it. That was all he wanted. The only reason he'd come to Natchez, the only reason he wanted

Samantha. Revenge. And he was tired of waiting. Bethany was long cold in her grave, and Lillian had made his life a living hell and probably would continue to do so if she could find him, and it was all because of Cord Rydelle.

The old fire, the need for vengeance, burned deep inside of Reid and ached for release. He had waited a long time, but now the time was right, and Cord would finally know what it was like to lose everything and see the woman he loved in torment, if not actually dead. Reid turned toward the door to leave, then paused as he remembered the look of bitterness that had darkened one of his opponents' eyes earlier that evening. The man had lost big, and that could do crazy things to a person's head, make them do things they might not ordinarily do. Like kill.

Reid palmed the derringer from his cuff before stepping outside.

Chapter Seven

Reid stepped into his hotel room and slipped out of his jacket, tossing it onto a nearby chair. He was tired, yet nervous energy seemed to course through him. Getting to sleep wouldn't be easy, and he definitely needed to get some rest. He turned toward the bureau and grabbed the bottle of whiskey he'd placed there earlier.

Someone knocked on the door, the sound ripping through the quiet room like a jarring snap of thunder.

His hand paused in midair, the bottle in his grip balanced over a shot glass.

Startled, Reid jerked around and stared at the door. Who in hell would be banging on his door at this hour? It was after three in the morning. He quietly and deliberately set the bottle down, and turned to fully face the door, moving to stand to one side of it in case whoever was there decided to shoot first and answer questions later. Instinctively he moved a hand toward the gun still holstered against his rib. "Who is it?"

"It's me," Clarissa whispered.

Reid frowned and jerked the door open. "Clarissa, what in the hell are you doing here at this hour?"

"Shush." She thrust her gloved hands against his chest and pushed him back into the room. She closed the door behind herself and pressed against him, a pout pulling at her pretty features as she looked up at him. "You didn't kiss me good night, Jonathan," she said playfully, "and I just knew I'd never get to sleep until you did."

The light from the lamp on the small table next to his bed turned her dark hair to shimmering waves of burnished red, her blue eyes dark and fathomless. Clarissa's bottom lip quivered slightly.

Suddenly it was Samantha who Reid saw standing before him, Samantha pressing her body against his. The yearnings that had been tearing at him all evening rushed in on him. Desire flared hot and overwhelming, engulfing him within its tide. He pulled Clarissa into his arms, crushing her petite form against his tall length. His mouth covered hers, his tongue hungrily pushed between her lips, savagely demanding, exploring as his hands roamed her back.

Clarissa's arms wrapped around his neck and she pressed herself tighter against him, her body begging for more.

His hand moved beneath her cape to cup her breast. He heard her soft gasp, felt her shiver of surprise, then a small moan of pleasure broke from deep within her throat and her arms tightened their hold on him.

His thumb moved in a rhythmic circle upon her subtly curved nipple, caressing, drawing the taut peak to its fullest, teasing it, and feeling it strain against the thin fabric of her day gown.

She pressed her hips against him; another moan slid

from her mouth into his. "Oh, yes, Jonathan," she breathed against his lips. "Love me."

His desire died as abruptly as a flame doused with water.

Reid tore his lips from hers and he looked down into her eyes. Clarissa, not Samantha. He fought the frustration welling up within him.

She clung to him. "Oh, Jonathan, kiss me again. Please, love me, Jonathan. Please."

But he couldn't. He felt nothing. She was a beautiful woman. She was willing. Begging him to take her, and he couldn't. Dumbfounded, he stared down at her. He'd made love to dozens of women, some he'd cared about, many he hadn't, but this had never happened. Not with any of them. His passion seemed to lie dormant, like a cold lump within his loins, refusing to emit even a spark of life.

Angry with himself, furious with Samantha, he lashed out at Clarissa, reasoning lost to his self-loathing and outrage. "Do you know what you're doing, coming to my room late at night like this?" He released her, practically pushing her away from him, suddenly needing to be away from her, to be free of her cloying touch, away from her seductive gaze. Reid stalked across the room and stopped to stand at the window, his back to her. "If the desk clerk or any of the hotel maids are any kind of gossips, you'll be lucky if you have any reputation left at all by tomorrow morning."

"I don't care," Clarissa cried, moving up behind him and throwing her arms around his waist.

He instantly wrestled himself free, then turned to glare down at her. "Go home, Clarissa, dammit," he said, his voice hard and cold. *Go home before I forget you're not Samantha again,* his thoughts whispered, *and do something we'll both regret.*

* * *

Samantha yelled good night to Clarissa through the door to her bedchamber, which she'd found locked.

Clarissa didn't answer.

"Never mind," she said to Dellie. "I'll come back in a day or two and try to talk to her again."

She kissed her aunt and slipped out through the back door.

Rogue pawed the ground anxiously as she approached and mounted. The games would be long over by the time she got back to the saloon, but hopefully Cord had realized where she'd gone and hadn't sent a posse out searching for her.

Samantha saw the carriage approaching Dellie's house just as she started to urge Rogue down the carriageway toward the street. Hurriedly backing him up, they stood within the shadows of the trees that fronted one side of the property, hidden from view by both the darkness of night and the long, draping strands of Spanish moss that hung from the trees' gnarled branches. A saddled horse was tied to the rear of the carriage.

The last thing she needed now was to be recognized by someone as she left Dellie's house. That would ruin them all, especially Clarissa.

The carriage pulled up before the house.

Samantha frowned, trying to see into the covered carriage, but it was too dark. Who in heaven's name would be calling at this hour? Then she thought again of Cord. He was the only one who knew about Dellie's house, and Sam's late night visits. Had something happened at the Goose? Something so bad that he'd sent someone here to get her? Visions of Molly, Jake, or Cord himself lying hurt flashed through her mind and brought a stab of panic to her heart. What if a fight had broken out over the games?

A sense of dread seized her. She was just about to move from the shadows and call out to whomever was in the carriage when she heard her sister laugh.

Clarissa?

Samantha's gaze instantly turned toward the lighted bedchamber window on the second floor of the town house, then jumped back to the carriage. Clarissa must have sneaked out the back after she'd gone upstairs, knowing Sam and Dellie would visit for a while after she'd supposedly retired for the night.

A man stepped down from the far side of the carriage, but it was so dark Sam couldn't make out his face. He untied the horse and mounted.

"Until tomorrow," Clarissa called out as he turned the mount and began to ride back in the direction they'd come.

Clarissa snapped the reins of the carriage and the horse moved forward, turning into the drive.

Samantha fumed, and was about to move her horse to block the carriage, when she decided against it. If she confronted Clarissa here, now, she had no doubt her sister would make a horrific scene. One that all the neighbors would undoubtedly hear. In the long run, it would probably do a lot more harm than it would good. Sam clenched her hands tightly about the reins, desperately wanting to strangle some sense into Clarissa and exerting all the restraint she possessed to keep from doing so.

A long sigh slipped from Reid's lips as he walked up the hotel stairs toward the second floor, where his room was located. Frustration gnawed at him, anger roiled through his veins, and he felt desperately in need of smashing something. The problem was he didn't know if he was actually angry with Clarissa for showing up on his doorstep, or with Samantha for disappearing, or with himself for caring. He rounded the corner of the landing.

Phillip, leaning against the wall near Reid's door, suddenly pushed himself upright upon seeing Reid. He squared his shoulders and stood, feet spread wide apart, in a defiant stance, his hands balled into fists.

"Can I help you?" Reid said, recognizing Phillip and hoping this wasn't going to disintegrate into a physical fight. The look in the other man's eyes told him that was an all too real a possibility.

"You can stay away from Clarissa Beaumont," Phillip said. "That's what you can do."

"And why should I do that?" Reid challenged.

"Because I told you to."

Reid smiled pleasantly. "Isn't that a decision for the lady? And me?"

"Clarissa and I are to be married."

Reid reached for the door to his room. "Perhaps you should inform Miss Beaumont about that then."

Phillip grabbed Reid's shoulders. "I'm warning you . . ."

Reid flexed his arm and the derringer dropped into his palm. Ripping away from Phillip, and whirling around, his hand came up and he pressed the short, silver muzzle of the gun against the bottom of Phillip's chin. *"That,"* Reid said, "is not such a good idea."

Chapter Eight

Reid pulled the carriage up before the long entrance drive. Weeds grew everywhere, some high, some dead, others clinging to the two brick pillars on either side of the drive's rusting, wrought iron gate, which stood open, broken away from its top hinge and half mired in the ground.

"That's Riversrun," Clarissa said, pointing toward the house sitting at the opposite end of the drive. "My grandfather built it for my grandmother, but she died a month after they moved in."

Reid shook his head, then turned to look at her. "What happened to it?"

She shrugged as if it didn't matter. "My father grieved for my mother terribly after she died, and he began to drink, then gamble. He lost it."

Reid looked back at the plantation house. Gigantic camellia bushes, overgrown and scraggly, lined the curving drive, their unpruned limbs heavy with a colorful array of pink and white blossoms. Huge oak trees dotted the landscape around the house, their gnarled and twisted, wide-spreading branches laden with draping veils of moss that resembled fraying sheets of gray gossamer silk, fluttering ever so softly on the faint afternoon breeze.

"Do you miss it?"

Clarissa shrugged again. "I was only nine when we had to leave. I guess I don't really remember all that much about it."

The branches of the overgrown shrubs scraped the wheels as the carriage moved down the drive. Even from a distance the results of years of neglect were evident on the large house, and as Reid and Clarissa drew nearer, the faded signs of disregard became almost painful to note. Every window and doorway had been boarded over, walls that had once been a pristine white were now gray, and the tall cypress shutters that adorned each window, some hanging crooked on their rusted hinges, only hinted at the vibrant shade of green they had once been painted. Airy galleries ran the entire length of the front of the house, supported by eight Corinthian pillars, a sloping, slate-covered roof extended over the gallery to shade the second story, and brick chimneys rose high into the sky from each end of the house.

Time had not been kind to Riversrun. Dead, leafless vines of what had once been a huge wisteria wrapped around one pillar and entwined themselves within several rungs of the second-story balcony's railing and spindles. The roof had huge, gaping holes where the slate tiles had fallen away, and the once beautiful fanlight window above the double entry doors was broken, what glass still remained little more than ragged shards.

Several marble pedestals stood about the yard, their statues long ago having fallen to the ground. Most of the delicately carved figures were now little more than broken, unidentifiable pieces of stone. The lawn had been taken over by weeds, and one of the two magnolia trees that framed the entry steps was dead.

"Too bad your sister doesn't buy the place back and fix it up."

"Elyse?" Clarissa said, a scoffing look on her face. "Nobody would accept her Top-the-Hill now even if she did buy it."

Reid frowned. "Why?"

Clarissa suddenly realized she'd said too much. "Oh, ah, well she's married to a Frenchman and I, ah, doubt most of the men around here would cotton to him. He's very . . ." She waved a hand back and forth. "I don't know, too perfect, I guess. Too French. He's always talking about how wonderful France is."

Reid nodded. He knew exactly how wonderful France was. Some of the world's most beautiful women lived there. And some of the world's worst hellhole prisons were also there. It, along with England, was a place he had no desire to visit again.

Later that afternoon, after seeing Clarissa home, Reid rode back out to Riversrun. He didn't know why he returned; he just felt a need to see the old plantation by himself, without Clarissa's caustic comments ringing in his ears.

Sitting astride his horse, he looked at the house again, wondering if Rubies's suggestion wasn't so bad after all, or so far out of his reach. He had enough money in the bank to buy the place, he was sure of that, and probably just enough to get it profitable again. And with Clarissa as his wife, and Rubies vouching for him as an old and trusted friend, he would be instantly accepted into both the social and financial circles of Natchez, which meant the bank

would probably be more than willing to advance him a
loan. He rode toward the house. At the path that led from
the drive to the house, he dismounted and left his horse
grazing on weeds as he climbed the entry steps that curved
down from the main-floor gallery in a wide fan shape.
Stepping over broken tree limbs, mounds of dead leaves,
and windblown dirt, he approached the front door, but
instantly realized that the planking nailed across its front
was still too sturdy to dislodge. Moving to a window, he
grabbed one of the boards nailed across it, and yanked.
The nails pulled loose from the wooden shutters and the
board abruptly came away in his hands. Within minutes
Reid had freed the entire lower half of the floor-to-ceiling
window. Surprisingly its glass, though covered with dust
and grime, was still intact. Reaching down, he grasped the
sill and pushed up. At first the window resisted, but a
moment later it slid easily upward on its pullies.

Brushing away a cobweb that hung across the draperies
still framing the window, Reid stepped across its threshold,
following the stream of sunlight that had rushed into the
room when he'd removed the boards. Stale, musty air filled
his lungs and he coughed, momentarily choking. He shook
his head, and looked at his surroundings. The hardwood
floors were covered with at least an inch of dust and dirt;
the walls were dingy, and stained by ugly water streaks
where the roof had obviously leaked, but other than that
it appeared as if the residents of Riversrun had merely
stepped outside, boarded the place up, and ridden away.

Double settees still sat before a marble-faced fireplace,
over which hung a huge, gilt-framed mirror; a piano sat
off to one end of the room, its lid still propped open, as
if waiting for someone to sit down and press out a melody
upon its keys. An elegant étagère stood in one corner, its
shelves laden with procelain figurines, and a marble-
topped table held a silver tea set.

He walked into the parlor and stopped, his eyes caught by the portrait hanging on one wall. It was a life-sized portrait of a man and woman. He assumed they were Clarissa's parents, the Beaumonts, and the more he stared at the portrait, the more he could see Clarissa in the woman's features.

For the next hour Reid checked everything; he toured the rest of the house, finding every room fully furnished. Obviously the house had been taken over intact, then immediately boarded up and left to rot. But if Valic Gerard still owned Riversrun, as Clarissa thought, why had he left it to fall apart rather than sell it?

He shook his head at the waste, then left the house to inspect the rest of the property: the barn, manager's office, delicately designed *pigionnier*, devoid of birds now, naturally. He noted that the *pigionnier* had been build as a miniature version of the young and single men's quarters, the *garçonnière*. Reid smiled. Southerners were not very trustworthy when it came to their womenfolk and single men, preferring to banish the latter to a building completely separate from the main house. He rummaged through the ample-sized carriage house and stables, walked the pastures and corrals, and finally found himself at what had been the slave cabins. About forty of them made up a sort of small village several hundred yards behind the main house.

Every building was made of clapboard, each two rooms in size, with a packed earth floor and a rock fireplace. Ragged curtains hung at glassless windows that looked out upon sagging porches, and here and there was evidence of an old flower box, a chicken coop, a garden.

Some of the buildings here looked ready to fall apart; others already had.

Reid turned to go, having seen enough for his purposes, when he was startled by the sight of an old black man sitting on the porch of one of the cabins, whittling on a piece of wood and watching him. "I didn't known anyone was here," he said, approaching the man.

Jeremiah's old gnarled hand kept moving the knife over the piece of wood he held and his gaze remained on Reid as he drew near. When Reid spoke, Jeremiah stopped whittling, whipped a red rag from his pants pocket and wiped it across his face. "I been here nigh on forever," he said. "You lookin' for somebody special?"

"No, just looking the place over. I'm thinking of making an offer on it."

"Buy it?" The old man shook his head and looked down at his whittling, moving the knife over it again. "Doubt he'd sell it to ya."

Reid glanced back at the house. "Doesn't look like the man who owns it really cares about it much." He turned his gaze back on the old man. "What makes you think he wouldn't want to sell?"

"Spite," Jeremiah said without looking up. "Pure, mean, spite."

"Spite, huh?" Reid's assessing gaze moved over the old man. His face was little more than a swirling mass of deeply creviced wrinkles that encircled his eyes, framed his mouth, and made a map of his wide forehead. He was bone thin, and even though he was sitting down, it was evident he was tall, his arms and legs quite long. A cloud of white hair covered his head, but his brows and the stubble of whiskers on his lean face remained as black as the man himself.

Jeremiah looked up then, returning Reid's stare through eyes that seemed as old as time. "I been on this here land longer than I can remember, maybe since the day I was born, and I'll be here till the day I die." He nodded. "That's a fact, just like he ain't gonna sell this place to you or nobody else is a fact."

Reid would never have taken Gerard for somebody who'd waste a piece of valuable property like this one had obviously been wasted, all because of spite.

"Stole it from Mr. Beaumont—that's what he done," Jeremiah said. "Killed him good, then stole everything and tossed them poor little girls and Miss Dellie out."

Reid rode away from Riversrun trying to imagine himself and Clarissa living there together, as man and wife, but no matter how he tried, the image just wouldn't take hold in his mind.

Chapter Nine

Two days later Reid's patience was nearly nonexistent, and his frustration level was on the verge of exploding. The only good thing was that the cards were falling in his favor at the Goose and he was winning. But his desire to bed Samantha was beginning to play havoc with his concentration, and Clarissa's possessiveness was starting to seriously get on his nerves and remind him of Lillian.

Clarissa was like a bougainvillea, a beautiful flower that draped about his body, while beneath that beauty tiny, potentially lethal, little vines clung to him everywhere, cloying at his limbs, his throat, his mind, and threatening to strangle him.

He paced his room. Tonight's games had been over for less than an hour. All evening he'd sat, part of his mind on the cards in his hand, the looks on the other players faces, their mannerisms, the stakes on the table, while the other part of his mind had centered solely on Samantha. He'd watched her walk about the room, greeting people,

talking, laughing with this fellow, sympathizing with that
one. She fascinated him, intrigued him, and made him
think of things he didn't want to think about. It was getting
to the point he had to remind himself almost constantly
that the only reason he wanted her was as part of his
revenge against Cord.

Reid poured himself another shot of bourbon and
walked to the window. Everything was quiet. The saloons
had all shut down, the boats were docked for the night,
their decks mostly deserted, as were the streets. Occasion-
ally an owl hooted, a dog howled, or a cat screeched.
Otherwise it was as if every living creature on the earth
had ceased to be.

Reid sipped at his drink. The silence was getting on his
nerves. He was too edgy to sleep, and he knew why—
Samantha. Image of her face would not leave his mind,
the desire to touch her, hold her in his arms, taste the
exotic sweetness of her kiss would not leave his body.
"Dammit," he snarled, and threw the shot glass across the
room. It bounced off the wall and rolled across the car-
peted floor.

The woman in the room next door screamed.

Reid swore again. Grabbing his hat and jacket, Reid
stormed from his room, slamming the door behind him.
The sound echoed down the long hallway.

Reid's strides were long and quick. The last thing he
wanted was to be confronted with some self-righteous harri-
dan who wanted to rail at him for making noise in the
middle of the night and disturbing her beauty sleep.

Once outside he paused, breathing deeply of the cool
night air with its heavy scent of the nearby river, the stacked
cotton bales that lined the wharves, the whiskey that filled
the saloons, the horses that crowded the nearby stables.
Maybe he should just get on one of the riverboats and
head on down to New Orleans. He turned toward the end

of the bluff and walked down the steep incline of Silver
Street that led to Under-the-Hill.

Instead of heading for the docks, he stopped in front
of the Silver Goose. The saloon's windows were dark, the
doors closed. His gaze moved to the second-story windows,
in particular the one he knew was Samantha's bedchamber.
Was she there now? Having as hard a time falling asleep
as he'd been having ever since he'd come to Natchez?

Heat, need swept through his body.

He moved around to the staircase at the side of the
building and quietly climbed it, acting on impulse now,
refusing to give thought to his actions. The door at the
top of the stairs was locked. Reid smiled. Reaching into
his jacket he pulled out his billfold and flipped it open.
Within a small slit in the leather nestled a silver pin. He
slid it out and, kneeling, inserted it into the door's lock.
He twisted it about. Within seconds the lock's tumblers
fell into place and, as Reid slowly turned the doorknob
again, the door opened.

A wall sconce halfway down the hall glowed softly, the
tiny flame behind the sconce's crystal globe burning steadily against the darkness.

Reid saw that no light shone from beneath any of the
doors. He glanced toward the one he guessed was Cord's,
and stared at it for a long moment. It would be easy to
simply slip into that room, draw out the knife he always
kept sheathed in his boot, and slip it quietly and lethally
between Cord's ribs as he lay sleeping. He might gasp as
it entered his flesh, might even scream as it pierced his
heart, but that would be all. He would be dead, and the
last face he'd see would be Reid's.

It wasn't enough.

Reid closed his eyes. That wasn't why he was here. He
hated Cord and wanted to destroy him, not murder him.
Reid looked at Samantha's door, wondered if it was locked,

then decided there was only one way to find out. He reached out, his fingers circling the knob, closing around it. The knob turned easily in his hand and he pushed the door open, slipped into the dark room, and closed the door behind him.

The glow of a small lamp in her sitting room left the bedchamber in soft shadow rather than inky blackness.

Reid looked toward the tall, four-poster bed that dominated the room. It was empty. He started, surprised, not having giving thought to what he'd do if she wasn't there. Or wasn't alone. Suddenly, as he glared at the empty bed, he felt a rush of anger. She was in the next room, with Cord. Reid was just about to reach for the doorknob to leave when a faint rustling sound in the sitting room caught his attention. He whipped around, then froze, listening again, trying to make out if it had actually been a sound he'd heard or merely something in his imagination.

As he stood still, trying to decide, a shadow moved across the sitting room's far wall.

Reid walked to the open door that adjoined the two rooms.

Samantha stood by the window, almost in profile to him, looking out upon the river. Moonlight flowed through the window where she'd drawn the curtain back and penetrated the thin threads of her nightgown, filtering through their delicate weave and outlining every curve and line of her body for his eyes. It touched the slope of her shoulders, the swell of her breasts, the turn of her hip.

She reached up and brushed the hair from her neck, then shook her head, sending tendrils of red, silky fire spreading across her back and shoulders.

Reid stepped farther into the room, not knowing what he was going to say, what he was going to do, only that he had to be near her.

Samantha sensed a movement in the room, and instinctively knew it wasn't Blossom. Forcing herself to remain calm, she reached toward the table beside her. Both the dagger she always kept sheathed in her garter and the derringer she carried whenever she left the saloon, lay there where they always did when not on her person. Her hand closed around the smooth pearl handle of the gun and her finger embraced its trigger. Samantha slowly slid it from the table and whirled around to face her intruder.

She recognized him instantly. He stood on the opposite side of the room, near the door. Blending with the shadows, he was more an obscure presence than a distinct form, but she knew it was him. It wasn't the pale glint of firelight coming from the dying embers in the grate of the room's fireplace that seemed to dance a brief reflection in the dark eyes she couldn't really see, or the faint golden glow that momentarily settled upon the pale wave of hair, or even the wide shoulders and arrogant stance that identified him to her. Rather, it was a sudden charge of sensual tension that fairly sizzled in the air between them, the animal magnetism he so effortlessly projected, and which reached out now to wrap around her now like a warm, inviting cloak of forbidden desire.

Every nerve within Samantha's body screamed to be in his arms, urged her to cross the room and slip into his embrace. It was an unreasonable feeling, and one she didn't relish having, but it was also undeniable.

She stared at him, her eyes straining to pierce the shadows that obscured the distinction of his features from her sight. Her finger remained wrapped around the trigger of the gun she held pointed at him, but she was no longer conscious of the weapon's existence within her grasp. Part of her ached to feel his hands on her body, while another part of her knew she should run as far and as fast away from him as she could before it was too late.

Instead she stood still and waited, for what she wanted,

for what she didn't want, because it was already too late to run. He was her fate, good or bad, and she couldn't avoid him. He moved toward her, then stopped and looked down at the gun. "Are you going to shoot me?" he asked softly.

She fought for breath, for reason.

Reid gently took the gun from her hand and set it on the table behind her. "I couldn't sleep for thinking about you," he said, the deep, whispery drawl of his voice caressing her senses. His hand brushed lightly over a long lock of her hair. "You've possessed me, Samantha. Left me with no will or thought of my own."

She looked up into his eyes and time suddenly stood still. Reason vanished. It wasn't his sweet words, or his handsome face . . . it was him. He drew her, intrigued her, mesmerized her. Animal magnetism, or something more? She didn't know. And didn't care.

An exotic, intangible sense of passion filled the room, drawing them together, flooding their senses, stoking the desires neither was able to deny any longer.

Without thought to what he was about to do or to whether the gnawing hunger that raged in him, the aching need to possess her really had anything to do with the vengeance he had sought for so long, Reid's arms crushed her body to his. He needed to feel her against him, her warmth pressing into him, her flesh touching his, and as he did, he found it almost more than he could bear. When she didn't resist him, he knew he was lost to her, maybe for only the moment, maybe for forever. It didn't matter.

"I don't want you," she whispered, slipping her arms around his shoulders.

"I don't want you either," he said, her scent filling him. "Reid."

The sound of his name on her lips was like a taunting whisper of seduction, a beguiling caress that fanned the flames of his mounting desire and threatened to pull him over the edge of reason.

Samantha watched, enthralled, afraid, helpless as his head lowered toward hers. She felt his arms tighten around her body, and refused to listen to the soft little words of caution slipping through her mind.

Run. Flee. He'll hurt you. You'll be sorry.

She tipped her head up to await the possession of his kiss.

She was his. Reid's arms tightened around her, crushing her to him.

His lips descended upon hers with a savage virility that turned her knees weak and robbed her of breath. The beat of her heart turned to a frantic throb, a lightning flash of sensations attacked her body, and his arms around her were suddenly the only reason she remained standing.

His breath became hers, the warmth of his body heating her own, the pounding of his heart against her breast the cadence her own needed to keep up its steady beat, rather than stop.

Logic, rationale, common sense told her that Blackjack Reid Sinclaire was everything in a man she didn't want, everything she didn't need in her life ever again—but her heart and body were not listening to that argument, and for the moment at least, they were in control of her senses.

She returned his kiss, slipping her tongue between his lips, into his mouth, twisting it about his own seeking one. The last lingering shreds of inhibition left her as a moan of pleasure tore from his throat. At that instant all the fears and uncertainties she'd carried deep within her, born from her father's guileless deception, Loren's betrayal, and Dante's treachery, fled as if they'd never existed. Nothing else mattered now but that this man who held her in his arms gave her everything of himself. His touch made her feel alive again, his kiss made her feel desirable, and she never wanted to lose those sensations again.

"I want you, Samantha," Reid breathed against her lips. The torment of his need had turned his voice as ragged as his body was hot. His need for her was greater than anything he'd ever felt, any emotion that had ever flowed through him, possessed him. It was as if he had merely gone through the motions with other women, as if all of his experiences, all of his desires, his defeats and conquests had been leading him toward her.

Samantha clung to him, her arms tightening about his neck, her fingers slipping within the golden hair at his nape. She knew what she was about to do would leave her a permanent scar, hidden and invisible upon her heart. He would use her, and he would leave her ... just like Dante had. She knew this as well as she knew that at this moment she didn't care.

His tongue filled her mouth.

Fire erupted in her veins, and every cell within her body yearned for his touch. It swelled within her breasts, and burned deep within her loins. What had happened in her past was over, what was to happen in the future was unknown, but what was happening now was what mattered to her the most. Her time with this man was meant to be ... whether for a moment or for forever, he was eveyrthing she'd always thought she didn't want, and everything she did.

Reid's mind spun with the myriad of pleasures assaulting his senses. At the same time, a voice called to him from the back of his mind, urging him to listen and understand the possible consequences of what he was about to do. But he refused to listen. Reality could be faced later. Pain, vengeance, whatever feelings assaulted him tomorrow, he would deal with then. Now all he wanted to do was make love to Samantha, to hold her in his arms and feel her naked body, hot and pliant, moist with a veil of passion.

A tiny gasp of pleasure slipped from Samantha's throat, and fiery waves of need ripped through Reid's veins, stabbed at his loins.

His tongue sensuously licked at the corners of her mouth, teasing, taunting, then closing over hers again, the intensity of his kiss stealing the very breath from her lungs, plunging her heart into a frantic rythym.

Samantha reveled in his possession of her, in the ravishment of his desire. *Remember Dante,* her mind whispered. *Remember Loren.* But she pushed the thoughts aside and refused to heed the nagging voice. Tomorrow she might, tomorrow she might regret everything, but not tonight. Tonight all she wanted was for him to hold her in his arms, to kiss her and love her and stay with her. "I want you, too," she said finally, surprising even herself at the brazen admission.

She felt his hand instantly move to cup her breast, felt the gentle kneading of his fingers, teasing her nipple, drawing it to a hard peak of desperate need until she arched against him, aching to be touched everywhere. His hand slipped to the ribbon that held the front of her sleeping gown secure, and his fingers deftly released it, first from one small loop of fabric, then another, and another and all the while his lips continued to work their dark magic upon hers. Finally, he pushed the gown from her shoulders. Samantha felt the sheer garment flutter from her body and fall to the floor, pooling in a glimmering white softness around her feet.

Drawing his lips from hers, Reid stepped back, his hands holding hers, guiding her from the fallen gown. His gaze traveled the length of her body, as the haze of moonlight that filtered into the room from the window bathed her in a silver glow.

A flush of embarrassment suddenly seized her, and Samantha tried to turn away.

"No," he said quietly, gently lifting both of her hands to his lips. He kissed each one, his gaze locked with hers; then his eyes dropped away and moved over her body again.

She was far more lovely than he'd ever imagined. Her skin was the soft whiteness of a newly opened magnolia blossom, touched by just a hint of honeyed goldness, and her breasts were supple and full, the darker flesh of the nipples pebbled from both their exposure to the air and the raging emotions of desire coursing through her veins. Her waist sloped gracefully, her hips rounded tantalizingly, and the dark, red touched patch of down at the apex of her thighs was an exquisite triangle that hinted at passions like none he'd ever known.

He leaned forward, his head lowering slowly toward her breasts.

"No," Samantha said.

He looked up and she saw the uncertainty in his eyes, the fear that she was sending him away.

She smiled. "Now it's my turn." She slipped her hands beneath his jacket, pushing it from his shoulders and feeling the corded muscles it hid, the heat of his flesh as it penetrated the thin threads of his silk shirt. Even before the jacket dropped to the floor, Samantha's hands had invaded his shirt, pulling each button free, slipping inside, sliding over his hot flesh.

A startling jolt of need attacked Reid's body as her hands moved over him, inciting his sexual hunger for her to a height he'd never thought possible. He ripped the shirt from his arms and threw it to the floor even as his lips threatened to devour hers. His body was about to explode with the want of her, the volcanic forces churning within him building to a cresendo he was powerless to stop.

But Samantha's explorations continued. Her hands moved along the rippling curves of his shoulder muscles, down the ropey length of his arms, over the sloping plane of his spine, then dived within the confines of his trousers. Her fingers kneaded the rounded curves of his buttocks.

A strangled groan of pleasure ripped from Reid as his desire for her dived to new depths, slicing through him like a knife and threatening to bring him to his knees. "You're going to kill me," he said against her temple, his voice ragged with the emotion cutting into him.

Samantha smiled. "Not yet," she said, then pulled her hands free. "Take them off."

It was an order he was more than glad to obey. Seconds later he dragged her back into his arms, his kiss more demanding, more savage than anything she had ever experienced. But she loved it. His hands roamed her naked body, burning her flesh where they touched, searing her with his need and leaving her no doubt that she was his forever.

She had never desired any man so completely, so wantonly, so desperately. She had desired Loren as an innocent schoolgirl, filled with all the dreams of what a husband and wife should be to each other. Loneliness had left her vulnerable to Dante, and blind to the dark edge of his rakish charm and lifestyle. But her feelings toward Reid were all fire and passion, the emotions of a woman with no more fantasies about what life and men should be like. She pressed against him, needing to be closer.

Reid pulled away from her again, and for the briefest of moments Samantha felt desertion, and a cry of denial rose to her lips. But before its sound slipped away from her, Reid's arms swept around her and she felt the floor disappear from beneath her feet.

He slid down onto the bed beside her. If he'd had any doubt that his desire for this woman was real, and not just a thing born of his need for revenge against Cord, it was dispelled as thoroughly as her caressing hands dispelled what little physical control he still maintained over his own body. He couldn't get enough of touching her, kissing her, feeling her body pressed to his.

She sighed his name, and his desire flared.

He had wanted their time together to last long into the night, to be like a wave that moved ever forward, slowly, building, growing until it crested in magnificense. But he was drowning in his need for her, and restraint was slipping from his grasp.

Samantha felt as if their bodies moved as one, as if they'd melded together, and each caress of his hands upon her, of her hands upon him, brought them ever closer, bonding them each to the other for all time. He thrust fiercely, caressed with demand, kissed with ruthless conquest. Samantha felt fire unfurl in her veins, explode somewhere deep within her, and sear every molecule of her body. The gnawing, building, hungry wanting that had dwelt within her since the moment she'd first seen him, that had nearly torn her apart over the last few minutes, suddenly shattered into unbelieveable fulfillment. Her body felt as if alive with a thousand needs of pleasure, each trembling and throbbing with the ecstasy of his touch, and for the very briefest of moments, she knew that his soul had touched hers.

Reid held her tightly to him, her name spilling from his lips over and over.

She trembled within the throes of climax, clutching at him, holding to him, screaming out his name.

Lost, he thought numbly—he was lost. Passion, white hot and fiery, erupted deep within him as he pushed himself into her one last time and tumultuous waves of pleasure that were nearly decimating in their surge through his body engulfed him like a fire that threatened to leave him nothing but a cinder. For one brief second, he had no breath left in his lungs, his heart had no will to beat, nor his mind the energy to hold thought.

"Reid," Samantha said, the word a gentle caress that floated warm and vibrant across his neck.

At that instant everything he believed, everything that had held his life together and gave him reason to go on disappeared, leaving him with only one desire—to keep her by his side for the rest of his life. It was a carnal need, a physical desire, an emotional dream. She was an enchantress, and he wanted to make love to her every night, wake to her smile every morning, and walk the fields of his land with her hand securely tucked within his. He wanted his children to have her smile, he wanted to grow old beside her, and he wanted her face to be the last one he saw when he closed his eyes for the final time.

Samantha made no effort to move from the circle of his arms, relishing the security she felt within that strong embrace. But soon, as she lay quietly beside him, she felt his ragged breathing turn steady and knew he'd fallen into a light sleep.

Moments later, unable to resist the temptation, she ran her fingers down the naked length of his body, the need to touch him more than she could resist.

Reid's arms instantly tightened around her, startling Samantha. Rolling on top of her, he caught her hands and thrust them above her head, pushing them into the pillows and pinning her in place. His brown eyes caught hers.

"Love me again," Samantha said boldly. "Now."

It was an invitation he had no desire to refuse.

Reid stood by the window. The sky was still dark, but he knew the sun would be coming up soon enough. Already several dozen roustabouts moved about the docks, loading cargo onto the the riverboats. The doors to Petries Warehouse, a huge building halfway down Falconer's Landing, stood wide open and two men were stacking crates onto a cart intended for one of the flatboats.

Get out. He sighed. His conscience was at work again, nagging at him. *Get out now, before she wakes, before things get messy. You've done what you intended to do, taken Cord Rydelle's woman. Leave now, before you say or do something stupid.*

He glanced back at Samantha, still asleep on the big four-poster bed. Her hair spread out around her like a halo of dark fire against the white pillow, and one bare breast peeked from beneath the sheet that covered the rest of her body.

Desire surged through him. Fresh. New. Hot. Dammit. He turned away and forced his gaze back to the street. He had made love to Cord's mistress. Part of his revenge was complete now, or soon would be when he let Cord know about last night. So why didn't he feel good about it? He should feel satisfied. Avenged. But he didn't. He felt miserable. Guilty. Even angry with himself.

With another cavalcade of curses slipping softly from his lips, Reid grabbed his hat and jacket from a chair and walked to the door. The best thing he could do for himself now was to get the hell away from her.

Chapter Ten

Samantha felt the warmth of the sun touch her cheek, then her eyelid. She stirred. A smile pulled at her lips and she reached out for Reid, wanting to feel the heat of his body next to hers, to run her hands over the smooth muscles of his arms and feel them around her again.

Her eyes shot open as all her hands felt was bedsheet. She sat up and looked around, her heart thumping madly. The sheet where he'd lain was cool to the touch. He was gone, and evidently had been for some time. She closed her eyes to hold back the tears that rose to her lids, hot and burning. She had known he would leave her, she had known he would walk away, most likely without even a backward glance, but she hadn't thought it would be quite so soon, or that he wouldn't even say goodbye.

She threw the sheet aside and slid from the bed, grabbing her robe. "Well, what did you expect?" she growled at herself. "You knew he was no-good. A drifter. A gambler. Rake. Murderer. Lord," she shrieked softly, "he's a married man, and you fell right into his arms anyway like some love-starved ninny." She stalked to her dressing table and grabbed the pitcher of lukewarm water that sat there, then poured it into the washing bowl. "Stupid," she muttered, splashing the water onto her face. "Stupid, stupid, stupid." She grabbed a towel, wiped her face, then threw it onto the table, nearly sending the pitcher flying against the wall.

Molly entered the room a few minutes later carrying a tray of coffee and pastries. "Good morning," she fairly sang.

Samantha whirled. "What's so good about it?"

Molly frowned. "You have a bad nightmare last night or something?"

"Yes," Samantha snapped. "Exactly." She grabbed a cup of the coffee.

"So," Molly said cheerfully, "which gown do you want to wear today?" She threw open the doors to Samantha's armoire.

"What blasted difference does it make?" Samantha growled. "Blue? Red? Green? I don't care. Just choose one and leave me alone."

Molly's brows soared in indignation. "Well, fine, missy," she said, hurrying toward the door. "Maybe you can just get your own things together this morning." With that she stepped into the hall and slammed Samantha's door behind her.

"Fine," Samantha said, stalking to the armoire. She grabbed a yellow day dress with a high collar, white sleeves, and a thin belt. Maybe the cheerful color would help dispel the black cloud she felt was hanging over her head.

Guilt at the way she'd treated Molly joined her bad mood.

* * *

Samantha heard Molly and Curly talking downstairs as she stepped from her room, then the back door slammed shut and the place was silent. She closed her door and turned to walk toward the stairs.

"Hello, is anyone here?"

Samantha stepped to the railing and looked down into the saloon.

A woman stood just inside the doorway.

"I'm sorry, we don't open until seven this evening," Sam said.

"This evening?" The woman did a little shake of her head and shoulders and chuckled softly. "My heavens, I don't think I've ever heard of a saloon that wasn't always open. How very quaint."

"Whatever," Samantha mumbled, her mood too dark to offer anything even halfway more congenial. She turned toward the stairs.

"I'm looking for Blackjack Reid Sinclaire," the woman announced loudly. "Do you know where I can find him? Tall, blond, good-looking?"

Samantha stopped and turned to stare down at the woman. "Pardon me?" she said, though she'd heard exactly what the woman had said.

"Oh, my heavens." The woman whipped open the fan that had been dangling from a cord around her wrist and fluttered it rapidly in front of her face. "However can you people stand this dreadful heat? Why, it's like hot water floating in the air around here. And Reid told me it wouldn't be like this down this way for at least another month or so, and he promised by then we'd be gone."

Samantha grasped the railing with one hand, raised the hem of her gown with the other, and began to descend the stairs, her gaze never leaving the woman's face. A nagging curiosity had gotten the better of her, and though she might loathe herself for it, and it was really none of her business, she had to know who this woman was, and *what* she was to Reid. "Yes, it can get quite warm. I take it you've never been to Mississippi before?"

The bright sunlight shining into the room from the unshuttered windows on either side of the entry door and the fanlight overhead made it difficult for Samantha to see the woman's face clearly.

"Oh, I just arrived on one of the packets, the *Magnolia Queen.*" She chuckled. "Silly name. Anyway, I'm Rhonda Sinclaire. I was supposed to wait in Boston until Reid got settled down here, but . . ." She shrugged. "As usual, he's taking too long, and I just had to come on ahead. Anyway, it was important." The swift breeze caused by the furious movement of her fan lifted the gold-brown curls of hair at her temples to wisp about her face and sent the giant ostrich plumes on her hat to waving frantically, as if in an effort to take flight.

Samantha drew closer and her view of the woman became clearer. Rhonda Sinclaire was extraordinarily beautiful. Everything about her seemed as if perfected by the hands of a sculptor. Dramatically arched brows rose above large, inky brown eyes that were framed by a luxurious ruche of dark lashes. High cheekbones, a thin, perfect nose, and exquisitely shaped lips combined to complete the regal look.

Her traveling suit was of a chocolate brown hue, the color the exact shade of her cool, assessing eyes, and the cut accentuated her narrow waist.

Samantha took an instant dislike to her, but whether it was because Rhonda had inquired after Reid, because she was obviously his wife, or because of her magnificiently perfect beauty and haughty countenance, she didn't know. Nor, she thought guiltily, did she care. "I'm sorry," she said finally, her voice as frosty and composed as the feelings churning with her breast were hot and seething. "Who did you say you were looking for?"

"She asked for Sinclaire, Sam," Cord said, stepping from his room. "Even I heard that." Light sarcasm edged his deep voice.

Samantha looked up to see Cord staring at them from his vantage point on the balcony. The bright rays of the afternoon sun streaming in through the open door of his room behind him, surrounded his tall, muscular, and shirtless body in a soft haze of yellow light.

Even at fifty years of age, her father was a beautiful man.

"Oh, ah, yes." She thought she detected a knowing gleam in his eyes and felt a rush of discomfort. Had he seen Reid come to her room last night? Did he suspect what had happened? She pushed the thought aside. No, he would never have allowed it, or remained silent. She was just being paranoid. And ridiculous. She forced a smile to her lips and turned back to the woman still standing by the door.

"I'm sorry, Miss . . ."

"Sinclaire," Rhonda said.

Samantha gritted her teeth. "Yes, Sinclaire. But as you can see, Mr. Sinclaire is not here." An unreasonable surge of resentment, not unlike jealousy, swept through Sam, quickly followed by a rush of anger as she saw the woman's gaze fixed on Cord.

"I can see that," Rhonda said, a tart sweetness to her tone. "Unless you have him hidden in your room."

The words gave Samantha a momentary start.

Rhonda's hungry gaze seemed to devour Cord, feasting on the sight of his well-honed shoulders and bare chest.

Samantha felt like slapping the woman's face. Did she have no modesty at all?

"He's staying at the Durante, Top-of-Hill," Cord said,

and nodded to the woman. He turned away and reentered his room, closing the door behind him.

"Well, that certainly is a handsome one," Rhonda purred. "Is he yours?"

"No, but I'm sure his wife shares your opinion," Samantha said coolly, the lie rolling off her tongue with amazing ease. She smiled, though she knew the warmth of the friendly gesture didn't make it to her eyes, and she made no effort to correct the lapse.

"Wife?" Rhonda snapped her fan closed and slipped it into the beaded reticule that hung from her wrist. "What a pity." She turned toward the door, then paused and looked back. "If it's not too much trouble"—her tone dripped with scorn—"could you possibly direct me to this, uh, what was it? The Durante Hotel?"

Samantha's smile remained a frozen fixture of her face. She'd much rather direct the woman to the fiery pits of hell. "Straight up Silver Street. When it crests the hill you'll see the hotel."

"Thank you. I assume I can get a carriage at the docks." Rhonda turned and opened the entry door.

"I assume you are Mr. Sinclaire's wife?" Samanth asked, hurriedly, wishing she hadn't asked the question, but unable to stop herself.

But Rhonda was already out the door and halfway across the boardwalk.

Reid left the hotel and saw Clarissa's carriage across the street. He didn't particularly want to spend the day with her; in fact, he'd awakened this morning trying to think of some way to get out of it. Then he'd come to his senses and remembered just how many benefits could be his with Clarissa Beaumont at his side, and how many more would open up to him with her as his wife. Wealth, respectability, and a new start in life, with a lot more alluring prospects than he'd ever imagined possible.

Rubies had made life in Natchez Top-the-Hill sound very appealing.

Anyway, didn't most men have a wife who was a shrew, and a mistress who was their goddess? Why not him?

Chapter Eleven

Reid approached the door of his room. He'd intended to be back much earlier and get a few hours' sleep before the games were scheduled to start that evening, but Clarissa had insisted on his accompanying her to a luncheon at the Briers. The planation was on the outskirts of town, and the luncheon had not only lasted all afternoon, but threatned to run through half the night, which was something he could not do unless he wanted to forfeit his seat in the games at the Goose, and he didn't.

He remembered the angry spark in Clarissa's eyes when he'd insisted on leaving. Instead of letting him escort her back to town, she'd stayed at the Briers, haughtily intimating she could find someone else to take her home. Reid assumed she meant Phillip Lethrothe. Or maybe even Valic Gerard, but there could be someone else. There had been any number of men at the luncheon who would have consented.

Reid sighed. Her pouting had been annoying, and her

threat meant to arouse his jealousy. It hadn't, and he'd merely agreed to her plan and left, which he knew probably did nothing more than intensify her pique of anger.

Following in Rubies's footsteps, at least the part that included marrying one of Natchez's belles, namely Clarissa, in order to more firmly and quickly cement his position in the elite society, was beginning to look a bit less appealing than it had only a couple of days earlier.

Reid stepped into his room, shut the door, and instantly stiffened. He was not alone.

The room was cloaked in shadow and his eyes were slow to adjust, but he trusted his instincts. They had kept him alive through a dozen close calls and a myriad of skirmishes over the years, and had never been wrong. His left hand went for the gun tucked into the holster that was nestled against his right rib cage, while he flexed his right shoulder and the hidden derringer dropped into his palm.

A slight movement to one side of the window drew his gaze. The dark silhouette of a person became visible to him.

Reid raised the derringer.

"Well, that's a wonderful way to greet me, even if there are times you'd like to kill me."

"Rhonda?" His alarm instantly turned to fury. Reholstering his Colt, and drawing the derringer back up his sleeve, Reid picked up a lucifer from the table near the door, struck it against the doorjamb, and held the small flame to the wick of a lamp.

Light filled the room in a soft glow.

He turned to glare at her. "What the hell are you doing here?"

She rubbed the sleep from her eyes and stood. "Oh, it's nice to see you, too, Reid. Thank you. And my trip down from Boston was just fine. No mishaps, muggings, or murders."

He ignored her sarcasm. "What are you doing here?"

"Well, until you pulled out your guns and prepared to blow my head off, I was sleeping," she snapped, her own anger flaring to life.

The urge to throttle her was almost more than he could bear. "Dammit, will you simply answer me? What are you doing in Natchez, Rhonda? You were supposed to wait in Boston until I sent for you."

She sulked. "Things changed and I had to . . ."

His dark eyes bore into hers. "Your being here could jeopardize everything."

"Everything? I thought you came here to play poker in that challenge thing you heard about. How can me being here jeopardize that?"

"There are things happening you don't know about." He hadn't wanted to tell her about Cord and his own bent for revenge because he knew she'd try to talk him out of it, and he hadn't wanted to be talked out of it. "And if anyone saw you, or finds out who you are, none of my plans will be worth a damn."

Rhonda waved off his concerns with a flippant sweep of her hand. "Oh, stop huffing. Your precious plans are intact, whatever they are. I haven't spoken to anyone here except that silly ol' desk clerk downstairs and some saloon hussy Under-the-Hill."

Reid's thoughts splintered toward panic again at mention of a Rhonda being in a saloon Under-the-Hill. "Who, Rhonda? What saloon? Who did you speak to? What did you say? Tell me!" he demanded.

"Oh, for heaven's sake, Reid, calm down. Some woman with red hair. All I did was ask after you and she wouldn't answer me. A man came out of his room and said you were staying here, so I came right up."

But Reid wasn't listening anymore. He'd stopped hearing her the moment she'd said some woman with red hair in a saloon Under-the-Hill.

Visions of a fiery-haired seductress filled his mind, his senses, pulling at him. A gnawing sense of emptiness ate at his chest, while hot longing filled his loins. God, he'd thought bedding her would finally rid him of the desire that had been simmering in him since that first night he'd walked into the Silver Goose. His desire would be satiated, and he'd have at least part of his revenge against Cord Rydelle. Then all that would be left would be to win their money, and let Cord know that his woman wasn't quite as true to him as he thought.

Reid almost laughed aloud. The joke was on him. Instead of feeling satisfied, instead of his desires being satiated, his hunger for Samantha was stronger than ever, and satisfaction and revenge weren't playing any part in his feelings.

He should have just walked into the Silver Goose that night and killed Cord Rydelle on the spot. Quick and easy. He was already wanted for murder in one country, why not make it two?

But it was too late for that. He had a lot more at stake now, for both Rhonda and himself, than merely satisfying the need for revenge that had been eating at him for all these years.

Being with Samantha had done more than merely stir his desires and leave him needing more of her, however. It had also proven that he couldn't spend a lifetime with a woman like Clarissa. Not unless he procured an awful lot of diversions on the side, and Reid had a feeling that quietly allowing her husband to have "diversions" was one thing Clarissa Beaumont would not be good at.

He turned back toward the bureau and poured himself and Rhonda a drink.

Leaving Samantha's bed that morning had been one of the hardest things he'd ever forced himself to do. He could still remember the sensually delicious feel of her flesh pressed to his, her skin as smooth as marble, as soft as velvet, as hot as fire.

He handed Rhonda her drink, then turned toward the window, his back to her.

His body still felt her warmth, his lips still tasted her kiss, and his mind was still filled with the image of her face.

With a half smothered oath he was not even aware he uttered aloud, Reid downed his whiskey in one gulp and slapped a hand against the window's sill. He had been a fool. He was a fool.

"Reid Sinclaire, for heaven's sake, are you even listening to me?" Rhonda said, slamming her glass down hard on the table beside her chair.

He whirled around. "Yes," he snapped. "You were bored. You didn't have anything to do. All the usual excuses, Rhonda, for doing whatever you want. So you packed up and followed me, even though you promised me you—"

"I said," she interrupted, her eyes flashing fury at him, "Lillian was in Boston looking for you."

Shock, ice cold and instant, raced through him. "Lillian?"

"Good, you haven't gone deaf." Rhonda smiled smugly. "Yes, Lillian was in Boston. That's why I left and came down here, to warn you."

He turned back toward the window and stared out at the night. It had been inevitable. He'd known Lily would come sooner or later. His wife was nothing if not persistent, and vengeful. She wanted a piece of his hide for killing her lover and soiling her reputation, not that it wasn't really her own fault. Nevertheless, she was intent on seeing that Reid suffered the consequences, even if she had to track him all the way to hell and back.

A vision of the rest of his life, always on the move, always looking over his shoulder for her, ruining his life, destroying everything he did or tried to do weighed down on him.

He turned back to Rhonda. "Did she see you in Boston? Did she follow you downriver?"

"She saw me in Boston, yes." Rhonda shook her head. "I don't think she followed me though. I was pretty careful when I left. I even took a circuitous route to the boat." Rhonda inhaled deeply. "But she's scary, Reid. I didn't want to stay there with her in town. I was afraid she'd try to do something to make me tell her where you were."

He nodded. "It's okay." He pulled her into his arms and hugged her close, then stepped back as he released her and smiled. "Sorry I snapped at you. I've been having a few problems, and you just surprised me, that's all. Do you have a room?"

She shook her head. "I didn't know how to register, what name to use, or what to tell him about who I was, so I . . ."

"Made something up?" Reid said, smiling.

She nodded. "I showed him that tintype of you in my locket." She touched the silver, oval-shaped locket that hung from her neck that was the only thing they had of their mother's. "And told him I didn't know what name you were using because you worked for the government and sometimes had to use an alias."

"Oh, Lord," Reid groaned, trying not to laugh.

"He still wasn't going to tell me anything, the louse. I had to bribe him."

"And he didn't ask who you were?"

She laughed softly. "No. For all that idiot knows I've been patiently waiting up here to kill you."

Reid smiled wryly. "Or seduce me."

"Oh!" Rhonda's eyes widened in shock. "You don't think he thought I was a . . ."

Reid couldn't hide his amusement at putting into words the most probable of what the man had thought. "Most likely."

"Oh, drat. I've done a lot of things," Rhonda moaned, "but selling my favors is not one of them. My reputation will be ruined." She began pacing the room. "Utterly ruined." She suddenly stopped and, whirling abruptly, looked at him with that sly look in her eyes that always warned him trouble was on the way. "Unless . . ." she said, letting the word slowly roll off her tongue.

Reid shook his head. "No. Whatever you have in mind, the answer is no." But even as he said it, Reid knew it was too late. Saying no to his little sister never worked, and he didn't have any hope that this time was going to be any different from all the others.

Samantha looked up from her ledgers as the door to her office opened. Cord paused for a moment, framed by the doorway, then stepped inside and shut the door firmly behind him.

"Okay, Sam, what the hell is bothering you?"

Her gaze instantly dived back to the ledgers and she shrugged her shoulders. "Nothing."

"Yeah, right." He dropped a foot onto a chair before her desk and leaned an arm on his knee. "C'mon, Samantha, out with it."

She set the quill carefully on the blotter and sat back in her chair.

"You're mad because I didn't ask Suzette to marry me like you want? Is that it? Because if it is, forget it. I told you before. I'm not getting married."

She smiled, relieved that he hadn't asked her about Reid.

"All right, fine, if that's what you want. But I have to do something about Suzette."

A frown dug into his brow. "What do you mean? What something?"

She shook her head, as if helpless against the decision. "Suzette is supposed to be pushing drinks to the gamblers—that's her job," Samantha said, "but she isn't, because she only has eyes for you."

"Sam . . ."

"No. It's your choice. Either Suzette does her job, which I honestly don't think she can, not here anyway, or she goes."

Cord glared down at her.

Samantha struggled to keep a serious expression on her face. She knew if he even suspected she was bluffing, he'd try to talk her into letting things remain exactly as they were, and she wasn't going to do that. If he didn't do something, he'd lose Suzette. Sooner or later she'd get tired of the way things were and she'd leave. Maybe it would just be a stab at forcing Cord's hand, but maybe it would be in search of something more than working in a saloon and loving a man who loved you but wouldn't make you his wife. Samantha knew if Suzette left, it would break Cord's heart, but if he remained pigheaded, she wouldn't blame Suzette a bit. "Well?" she demanded, as the silence between them threatened to drag on forever.

He straightened and his foot crashed to the floor. "I'm half owner in this place, right?"

Samantha nodded. "Yes."

"Then hire someone else to help out, and take her wages out of my cut."

Damn. She'd hadn't thought about that.

Cord smiled, knowing he'd won this round. "Come on, I'll take you to supper."

Samantha shook her head. "No, I have to finish the accounts."

"The accounts can wait." He walked around her desk and took her hand. "Come on."

"I'll have to change first. There won't be time when we get back."

He stepped aside as she rose. "I'll wait for you in the saloon."

Twenty minutes later Samantha was back downstairs. "You two don't have to take me to supper."

Cord offered his arm as Jake hurried to open the door. "We know we don't have to—we want to. And we don't have to hurry. Suzette and Molly and Curly are going to get things ready for tonight."

"Yeah. Anyway, they're having roast beef at the Carlisle tonight," Jake said. "And you been in a bad mood, so we figured that might cheer you up."

Jake's words stung, but she knew they were true. She'd been thinking of Reid. And not being able to stop thinking about him had soured her mood to the point she was probably more bitter than a lemon. She'd been a fool . . . again. "You're right. I have been rather peevish." She smiled. "So now I'll stop."

"Just like that?" Cord said, looking at her warily.

Samantha slipped a hand through Cord's offered arm, then turned and placed her other on Jake's arm. "Yes, just like that."

They headed down the street toward the Carlisle, which stood at the opposite end of Under-the-Hill from the Silver Goose saloon.

Huge drays, heavily laden with cargo, rumbled their way down the street past them as the three made their way toward the hotel and restaurant. The wagons' wheels stirred up clouds of dust on the unpaved street, but no one seemed to notice. Several children scampered past, chasing a ball, a ragtag dog at their heels.

At least a dozen paddle wheelers were docked at the landings, half of them heavily laden with cargo and readying to depart. Suddenly the loud boom of a cannon filled the air and the woman walking in front of them jumped to grab the wall of the mercantile and screamed.

Samantha hurried to her side and touched her arm gently. "It's only Old Saratoga," she said, trying to calm the woman and pointing toward the bluffs. "It's a cannon."

"Well, whyever did it go off?" the woman asked nervously, looking about as if she expected to see an army of savages riding down on them in attack.

Sam smiled. "It's set off to announce a riverboat's approach."

"Goodness gracious," the woman said. "It's enough to scare a body to death."

"I guess we're so used to it, we don't even notice it anymore."

The woman walked off muttering to herself, and Samantha stifled a laugh as Cord and Jake didn't bother to even try to quiet theirs.

An hour later Samantha watched Jake gulp down a third piece of apple pie. "Do you ever fill up?" she asked teasingly.

Cord reached into a pocket of his vest. "Well, you're in a better mood, our difference on that little matter we discussed earlier is settled, and Jake's stomach is finally full, I hope." He pulled out his pocket watch and flipped its case open. "And I'd say it's just about time we get back to the saloon and make sure everything's ready for tonight's games."

Samantha rose, and as she did her gaze swept the room. She was just about to turn toward the door when she saw him. He was sitting at a table near one of the dining room's wide windows, a view of the river beyond its panes.

But it wasn't merely the sight of Blackjack Reid Sinclaire that gave Samantha reason to pause—it was the woman sitting across the table from him.

"Sam?" Cord said. "You all right?"

"Yes." She struggled to maintain her composure. Damn him. She wanted to cry, and scream, and throw something. *He's no-good,* she told herself quickly. She'd known that from the beginning. He was just like Loren, just like Valic and Dante. Scoundrels, every one of them. And she was better off without him.

Liar, a little voice in the back of her mind whispered.

She whipped away from the table and walked toward the door.

Cord followed Samantha, watching her make her way across the crowded room, her back stiff, her gaze stubbornly fixed straight ahead. An air of coldness emanated from her. He glanced around for the cause of her change of mood, and found it almost instantly. Sinclaire! Curse the man to hell. Fury welled up inside of Cord. Once, long ago, Reid had been like a son to him, but if he ever found out the man had hurt Samantha, he'd kill him, and he wouldn't even bat an eyelash while doing it.

"Reid, whatever is the matter with you?" Rhonda asked, reaching across the table and nudging his arm.

He threw her a cursory glance, but did not answer. He was too busy watching Samantha. She had looked at him once, as she'd risen from her table, but it had been a look of pure ice. He thought of going after her, but held himself back. There was nothing between them. She was a saloon whore, and he was a gambler. They'd spent an evening together, and enjoyed each other's company and bodies. So what?

But something hovering deep in the far back, dark

recesses of his mind told him that there was much more between him and Samantha than a few hours of shared pleasure.

"That's the woman I talked to in the saloon," Rhonda said, her gaze following Reid's.

Reid had already known that. The problem was, he wasn't certain that Rhonda had told him "exactly" what had been said. Rhonda was impulsive, impatient, and outspoken, and he feared she would become quickly bored with the few social activities she'd be able to find around Natchez to amuse her.

He turned back to his sister. "Rhonda, exactly what was said between you two?"

"What?"

"What did you say to Samantha?"

"I told you," she snapped, instantly vexed. "I asked where you were, and she wouldn't tell me."

"And then what did you do?"

"Nothing."

"Rhon?" he said, his disbelief heavy in his tone.

"Why do you always think I've done something?" she flared, reaching for her wineglass. "Every time one of your little schemes goes awry you always think it's my fault. Just like with that situation in France, and then Lillian."

Chapter Twelve

The sun had nearly disappeared over the horizon, leaving Under-the-Hill steeped in the shadows of dusk, while painting the sky with a swash of gold-tinged pink.

Old Saratoga boomed.

Samantha didn't even notice. She slammed a hand against one of the Goose's louvered entry doors and stalked into the saloon. It was still empty; the games were not scheduled to start for another hour and a half. "Curly," she said, and paused at the bar. "The good stuff."

The bald bartender set down the tray of glasses he'd just carried in from the storage room and looked at her as if she'd just asked him to shoot himself. "What?"

"Give me Cord's bottle and a glass."

He stared at her, still struggling with disbelief. "Excuse me?"

"A bourbon," Samantha demanded again. Her anger was building stronger with each passing second. Was she mad at Reid for leaving her without a word? For having another woman, which she'd already known? Or was she just plain mad at herself for caring at all.

She decided it was all three.

He could have at least said something to her before leaving, instead of sneaking out of her room in the middle of the night while she slept.

And he didn't know that she knew that he was married. He could have told her. It would have been the honorable thing to do.

She nearly scoffed aloud. Honor? Blackjack Reid Sinclaire didn't have any! She glared at her bartender. "Curly, where's my drink?"

The frown cut deeper into his forehead and drew his bushy black brows together so closely over his nose they seemed to become one long and unbroken dark line.

"Sam," Cord said, his tone reproachful as he moved to stand beside her. "Why don't you take it easy? Go up to your room and lie down for a while?"

Curly glanced at Cord, not certain what was going on, or what he should do.

Samantha slapped a hand on the bar. "I want that drink. Now!"

Curly hastily reached under the bar, where he kept Reid's "good" stuff, and grabbed a bottle.

Cord motioned for Curly to wait. "Sam, why don't we talk about . . ."

"If I have to, I'll go down the street to Jubilee's to get a drink," Samantha threatened. She wouldn't, but she figured the threat sounded good. Jubilee's, and a couple of the other saloons along the river, had a little secret that wasn't much of a secret anymore; they watered down their whiskey, then dropped a dead rat into it to give it back a "sting" and let it sit for a while, fermenting. The thought of drinking that stuff sent a shudder through Sam. She'd rather die of thirst.

Cord sighed. "Fine." He looked at Curly. "Give her the damned drink."

Samantha watched Curly set a shot glass on the bar in front of her then fill it. She grabbed the glass and downed the golden liquor in one gulp. Fire swept its way through her throat and brought tears to her eyes. She instantly coughed and gasped for air.

"You okay?" Curly asked instantly, his eyes full of concern.

Samanatha nodded, unable to talk. She could count on one hand the number of times she'd actually taken a drink of anything stronger than sarsaparilla. She gasped again, hanging on to the bar with both hands, then straightened. "I'll be in my office," she said, her voice raspy, her entire body feeling as if invaded by a flow of hot, volcanic fire. "And I don't want to be disturbed"—her gaze pointedly moved from Curly to Cord—"unless this place is on fire and falling down around our ears."

They watched her stalk from the room.

"I knew Sinclaire was trouble the minute he walked in here," Cord grumbled under his breath.

The *Mississippi Belle*'s gangplank lowered. Several men on the wharf hurried to secure it in place, while another drew a large dray up nearby, preparing for whatever cargo would be unloaded after the passengers debarked.

Lillian turned to address the ship's servant who'd stumbled down the corridor after her, laden down by her bags. "I'll need a carriage."

The man nodded. "Yes, ma'am." He set her bags down and hurried toward the gangplank.

Grasping a fold of her skirt, she raised it slightly and followed him, the white and green plumes attached to her hat, which she'd purchased in Paris because it so perfectly matched her traveling suit, danced softly over her shoulder with each step she took. "What an absolutely disgusting place," she murmured, pausing on the wharf to look around. She turned back to the servant. "This is Natchez?"

"Yes, ma'am," the servant said. "I'll get your bags, ma'am, and"—he motioned toward a nearby carriage—"he'll take you Top-the-Hill to the Durante Hotel."

"Is that the best place in town?" Lillian asked, staring down her nose at the man as he struggled to pick up her bags again.

A forced smile pulled at his lips. "It's the only hotel Top-the-Hill, ma'am, at the moment, that is. The Pierson-Montague is newer, and bigger, but that had a fire last month, so it's closed for repairs."

"Wonderful," Lillian grumbled uner her breath. She allowed him to help her into the carriage. Well, at least they had carriages here, she thought, as the driver snapped his whip and they began to roll forward. By the looks of the shabby clapboard buildings they were passing, she'd probably been lucky they hadn't just given her a mule to ride.

She looked at the passing scenery with disdaing. Valic just better know what he's doing, she thought, or she'd have his head on a platter for dinner, and that would only be for a start. She snapped open her parasol and held it over her to block out the sun. Heavens, but it was hot. She'd fully intended to follow Reid, but not to some hot, run-down little river town. If she'd know it was like this, she just might not have come. She glanced into her reticule, making certain the money Valic had sent her was still there. If Avery Brontiff hadn't been such a cad, she wouldn't be in this fix now. But, she smiled to herself, a handsome face always had been her downfall, among other masculine attributes, and Avery's attributes had been quite substantial. It was just too bad she hadn't realized earlier he was also a thief. But that little talent of his she hadn't realized until the morning she'd wakened up to find herself having been relieved of just about every cent she possessed, her home stripped of every valuable that had been in it, and a threat of debtors' prison hanging over her head. Suddenly having Reid Sinclaire for a husband didn't seem so bad ... and who was to know her petition for divorce had been granted? Certainly not Reid—he'd already been long gone from England when that had happened.

But, of course, her plan to reunite with Reid was on hold until she talked to Valic. He obviously had something in mind he wanted her to do, and his correspondence had indicated that he would pay handsomely.

The carriage stopped before a three-story brick building at the crest of Silver Street. A small sign proclaiming it the DURANTE HOTEL hung over the door, and its front windows and entry looked across the bluffs to the river below.

Well, it certainly wasn't the Drake in London or Paris's Julian, but it was much better than what they'd passed before coming up the hill.

The hotel's lobby was spacious and, Lillian thought, the decor a bit understated. The walls were white, the ceiling quite high, long green drapes framed floor-to-ceiling windows, tapestry-covered settees were set about here and there, and the desk and stairs took up one entire wall of the room.

"Ah, madam, you have a reservation?" the desk clerk said, smiling happily and causing his already full cheeks to puff out ever further.

"No," Lillian said coolly, "and I don't expect that to be a problem. I am Lady Moreleigh."

The clerk's eyes widened. "Oh, but madam, we do have

a reservation for you." He handed her a sealed note, then swiveled the register book toward her so that she could sign it and turned to retrieve the keys to her room.

Lillian smiled. Valic was proving quite competent. She signed the book with a flourish.

The desk clerk clapped his hands and a porter hurried to Lillian's side.

Moments later she followed him to her room, tipped him, and told him to have someone sent up to prepare a bath for her. The moment he left the room, she pulled the note the desk clerk had handed her from her reticule. He'd said it had been left for her earlier that afternoon, and since no one knew she was coming to Natchez except Valic, she assumed he'd seen to her room and left the note. Lillian broke the wax seal and unfolded the thin piece of paper.

The writing was an exaggerated slash of swirls and elegant lines. Valic's. She had seen his handwriting enough times to recognize it instantly. He wanted to meet her in the morning, at nine o'clock, but they couldn't be seen together. She was to rent a carriage and drive it toward a plantation called Elmwood. She could arrange for the carriage rental through the desk clerk and also get directions to Elmwood from him. Valic would intercept her along the way.

Lillian smiled. She just loved games, and this one just might prove to be the most intriguing and fun she'd ever had. Especially if it meant destroying Reid, which Valic had hinted that it did.

Reid looked about the Silver Goose. His thoughts were in chaos, but then that was nothing new, so was his life, and had been for the past five years. Everything had begun to go wrong for him the night Bethany had been killed.

Reid pulled a cheroot from his pocket and clipped off one end. If he was lucky the games would end before Lillian made it to Natchez. If he wasn't, he could expect all hell to blow up in his face. The thought of seeing his wife again left a decidedly bad taste in Reid's mouth. The prospect that she might be accompanied by a bounty hunter or two made it worse. He drew a lucifer from the pocket of his silver threaded black vest, struck it against the edge of the table, then held it to the end of the cheroot and cupped the flame with his hand. All the while he looked at Cord, standing across the room at the bar. What would his old friend say now, Reid wondered, if he walked up to him and said he'd had his way with Samantha? If he explained, in detail, how Cord's mistress had gladly, even passionately, invited Reid into her bed? And with Cord quite possibly right in the next room.

An ugly oath ripped through Reid's mind. A week ago the thought of seducing Samantha and then throwing that conquest in Cord's face had given Reid hours of intense pleasure, the anticipation of actually doing it something he'd looked forward to with relish. Now . . . thoughts of Samantha lying naked beside him, her warm body pressed to his, the way she'd cried out his name when he'd been inside of her, satisfying her, filled his mind. And just the thought of telling Cord that he'd made love to Samantha disgusted him.

"So, you gents ready to lose your money tonight?"

Reid dragged his attention from Cord and looked back at the men at his table. "No, that's not why I'm here," Reid said to the man who'd spoken, "but I am ready to play poker and take your money." He smiled easily.

As the dealer took his place at the table and began shuffling the cards, Reid's gaze wandered the room again. The flickering light of the ornate brass and crystal chandeliers overhead turned the white smoke from the men's cigars and cheroots to a sickly gray that hung on the air, giving the room a pale eeriness.

As the cards were dealt, Reid felt them hit the hand he had lain on the table. At least the game would take his mind off of Samantha . . . and Lillian . . . and Clarissa . . . and Rhonda. He looked down and slid the cards into his palm. Women were going to be the death of him, and he was barely thirty years old.

Before the evening was half over Reid had managed to win twenty-five thousand dollars, and his present hand was a good one.

"You rotten skunk! You're cheating!"

Reid whipped around and stared at the man who'd slammed a fist onto his table and shouted. He was seated at the table directly behind Reid, a tall, burly man and one of the few in the room that Reid didn't recognize.

He suddenly jumped to his feet, nearly knocking the table over.

Three others at the table also bolted to their feet. A derringer instantly appeared in one man's hand, another reached for the gun holstered at his waist, while the third threw back the tail of his long coat and went for the Peacemaker strapped to his thigh.

"Hold it!" Jake grabbed the tall man's arms and jerked them behind him. "Ain't no cheating in here," Jake growled, "and we ain't having no trouble either." He ushered the man toward the door. "You just got eliminated, friend." He shoved him outside.

"You can't do that!" the man screamed. He barged back through the swinging doors. "I paid my fee, and I wasn't the one cheating."

Jake's fist slammed into the man's jaw and he dropped instantly to the floor.

Everyone went back to their game.

Cord said something to the bartender, then approached

the table where the trouble had ensued. He picked up the tall man's cards, then those of the man he'd accused of cheating. He set both down and glanced at each man seated at the table, his gaze finally locking on the accused. "You want to say anything about what happened here, Gerard?"

Valic shrugged. "The man was a sore loser. What else is there to say?"

Cord's eyes narrowed and he looked at the dealer. "I'll take over the deal at this table for a while, Sean."

The man nodded and relinquished his seat.

Within the next hour three men from Reid's table dropped out of the game. They'd lost their money and the challenge, but wished those still playing luck.

Samantha called for a five-minute break.

Men rose immediately, pocketed their stakes, and wandered about. Some headed for the john, others stepped outside for some fresh air, and still others merely walked around the saloon, stretching their legs.

Reid approached Samantha. He should have approached Cord—should have already told him what he'd intended to say—should have already enjoyed the look of anguish he knew his words would bring to his old friend's face, and heart. But some time during the last few hours he'd decided he wasn't going to say anything. It bothered him that he'd made that decision and he wasn't sure why, but he just knew he couldn't say anything to Cord. And that punched a big hole in his plays for revenge against the man. "You look beautiful this evening," Reid said softly, pausing beside her.

Samantha started. In her preoccupation with watching Cord handle the problem at the table, then answering a question Curly had asked just after she'd called for the five-minute break, she hadn't noticed Reid's approach. She turned toward him. Hurt, humiliation, and indignation flared in her instantly, combining, melding, fusing, and turning to a white hot fury. He had actually approached her. Was actually making small talk, as if nothing was wrong. As if nothing had changed between them. The man had more audacity than a sex-starved bull. Samantha's hand ached to slap his face. Instead, she forced her lips into a cool smile. "Isn't that something you should be saying to your wife, Mr. Sinclaire?" With that, and an intense sense of satisfaction, she turned abruptly and walked away.

His wife? Reid's heart felt suddenly gripped by the icy fingers of dread. He whipped around, his gaze skipping hurriedly around the room in search of Lillian.

Samantha ran into her office and slammed the door behind her. Damn, but she hated him! He had charmed her with sweet words, made love to her in her own bed, and left without even a good morning or a goodbye. That was bad enough, but then he'd brought his wife to town and actually paraded her down to the Carlisle, right in front of Samantha. She pounded a fist on her desk. Why, when it came to men and her heart did she always end up being such a fool? Didn't she ever learn anything? She paced the office. Swore a cavalcade of oaths that would turn her aunt Dellie's gray hair to snow white. Fought back her tears. Kicked a chair and sent it crashing against the wall, and swore some more. Finally, she pulled herself together. If she hid in her office much longer, Cord or Jake would come looking for her to find out what was wrong. She checked her appearance in the mirror that hung on one wall and left the office.

She no longer felt an urge to murder Reid Sinclaire, she told herself. Now she'd be satisfied to merely see him tarred and feathered.

She brushed a wayward curl from her forehead, held her chin up defiantly, and squared her shoulders as she walked into the saloon. The very last thing she intended to do was let Blackjack Reid Sinclaire see that he'd had any effect on her life whatsoever. She didn't need him, didn't want him, and the sooner he was gone from Natchez and out of her life and sight the better.

At the end of the bar she stopped short, her enforced calm instantly destroyed as fury and jealousy assailed her. Samantha swallowed hard as her gaze riveted itself upon Rhonda Sinclaire. Her golden brown curls shimmered beneath the chandelier's glow, accentuated by a gown almost the exact shade and trimmed with dark brown velvet that seemed to intensify the inky color of her dark eyes. She stood next to Reid, one hand on his shoulder possessively as she leaned over him and whispered something into his ear. Leaning forward like that, the deeply cut décolletage of her gown revealed far more of her attributes than Samantha would ever have thought a "lady" should or would reveal. But then she was a gambler's wife, Samantha reminded herself derisively, so she mostly likely wasn't a lady in the true sense of the word, in spite of the fact that according to what Cord had said, Reid's wife was a titled Englishwoman.

Reid held his cards against his chest as he looked up at Rhonda. "Are you sure?" he growled softly.

She straightened and rolled her eyes, giving him a sardonic grin. "Of course, I'm sure. I was just about to leave the room when she walked past and a porter showed her into one of the others down the hall."

"Which one?" Reid asked.

"Room 312."

"Did she see you?"

Rhonda shook her head. "I stepped back into the room and closed the door before she could."

"I should have known things were going too smoothly the moment you showed up." Reid threw in his hand. He was up thirty thousand dollars.

The rest of the evening passed with excruciating slowness, but finally it was time to leave, and even though his mind had been haunted with thoughts of Samantha and the prospect of seeing Lillian again, which he dreaded, he managed to win.

"Come on." He rose and grabbed Rhonda's arm. After depositing his money with Curly, a game rule, Reid practically hurtled his sister from the saloon.

"That woman is not going to keep messing up my life," Reid snarled, as they walked into the hotel lobby.

Rhonda hurried alongside of him. "What are you going to do?"

"I don't know."

They climbed the stairs in silence and walked cautiously down the hall and past the doors to their own rooms until they were nearly in front of 312. "There's no light coming from beneath her door," Reid whispered, staring down at the narrow space between the bottom of the door and the floor.

"She's probably asleep."

Reid looked at his sister. "Yeah, but with who?" Before she could respond, he motioned her back toward their own rooms. "I don't much feel like getting into another shooting match over Lillian, and having another wanted poster on my head."

She looked at him sharply. "Do you care what she's doing?"

"No. I just wish she was doing it on the other side of the world."

"I could confront her," Rhonda offered, praying he wouldn't take her up on the offer. "Find out what she wants. Why she came here."

"No. It's obvious why she came here—she's after me." He stopped, his door half opened, and looked back at Rhonda. "Do you know if she checked in alone?"

Rhonda shrugged. "I didn't see anyone else with her."

Reid frowned. "Well, if there were any bounty hunters with her, knowing Lillian, she wouldn't exactly want to keep their company all that close."

"So what do we do?"

"Nothing that won't keep till morning," Reid said, not quite sure himself what he was going to do.

Lillian whipped the carriage reins, feeling a delicious sense of adventure. Valic always had been especially wicked. She wondered just what his scheme was this time. Something daring she knew, and dangerous, since he didn't want them to be seen together. But that was just as well. If this didn't work out, she would need to be on Reid's good side, so she couldn't take any chances.

The mansion he'd told her to watch for—Elmwood—came into view, a delicately elegant but modest two-story white structure with balconies that ran the entire front of the house and were framed by intricately designed wrought iron railings and balustrades.

Lillian didn't know what to do. Stop or keep going? His note had said drive toward Elmwood, not past it. Where was he? She looked around, but decided not to stop the carriage. After all, she couldn't just sit there in the middle of the road without attracting attention. Within seconds the mansion was behind her. Lillian sighed. She'd kill Valic if this was some sort of wild goose chase. The road was narrow and framed with a profusion of shrubs and trees, casting cool, hazy shadows everywhere. The sudden thought that she could be attacked by a highwayman, that she could be robbed, or . . . or her person taken advantage of sent a sweep of icy gooseflesh skipping over her arms.

A horse and rider suddenly darted into the road from the bushes.

Lillian's heart nearly stopped. She jerked on the reins and let out an involuntary shriek. The carriage horse reared.

Lillian was thrown against the back of the seat. Her fears were coming true! She was going to be robbed . . . raped . . . maybe even murdered!

Valic laughed and grabbed the horse's harness to still him. "Lillian, my dear, you always did know how to make an entrance and greet a man."

"Good Lord, Valic, you beast," she snapped, pressing a hand to her breast and straightening herself on the seat, "whatever is the matter with you? You nearly frightened me half to death."

He dismounted, tied his horse to the rear of her carriage, and climbed in beside her, taking the reins from her still trembling hands. A moment later he drew the carriage to a stop in a small clearing that sat well off the road and out of view of anyone passing by.

"Lillian," Valic said. He dragged her into his arms and caught her lips with his. "Ah, but I have missed you, *chérie.* Terribly."

A hot wave of desire instantly surged through Lillian, but she fought against it and pushed him back. There would be time for that later. "Oh, Valic, please, it's been over two years," she said impatiently, and straightened the front of her dress. "And we both know very well that you didn't contact me in Boston and request I come to this horridly uncivilized place just because you missed me."

A lascivious smile played upon his lips. "But I have missed you."

Charm, good looks, and a devious mind. She found him delicious. And almost irristible. "And?" she demanded, feeling the flush in her cheeks and hating it for giving her away.

He settled comfortably back in his seat and smiled. The curve of his lips was wickedly sensual, but the look in his eyes was just plain wicked. And Lillian loved it. In fact, there wasn't another man on earth, at least whom she'd met, who excited her quite as much as Valic always did. "Remember that earl, Lillian? What was his name? Wentworth? Kennyworth? Dockworth? Something like that?"

"His name was Kenilworth," Lillian said frostily. She had been in the process of seducing the earl and relieving him of his jewelry when she'd had the misfortune to be spotted by Valic. They'd been strangers then, but that situation had been quickly remedied.

She'd owed Valic a favor for not turning her in ever since, and she knew that, in his own way, he was calling in that favor now. But she had no intention of doing anything for free, debt or no debt.

"Ah, yes, the Earl of Kenilworth," he mused. "James, I believe his name was. Liked to be called Jamie, as I recall." He shook his head. "What a sorry one he was." He laughed. "By any chance, my dear, do you still have the diamond stickpin you stole from him that night?"

"No."

"Too bad. I liked it. And it would have gone so handsomely with this suit, don't you think?" He sighed. "Oh, well."

"Oh, well what?" Lillian said, her patience about evaporated. She wanted to know what he had up his sleeve, and she wasn't going to be in the mood for any of his charm and kisses until he told her.

He turned in his seat, took one of her hands in his, and began to play with her fingers, running one of his seductively up and down between hers. "Do you still like to play games, Lillian?"

She smiled. Now they were getting down to business. "Of course."

"Good. Then you'll enjoy what I have in mind."

"Which is?"

"You remember the poker game I mentioned in my earlier note to you, and its one million dollar prize?"

She nodded.

"I cannot afford to lose it."

Lillian laughed then. "So don't," she said simply. "You can bottom deal, sleeve slip, and palm a deck of cards better than anyone I've ever seen. Just do what you do best, Val."

"Your husband . . ."

"Ex-husband," Lillian reminded him.

"Has a reputation for being the best at spotting those little tricks."

"So?"

"So I need his mind preoccupied. I need him at his worst, not his best. Seduce him, Lillian. Get him back in your bed and play with his mind. Destroy his ability to concentrate, to think of anything but you."

She smiled coyly. "And what makes you think he still desires me, darling? We are divorced, you know? And after that ugly little incident in London, with Sir Percival, I really . . ."

"You are a desirable woman, Lillian. I am sure you have your ways of enticing a man." His lips brushed her cheek. "Even when he doesn't want to be enticed."

He also needed Reid away from Clarissa, and if the man

was losing his money, and enjoying Lillian's favors, maybe he'd have no time or desire for Clarissa Beaumont. And that was definitely a little contingency plan he couldn't afford to have go awry just now.

The young woman was a virtual ninny, and the time he spent with her was pure agony, but if things with wrong at the saloon or with Samantha, he would need Clarissa more than ever.

Chapter Thirteen

Samantha looked at her image in the tall mirror, then adjusted her short, waist-length jacket. The soft orange and apricot hued riding outfit seemed pale compared to the colorful gowns she wore at night in the Goose.

She sighed, remembering a night long ago when she'd wanted a red ballgown and Dellie had been aghast at the very thought. Now she had half a closet full of red gowns as well as brilliant greens, dazzling blues, lavender, pink, black, and a myriad of other colors.

Turning to her dressing table, Samantha picked up her riding crop and left the room.

The tinkling sounds of piano music echoed through the Goose from the barroom, but she ignored it and left by the back door. Curly liked to play the instrument once in a while and usually picked day hours, when Holland wasn't there, since the old man acted as if anyone touching the piano but him was the world's worst sin.

Molly had sent word to the stables earlier and Rogue

was already saddled and tied, waiting, at the back door. Once mounted, Samantha pulled the thick brown veil from her hat and down over her face and headed up Silver Street, but she didn't go anywhere near Dellie's house. Those visits were reserved for late at night.

Heading out of town, she rode briskly, and it wasn't long before she was on the road to Riversrun. The previous night Valic had made a comment to her that he'd had a very tempting offer on the place from someone up north, and Samantha had awakened this morning with a desperate urge to see the place again. She didn't know why— maybe she just wanted to walk its grounds once more before someone else actually moved into the house and took the place over. Then it would be lost to her forever— no longer the Beaumont plantation, Riversrun, but someone else's, maybe even with a new name.

She maintained caution as she rode, turning her face or lowering her head whenever anyone passed. As she neared the property she cut off the road, following an old shortcut to the river. She stopped halfway to her destination and stared at the house, then quickly turned away before her sadness could settle too comfortably around her heart.

The small gazebo her father had built for her mother was still there, on the bluffs, but like the house, it was falling apart because of neglect. Most of its fancy wooden trim was broken and lying upon the ground; the structure's once pristine white balustrades and railings were now gray, and at least half of the pointed roof's shingles were gone, blown off by the wind, or having just lost their security and fallen to the ground.

Samantha dismounted and stepped into the small interior. Its shadows at once engulfed her.

A wild jasmine plant had begun curling its possessive tentacles around one of the balustrades several years ago, and now one entire side of the gazebo was covered in a tangle of vines. The scent of its blooms was a heady one, sweet and almost overpowering.

Samantha liked to remember her parents when they'd come here. She had been young, and they had seemed to be very much in love. That was why it was so hard for her to have any real ill feelings toward what her stepfather had done. She'd been hurt and dismayed and angry, but she had never been able to hate him, the way Clarissa seemed able. When their mother died, it had virtually taken all the life out of Staunton Beaumont. Nothing had mattered to him anymore. Not his home, his land, his sister, not even his children. It was as if when his wife's heart stopped beating, his had too.

She looked out at the river, letting her mind continue to wander wherever it wanted to go. Would she ever find a love that meant that much to her? Samantha wondered. That meant more than life?

"Hello, beautiful."

Samantha gasped and spun around.

Reid stood only a few feet away.

She hadn't heard him arrive. "What . . . what are you doing here?"

He shrugged nonchalantly and approached. "Enjoying the view. Taking a ride." He paused at the stairs to the gazebo and, raising a booted foot to rest it on one leaf-covered step, looked up at her. "Looking for you."

There was nowhere for her to go, no way to run from him, no way to pass him without touching him. She turned her back to him. "I don't believe we have anything to say to one another."

"Really?" Insolence tinged the lone word. "And why is that?"

She couldn't believe his audacity. "Go back to your wife,

Mr. Sinclaire," she said softly. "I don't want you, or anything to do with you."

"Really?" he said again, drawing out the word.

She heard him step into the gazebo and her heartbeat raced.

The wooden floor creaked softly beneath his weight.

He was too near. She whirled around to face him. "Yes, really." His smile instantly warmed her blood, fired her desire, and she struggled against the feelings. "I'm warning you—leave me alone."

"Too late," he murmured softly, bending to brush his lips across her cheek. One hand moved to caress her arm, sliding slowly between shoulder and elbow, teasing, tantalizing, soothing. The other rose to the side of her neck, a feather-light touch of the very tips of his fingers that sent a shivering ripple of yearning through her.

Her anger threatened to dissipate. She would not lose control. She would not.

He brushed her hair aside, and his lips pressed to the curve of her shoulder.

Why did he have such an effect on her? She struggled for composure. "What . . ." Her skin burned from his touch. "What is there between you and Cord?" she asked breathlessly. "Why do you . . . hate each other?"

Reid pulled back and looked deep into her eyes. It wasn't a question he'd expected from her . . . but then maybe he should have; after all, she was his woman. Anger, irrational, unexplanable, and unreasonable, threatened to overwhelm him.

A moment ago she'd seen fire in his eyes. Now there was nothing but a dark, empty coldness.

"What's between Cord Rydelle and me is none of your business."

She started at the change in him, and the curtness of his words. "Cord is important to me," she said. "I care about him very much, and whatever is between you two is eating him up inside."

His gaze bored into hers. "Don't," he said softly.

It sounded like a warning, and one she neither understood nor welcomed.

He was a gambler. He was married. And according to Cord, he was a murderer. He'd already hurt her once, and she had no doubt he would do it again if she gave him the chance. "I care about you, too." She hadn't meant to say the words aloud, hadn't even wanted to think them, but suddenly they were falling past her lips, and it was too late.

Reid's gaze held hers for a long moment. His features had turned as hard as cold granite, his shoulders rigid. He was no longer the man who had held her in his arms, no longer a man fired by desire. "Then you're a fool, Samantha," he said, his tone lifeless, cutting.

A craggy voice cut through the silence. "Catfish going down the river, mo dee doh doh, catfish lies and onion pies . . ."

Reid jerked around and stared toward a copse of trees. Jeremiah. He'd forgotten he had seen the old man moving about the fields.

Samantha pushed past him and grabbed for the reins of her horse.

"Wait," Reid said, as she hurriedly mounted.

She looked down at him. "Stay away from me, Mr. Sinclaire." Pulling her horse around she pressed her heels to his ribs and he bolted away from the gazebo.

Before Reid could do more than blink, horse and rider disappeared into the trees.

He swore. He was playing with fire, and he was getting good and burned, and dammit if he could stop himself. What the hell was there about this woman that brought out feelings in him he'd rather never feel again?

He turned and looked out at the river, and the vast landscape of Louisiana beyond it. What the hell was he doing? He'd come to Natchez for one reason, and one reason only: to get revenge against Cord Rydelle for getting Bethany killed. The challenge of the game, the seduction of Samantha—those had merely been a few added benefits. But they were fast becoming complications, as was this thing with Clarissa Beaumont. And now Lillian was in town, though she'd slipped out of the hotel that morning before he'd had a chance to catch her and confront her about why she was there.

He leaned against one of the old gazebo's pillars. Did he really want to settle down here anyway? Take Clarissa for his wife?

That thought led him right back to Lillian, and a whole new train of despair.

Chapter Fourteen

Reid stared up at the cloudless sky, though his thoughts were elsewhere. He knew if he stayed out on the gallery much longer, Clarissa would come looking for him.

Nearby a vine wound its way over a trellis in the garden, the fragrance of its blooms filling the night air and reminding Reid of the perfume Samantha had worn the night he'd made love to her.

Resignation washed over him on a tide of softly simmering self-anger. Why couldn't he stop thinking about her? Revenge. That's all his assignation with her was supposed to have been. Revenge. And he'd gotten it, so why didn't it feel good? Why wasn't he satisfied. Several pithy curses flashed through his mind. Why couldn't he just get on with things and forget about her?

"And why the hell can't I bring myself to tell Cord I've had my way with his mistress?" Reid growled softly into the night.

But just thinking of Samantha brought an ache of desire

to his loins he found hard to ignore, or deny. As much as he'd wanted her that first night, he wanted her more now.

"Jonathan, whatever are you doing out here?" Clarissa slipped up beside him and wrapped an arm around his. "We've missed you."

They'd driven out to the home of one of her friends who had invited them for a light supper, but after about two hours of listening to talk of upcoming soirees, banquets, and planting strategies and political talk about who should and should not be running for president of the country, Reid excused himself for a few moments and left the house, desperate for a cheroot and a little peace, quiet, and solitude.

He didn't care about their parties or planting strategies, and he cared least of all about politics. It was a game for fools.

"I was just about to come back in for you," Reid said. "I have to leave."

"Oh, Jonathan," Clarissa pouted. "Why?"

Because I have to be back at the Goose in an hour, he thought. "I have an important meeting with Mr. Bigelow in town," he lied, knowing he couldn't tell her the truth. "Business."

The night was heavy with humidity, but the heavy foliage of the gardens and the wide-spreading limbs of the oaks that grew here and then about the house left the landscape in deep shadow.

"Well, first we must have some of Sarah Jane's famous pecan pie, Jonathan. She'll be quite indignant if we don't, you know."

They walked toward the house. He hated pecan pie, and he really didn't care if Sarah Jane became indignant with him or not.

Could he really live among these people? He'd wanted to for years. Dreamed about it. Planned it. But then, Bethany had been killed, and he'd married Lillian. That had put an end to a lot of his dreams. Now, bringing those old dreams to fruition had looked promising again. His plans were proceeding well, considering the appearance of both Rhonda and Lillian, but he couldn't quite get rid of the nagging sensation that something else was terribly wrong. He didn't know what it was, but he couldn't shake the feeling, except that it didn't seem to have anything to do with Lillian, which puzzled him.

He looked down at Clarissa. A cascade of red-brown curls tumbled in wild disorder about her shoulders, and the faint flush of excitement on her cheeks complemented the blue eyes framed by long, dark lashes. Pausing, he let impulse dictate. Dragging her into his arms, Reid crushed her body against his length as his mouth caught hers. His tongue forced her lips apart, then dived between them. He held her tightly, desperately, as his tongue dueled with hers, probing, exploring, ravishing her senses and waiting for some sense of desire, some hunger or lust to assault him.

It had to come—it had to be there, somewhere.

Finally, even reluctantly, Reid tore his mouth from Clarissa's. She leaned against him, her hands holding tight to his upper arms, her lips passion bruised, a look of confusion and excitement in her eyes as she stared up at him, gasping softly for breath. "Oh, Jonathan."

Guilt, frustration, and anger assailed him. She was a desirable woman, and he'd felt nothing. Not a stirring of passion. No desire to caress her body with his hands. No hunger to make her want him. No need to feel her body naked against his.

Marrying Clarissa could bring him everything he'd ever wanted, everything he'd been trying to achieve on and off for the past fifteen years. But now he was beginning to wonder if he still wanted what he used to dream about.

He smiled graciously as they entered the house, as they

sat at the table with their hosts, and as they ate Mary Lynn's famous pecan pie.

What if his parents hadn't been killed in that fire when he was fourteen? Reid suddenly wondered. Where would he be now? Would his life have turned out differently? Would he be a gentleman farmer like his father had been? Or maybe a clerk in a bank, or some other New York company? Would Rhonda have already been married to someone their father had approved of, maybe even chosen, and have a house full of children?

But their parents had died, and Reid and Rhonda had been sent to live with a bachelor uncle in New York who hadn't wanted them. Rhonda had promptly been ushered off to a girls boarding school in Boston, and two months later, on the same day Reid turned fifteen, he'd run away. When Rhonda graduated from her school, Reid had returned and taken her on the road with him.

She'd worried for weeks that their uncle would send someone after them. Reid had known he wouldn't. The man didn't care enough. And now he was dead, having left all of his money to his mistress.

"Jonathan," their host said, breaking into Reid's thoughts, "have you given any more consideration to buying a place around here? The old Tagier place is for sale, you know. The house is a bit run-down and some of the fields have been fallow for the past couple of years, but I . . ."

"Oh, ekk," Clarissa said, a pout instantly forming on her lips. "That old creepy place. Why would anyone want to live there?"

"Actually," Reid said, thinking of the offer he'd made on Riversrun through a New York agent who had orders to keep his identity secret, "I hadn't . . ."

"Jonathan has been thinking of building us a house,"

Clarissa said, a sly smile on her lips as she hooked her arm through his and looked up at him. "Haven't you?"

Everyone stared, wide-eyed, since there had been no announcement of an engagement between Reid and Clarissa.

Would they gasp in horror if he strangled her? he wondered. Or would they applaud?

By the time he pried Clarissa away from her friends and returned her to the small town house on the hill, he had barely enough time to return to the hotel and freshen up before going to the Goose. And his mood was so black he was certain there was a thunderstorm following in his footsteps, or hanging over his head for all to see. Clarissa's little comment had been the same as declaring that he'd asked for her hand in marriage—and he hadn't. He'd been thinking about it. And maybe he eventually would have. Now he was beginning to wonder if he'd totally lost his mind even considering the idea.

He climbed the stairs to the hotel's second floor. The waning light of the late afternoon sun poured onto the landing from a tall window. Hopefully Rhonda had managed to stay out of trouble while he'd been out.

"Hello, darling."

He recognized Lillian's voice instantly, and the cold chill of dread that had been threatening him ever since he'd heard of her arrival in Natchez now snaked its way through his body. He'd known she was here . . . Rhonda had seen her in the hotel, in a room just down the hall from theirs, but still he felt a jerk of surprise at seeing her.

She was leaning inpudently against the wall next to his door, obviously waiting for him. As usual, everything about her seemed perfect. Her hair was coiffed in a profusion of ringlets that cascaded down one side of her head and over her shoulder, every strand in place, and the yellow gown she wore was a perfect accent to both her coloring and her lithe figure, fitting snug in all the right places and cutting just deep enough above her breasts to be daring, but not deep enough to be deemed scandalous.

A little white straw hat with a yellow plume gave her an air of sassiness.

Lillian smiled as Reid approached. She saw the coolness in his eyes, the wariness and disappointment. But mostly, she saw the anger. Valic's offer had been more than generous. He was convinced he could win the one million dollar challenge, but only if Reid were out of the game. If Lillian got Reid's attention off the cards, if she destroyed his concentration and he lost, Valic would pay off her debts and even give her a bit of a reward. But she was no fool. She'd nearly gotten Reid killed in England in order to save her own reputation there, and her lies had labeled him a murderer. A price was instantly put on his head, and he'd become a wanted man. It was highly doubtful his passions would be strong enough, or his forgiveness ready enough, to overlook that little bit of treachery. But she did have an idea all her own, and it had nothing to do with using her womanly charms on her ex-husband. Though as she watched him walk toward her and her eyes raked over his tall length, just for a moment, she regretted that she would never know the feel of his body pressed to hers again.

"What do you want, Lillian?" Reid asked, his tone surly now. He weighed the idea of talking to her in the hall, where who knew how many others could overhear them, or opening his door and entering his room, knowing she'd follow. Lillian was nothing if not brazen. He opted for privacy, and entered his room.

"Well, I could say I want you back," Lillian said, her tone teasing as she sauntered past him and paused near the window that overlooked the street.

"We both know that isn't going to happen."

"Well, we are married, you know."

"We shared a house, Lillian," Reid said, his tone as hard and cold as the spark in his eyes, "and sometimes a bed. But occasional sex and sharing a roof over our heads doesn't make a marriage. Or did you forget that you didn't take my name when we married? Or that you've had . . ." He screwed his forehead into a thoughtful frown. "What was it, three or four paramours in the past year alone? And then had me falsely labeled a cold-blooded murderer after I defended myself against one of your lunatic lovers?"

She smiled smugly and closed the distance between them. "Sir Percival wasn't a lunatic, Reid, merely overzealous and a bit possessive." Her smile turned slyly flirtatious. "And as I recall, sharing a bed always was the best part of our relationship." She reached out and ran her fingers lightly up his arm.

Reid jerked away as if touched by a hot iron. Six months after Bethany's death and two months after arriving in London he'd become involved in a three-day poker game, gotten so drunk he didn't known which way was up, and woke up the fourth day to find himself married to Lady Lillian Morleigh.

He'd still been grieving over Bethany's death, but he tried to make it work between himself and Lillian. At least, he thought he'd tried. Maybe he hadn't, really. Maybe their problems were his fault.

Lillian sighed as he pulled away from her, disappointed, but not really having expected much else. "I've heard you are seeing a young lady here, darling, that you're even thinking of settling down in these parts, buying yourself a little plantation, becoming a real 'gentleman.' "

She wanted something. He felt it in his gut, and it twisted sour. "So?"

She shrugged, whirled around, and walked back to the window. "Well, I assume you wouldn't want it to get around to all these oh-so-respectable people in Natchez that you're still a married man, now would you, sugar? I mean, that would certainly be frowned upon if you're courting someone else, now wouldn't it?"

"Lillian—"

"And I'm sure you don't want these genteels up here in their little plantations to know that you're still a professional gambler," she said, cutting him off. "Not a . . ." She laughed softly. "What is it you're calling yourself down here? An importer and exporter of fine European textiles, with interests in transportation?" Her laugh loudened, and she placed a hand to her breast, as if trying to contain her amusement.

He didn't know how she'd found out all of that, but he knew, for-the moment at least, he had to keep her quiet or she could ruin everything: the game, his relationship with Clarissa, and his chances of being accepted Top-the-Hill. "What do you want, Lillian?"

She smiled. "Now that's more like it, darling." She sashayed back across the room toward him, arrogance drawing her brows upward. "All I want is a paltry five hundred thousand dollars."

"I don't have that kind of money to give you, and you know it." Reid felt his temper flaring. He had it in the bank, but he had plans for that money, and those plans didn't include just handing it over to Lillian. How could he have ever stood living with this woman, calling her his wife for almost five years?

Because you spent most of your time either gambling, or lazing about in a drunken stupor, a little voice in the back of his mind whispered.

Lillian shook her head and smiled. The gesture reminded Reid of a cat who'd just caught a mouse. "But you will have the money," she said, "when you win the game down at the Silver Goose."

"What if I don't?"

She smiled, and wickedness shone from her eyes. "Then I'll just have to alert the authorities to where you are, and collect the bounty on your head instead."

Her answer didn't surprise him, and he had no doubt that she'd do it.

"Jonathan!"

Reid groaned upon recognizing Clarissa's voice. This really was turning out to be the most horrid of days. First Clarissa and her friends, then Lillian and her demands, and now Clarissa again. He had fifteen minutes to get down to the Goose and take his seat. If the games started before he arrived, he forfeited his entry as well as his winnings. Then again, the way this day had progressed so far, maybe he was destined to lose everything tonight, so it wouldn't really matter if he made it to the Goose or not. He turned as a carriage drew up beside him and stopped.

Clarissa leaned forward. "I forgot all about the masquerade ball."

He frowned, a sinking feeling in his stomach. "What masquerade ball?"

"The one I forgot to tell you about, silly. The Governor's annual masquerade ball. It's just going to be the biggest event of the season, and we're invited." Her eyes were alight with excitement. "It's being held at Auburn this year, and everyone who's anyone is going to be there." She suddenly looked stricken with panic. "Oh, we are going, aren't we, Jonathan? You don't have to leave town or something? You don't hate masquerades, do you?"

Reid struggled for patience. Could he really stand having Clarissa at his side for the rest of his life? She was beautiful, desirable, respectable, and she drove him to distraction. "No, I don't have to leave town or anything, and no, I don't hate masquerades. But I am late for my appointment. We'll talk about it tomorrow. Right now I have to . . ."

"Oh, but I have to know what you want to be?" she said, climbing down from the carriage and slipping an arm possessively around his. "We only have a few days to prepare, and I'm having Mrs. Pellerton come to the house tomorrow to start on our costumes. She really is the best seamstress in town. I was thinking of Romeo and Juliet, but that was so tragic, and I heard that the Parrimores are doing that anyway. Then I thought of Neptune and a mermaid, but Aunt Dellie nearly fainted when I mentioned a mermaid's costume, and then I thought . . ."

She continued talking, but Reid quit listening. Why did he feel as if Clarissa already had a ring through his nose and was walking down the aisle? He pulled his pocket watch from his vest and flipped it open. Ten minutes and he would forever lose the chance to win one million dollars. He steered Clarissa back toward the buggy, forcibly removing her arm from around his. "Whatever you decide, Clarissa, is fine. Now I really do have to go." The moment he heard his own words he knew he'd regret them, but it was too late to change them now, and he didn't have time to worry about it.

Moments later, as Reid walked down Silver Street, he wondered if this masquerade ball could have anything connection with Lillian's arrival in Natchez. It seemed a farfetched idea, then again, hadn't that been all the rage in England the year he'd left? There had been a flurry of masquerade balls over the holidays and during these, several royals had been relieved of some valuable pieces of jewelry. And Lady Lillian Morleigh had been in attendance at every one of the balls. He'd heard a rumor once that she had once worn a brooch that looked very much like one stolen several years earlier from the Duke of Reimoure.

Her explanation that it had been sent to her by a secret

admirer didn't ring true then, and it didn't ring true to Reid now.

He cursed softly. Trouble just seemed to have a way of following in his footsteps, and now, just when he thought he might have shaken it, Lillian was leading it right back to him in spades.

The moment he walked into the Silver Goose, his gaze sought out and found Samantha. She was standing toward the rear of the room, at the end of the bar, talking with Foxe Brannigan.

Reid felt a spurt of jealousy burn hot within his chest. Foxe was a ladies' man, through and through. He'd fleeced more women on riverboats than the night sky had stars, yet they all loved him anyway. Some were even foolish enough to come back for more. Samantha seemed to be hanging on his every word. Reid made his way toward them.

He had never seen a woman more beautiful. Her hair shone like fire beneath the light of the chandeliers, while the deep emerald satin of her gown seemed to play with the color of her eyes and accentuate the creaminess of her skin. "We need to talk," he said, ignoring Foxe and staring pointedly at Samantha.

She looked at him coolly. "I'm sorry, Mr. Sinclaire, but I happen to be busy at the moment, and frankly, as far as I'm concerned, we have nothing to say to each other. Unless you have a problem with the games?"

His anger burned hotter. "It's important."

The silence between them grew tight with tension, as each stared into the other's eyes.

Samantha found herself fighting to control the trembling that had attacked her body the moment she'd noticed him approaching her. She would not be played for a fool again. Never, ever again. "Maybe it's important to you, Mr. Sinclaire, but I can't think of anything you

might have to say to me that I would deem important."
She looked back at Foxe and smiled. "Sorry for the interruption. Now, what were you saying?' ""

Reid grabbed her arm, his fingers firmly encircling the
bare flesh just beneath the fringe of white lace that
trimmed the green satin bouffant sleeve.

"Excuse me," Samantha said, glaring at him and jerking
her arm back.

"Yes," Reid said, looking at Foxe, "excuse us."

Reid held firm, and suddenly propelled her down the
hall, past her office, and out the back door.

Samantha pulled herself free and whirled away from
him as they stepped outside. "How dare you!"

He leaned lazily back against the closed door, preventing
her from reentering. "You're angry with me because I left
your bed without saying goodbye."

Samantha stared at him, unable to believe what he was
saying. "You are the most arrogant, the most . . ."

He grabbed her arms and dragged her up against him,
crushing her breasts to his chest, his mouth to hers. His
tongue dove between her lips, the act conquering her
resistance, destroying the barriers she'd tried to rebuild
against him. Her senses spun.

Resist him, everything inside of her warned, but she
couldn't obey. His hands on her body, his lips on hers,
destroyed her common sense, made her feel things she
didn't want to feel, made her want things she knew she
could never have.

"I want you, Samantha," Reid said, his lips moving over
the curve of her chin, down the slope of her neck.

It took all of the willpower she possessed, but Samantha
pulled away from him. "You . . . you want me," she echoed,
staring at him. "What about your wife, Mr. Sinclaire? Do
you want her, too?"

"You don't understand. It's . . ."

"Did you know she came to the Goose?" Samantha said. "Rhonda Sinclaire. It has a nice ring to it. Rhonda and Reid. Sounds kind of like a stage act, doesn't it?"

"Rhonda?" Reid felt such relief he nearly laughed. She thought Rhonda was his wife. He grabbed her arm and hauled her back into his embrace. "Rhonda is not my wife," he growled softly. His mouth captured hers again, inflicting an assault that nearly left Samantha quivering. "She's my sister," he said, a moment later.

"I don't believe you." Samantha's breath was ragged, her heart beating so fast she felt faint. "You're lying. You're . . ."

Reid's head lowered and his lips brushed against the top of Samantha's breasts. "No," he whispered against her flesh, "I'm not."

A moan escaped her lips.

"I'll send for her, and you can ask her yourself."

Her knees trembled.

"I want you," he whispered harshly.

"Gentlemen, please take your seats," Curly yelled from inside the Goose. "The games are about to begin."

Reid cursed and straightened. He looked into Samantha's eyes. "We'll continue this later," he said softly, and brushed his lips across hers again, before turning and walking back into the saloon.

Chapter Fifteen

"Oh, dear." Dellie darted about her parlor, trying to decide what to do. "Oh, dear, oh, dear, oh, dear." Her eyes filled with tears.

"Miz Delphine, if you don't calm yourself," her maid said, coming into the room carrying a tray laden with a teapot, a plate of cookies, and a cup and saucer for Dellie, "you're gonna just up and keel over and die—that's what you're gonna do for sure."

She placed the tray that was nearly bigger than she was on a table and huffed with the effort.

Dellie ignored the woman and whirled about, charging for her small writing desk. Throwing herself onto its chair, her brown and white skirts flouncing about her, she grabbed a quill from its holder and plunked its end into the inkwell. "I just don't know what else to do," she mumbled, hurriedly scribbling a note to Samantha. Dellie turned to the maid. "Annie, you must go Under-the-Hill for me right away and deliver this." Dellie quickly sealed the note and held it out to the small, black woman.

Annie looked at Dellie incredulously, her yellow aged old eyes widening in disbelief. "Under-the-Hill?" she repeated. "Under-the-Hill? You want me to go down to that sinful place all by myself?"

"Oh, Annie," Dellie shushed, "it's not that bad. And I really need you to do this."

"What for?" Annie demanded, eyes narrowing, hands propped on her bony hips in defiance. The two women had been together for so long that propriety, or concern for who was the mistress and who was the maid, was not always a question between them any longer.

"I told you," Dellie said, clearly exasperated. "I need this delivered immediately." She stood and shoved the note at Annie. "Now, I need you to go down to the Silver Goose saloon on—"

"A saloon?" Annie screeched. "Miss Delphine, you can't mean that. You can't mean for me to go to a saloon down in that god-awful place. Oh, no." She shook her head wildly and huffed. "I'll be killed, or . . . or . . ."

Dellie stomped her foot. "Annie, stop all this nonsense. Please. This really is an emergency." She grabbed Annie's hand and shoved the note into it. "I'll buy you a new dress. I'll give you the weekend off. Anything! But I need you to do this."

Annie stared at Dellie in surprise, having never seen her mistress in such a state.

"Go to the Silver Goose," Dellie said, "but make sure to wear a shawl, no, a cloak." She grabbed her own full-length cloak from a hook near the front door. "Here, wear mine." Dellie swirled the garment around Annie's shoulders. The small woman nearly disappeared within the generous folds of lightweight wool. "Try not to let anyone see your face," Dellie said, pulling the hood up over

Annie's head and tucking it close about her diminutive black face.

"Ain't got no worry 'bout that," Annie grumbled, shoving the note into the pocket of the voluminous cloak. She looked up at her mistress, who was a good foot taller, and at least a hundred pounds heavier than she was. "I can't even find myself in here."

"Give the note to a man named Jake, Annie. You can't miss him. He's a very big man, with wild red hair and freckles all over his face."

Annie frowned.

"Brown marks," Dellie explained, realizing Annie didn't understand her description of the man who Samantha described as her friend, self-appointed protector, and peacekeeper at the saloon. "Hair the color of fire," she went on, "and little spots all over his face the color of café au lait."

"What if he ain't there?" Annie asked.

Dellie urged her toward the back door. "He'll be there. He's always there, and he'll know what to do when he sees my note."

"But what if he ain't there?" Annie insisted, hanging back.

Dellie let go an exasperated sigh. "Then ask for Cord and give the note to him."

"He got spots on his face, too?"

"Annie," Dellie shrieked, "go!"

Half an hour later, holding her cloak tightly about her shoulders, Annie made her way down the steep incline of Silver Street. "Ain't no decent woman never come down Under-the-Hill," Annie grumbled to herself, which she often did much to Dellie's consternation. "And I'm a decent woman. Wouldn't come neither, if Miss Delphine didn't have herself in such a snit. All because of Clari, too—I know it. That child's got the devil at work in her. Yes, sir, the devil. And it's gonna be the death of all of us."

Annie turned her face away from the brightly lit windows of Jubilee's Saloon as she passed. A woman in an outfit that Annie found disgraceful was dancing on one of the tables as several men roared their approval, and one kept lifting up what Annie assumed was supposed to be a gown, but looked more to her like a fancy camisole and a gown's skirt cut too short. "People ought to be ashamed what they do down here," she mumbled, tearing her gaze away from the scandalous scene and hurrying on.

Someone approached.

Annie hugged the hood of her cloak tighter about her throat and lowered her head. "Lord a'mercy," she prayed softly, "don't let him be no murdering thief." She missed her Jacob something terrible, but she didn't want to join him in the great beyond any sooner than need be.

The man passed, and the trembling in Annie's hands lessened somewhat. She hurried past several shops that were closed up and dark for the night. An alleyway separated two buildings. She said another prayer as she crossed it, hoping no one would jump out of the darkness and attack her.

She knew if that happened her old heart would just stop beating. There'd be no need for some scoundrel to kill her. She'd just drop dead all by herself. She glanced down Falconer's Alley, steeped in inky shadow. The dock was visible at the opposite end, moonlight having settled upon the paddle wheelers docked there, and the huge stacks of cotton and crates waiting to be loaded.

When she was younger Annie had dreamed about sneaking away from Riversrun and hiding on one of the river-boats, riding it up river, to the North, where everyone was free. Then she'd fallen in love with Jacob, and Mr. Beaumont let them get married and all her dreams had changed.

Annie sighed as she kept walking. She'd been happy most of her life. Her one regret was that she'd never had any children for Jacob. He would have been a good father.

She paused in front of the Silver Goose and looked in through the window. It was crowded, and there were only three women inside. One was handing a man near the window a drink. Another was leaning against the bar, just watching everyone else, and the last woman stood at the far end of the room, her back to the door.

Annie stared at the woman in the rear, appreciating the beautiful color of her gown, which reminded Annie of the lush lawns that had grown all around Riversrun when they'd lived there. And her hair, the color, reminded her of Clarissa's, and Dellie's, before it had turned gray. Could that be Elyse? Annie squinted her old eyes, but couldn't tell. She shrugged the thought aside and looked at the other people in the saloon. She didn't see anyone who looked like the man Dellie had described, but she walked to the door anyway, inhaled deeply, said a prayer, and entered.

Curly looked at Annie, his brows diving into a frown. If he didn't know better he'd have thought he was looking at a walking cloak, because he sure couldn't see a face anywhere within its dark folds. "You want something?" he asked hesitantly, suddenly wondering if he was staring the Grim Reaper in the eye.

Annie's chin dug deeper into her chest. "Got a note for Jake."

Curly started, but whether his shock was that someone was actually in the cloak and had spoken, or that they'd asked for Jake, he wasn't sure. And he didn't feel like examining the question.

Jake, having heard Annie, stepped away from the wall beside the door where he'd been standing and keeping an eye on everything. He tapped Annie on the shoulder.

She let out a faint shriek and, clasping the cloak with fingers nearly stiff with tension, spun to face him, her entire body trembling. Her eyes met his belt buckle. Annie gasped in a blend of shock and terror, hurriedly stepped back, then craned her neck back as far as it would go in order to look up at his face. "Lordy me, you're near big as a building," she said, her eyes large with disbelief, her heart still palpitating in fear.

Jake laughed, and the menacing aura that usually surrounded him when his face was set into a scowl suddenly vanished, revealing a big, friendly giant. "Depends on the building. You got a note for me, little lady?" he said, the play of his Irish-accented words like nothing Annie had ever heard in her life.

She dug Dellie's note from the pocket of the cloak and handed it to him.

The moment he saw it Jake's smile dived into a frown, but before he could say anything more, Annie slipped past him and ran out the door. If Dellie had written anything that was going to make that giant of a man angry, Annie didn't want to be anywhere around to see it.

Jake stared at the name written across the front of the sealed note, and felt an ominous foreboding. Resisting the urge to go to Cord, he walked to the rear of the bar and handed the note to Samantha. "Some little bitty thing of a woman in a cloak just delivered this for you."

Samantha was just as surprised as Jake had been, then her heart nearly stopped as she recognized Dellie's writing. Her aunt had never sent a note to her before, had never dared for fear someone would discover who it was from and their charade would be ruined, their lives destroyed.

Samantha hurried into her office, closed the door behind her, and ripped the note open.

> Samantha,
>   Please come as soon as possible. I fear C is about to do something horrid and I don't know how to stop her.

The note was unsigned, but Samantha didn't need a signature to know it was from her aunt. What was Clarissa about to do that Dellie found so horrid that she'd take the chance on contacting Samantha?

But as soon as the question took form in her mind, she realized there was no use speculating about it. With Clarissa, there was just no telling what her little sister would do.

Samantha waited until almost midnight, then left the saloon and hurried up Silver Street toward Top-the-Hill, all the way wondering why she'd ever listened to Clarissa's arguments and pleadings against being sent to a convent or girls' school.

"She's going to elope, Elyse. I just know it," Dellie said, pacing the room. "I overheard her talking with Sarah Jane this morning while they were getting fitted for their costumes for the masquerade ball. Whispering and giggling about marriage, and houses, and what not."

"But why do you think she'd elope?" Samantha asked. "I would think Clarissa would want the biggest, grandest wedding ever held in Natchez."

"Humph!" Dellie paused and stared at Sam. "I heard her tell Sarah Jane that she just knew her aunt and sister weren't going to approve of her beau, but she was going to marry him anyway, no matter what we said. Even if they had to run away to New Orleans to do it." Dellie threw herself into a chair with a wail. "Oh, Elyse, whatever are we going to do with that girl? She's going to ruin her life and bring scandal back to this family. I just know it, sure as I know my name is Delphine Beaumont."

"Calm down, Auntie," Sam said, trying to sooth her aunt. In reality, however, she was just as worried as Dellie. "Is Clarissa still seeing Valic Gerard, Aunt Dellie? Could that be who she was talking about with Sarah Jane? Because if so, she certainly is right that we'd never approve of her marrying him."

"Oh, Elyse, I'm not sure. Yes, I think she's still seeing him. And I know she's still keeping Phillip dangling on her line, but then there's this other one. I caught a glimpse of him the other day, when he came by. She practically flew out of the house before he could come to the door, which she's done several times, but I saw him when he helped her into his carriage."

Samantha sat forward in her chair, her attention focused solely on her aunt's words. "So, what did he look like, Auntie? Precisely."

Dellie sighed. "Well, let me think. He has kind of dark blond hair, quite attractive really. Tall, slender, and very well dressed. I think when he came this morning he was wearing blue trousers and waist jacket, a black vest that seemed to shimmer against the sun, as if there were silver threads in it or something, and a white shirt.

"Oh, and a hat, you know, wide brimmed. One of those . . . what do some of the men call them now? Phillip has one. A Stetson, I think. And it was black."

Samantha felt her heart skip a beat. If she didn't know better, she would have sworn Dellie had just described Blackjack Reid Sinclaire.

*   *   *

By the time Samantha got back to the Goose the games were nearly over for the night. They were down to only eighteen players now. It would soon be time for her to face the final six. Her gaze swept the men as they scooped up their chips, rose from their tables, and sauntered to the bar for a last drink before leaving, and to deposit their stash of winnings with Curly.

Foxe Brannigan, Valic Gerard, Rafe Santana, Tom Mowry, Bradley Simms, Corey Quait, Foster St. Leuve, and several she didn't know by name and had never met before they answered her challenge—Jack "Diamonds" Norrette, Luke Foster, Brett Morgan, and Blackjack Reid Sinclaire.

Her gaze swept over Reid as Dellie's words played through her mind.

Blond hair, quite attractive. Tall, slender, and very well dressed. Blue trousers and waist jacket, a black vest that seemed to shimmer against the sun, as if there were silver threads in it or something, and a white shirt.

Reid's blue trousers, held snug beneath the arch of his shoes by his sous pieds, delineated the long, lean line of his legs, while the matching jacket spread tautly over the wide breadth of his shoulders, then cut in to accent the narrow width of his waist. It was a color and cut that complimented him, and was set off further by the silver threads that were woven through his black vest.

And a hat. Wide brimmed. What do some of the men call them now? A Stetson. Black.

She glanced back at the table he'd vacated. A hat sat before the chair Reid had occupied all evening. A black hat, and she felt certain it was a Stetson. Samantha felt a knot form in her stomach. It couldn't be him. She shrugged the ridiculous thought from her mind. How would he have met her sister? It was impossible.

"Two or three more nights," Cord said, moving to stand beside her.

She looked up, puzzled.

He smiled. "I figure two or three more nights and we'll be down to our last group of players," he said. "Then it will be time for you to show them how the game's really supposed to be played."

"I need my sister followed," Samantha said.

The words hung in the air between them.

She hadn't meant to say the words aloud, hadn't even made up her mind that having Clarissa followed was the thing to do, but once the words were out, she knew it was exactly what had to be done. To her surprise, Cord showed no reaction. "Did you hear me?"

He nodded. "I knew something was wrong. I just thought maybe it was . . ." He let whatever he was going to say drop. "I'll get someone right on it." He studied her for a long moment before continuing, then turned and reached for the glass he'd set down on the bar. "What are they supposed to be looking for?"

"A beau," Samantha said. "She doesn't want Dellie or me to know who he is, and . . ." She glanced over her shoulder nervously.

"You figure it's not someone you and your aunt would approve of?" he offered.

She smiled, relieved that he hadn't caught her look at Reid. "Unfortunately, yes."

"Have Jake lock up. And tell Suzette I'll be back in a couple of hours. I know just who we need." Turning away, he walked past the small group of men still standing at the bar and left by the front door.

Reid watched Cord leave, then glanced back at Samantha. He'd been fighting the desire to go to her all evening, the need to drag her into his arms and make love to her having played havoc with his concentration since the moment he'd walked into the saloon earlier.

As if hearing his thoughts, and feeling his eyes on her,

Samantha's gaze met his. A coolness instantly came over her features and she turned abruptly. "Jake, Curly," she said, "lock up please. Good night."

Reid watched as she swept up the stairs without another look in his direction. She entered her room and slammed the door behind her. He walked to the table, picked up his hat, and, setting it on his head, turned toward the front of the saloon. But thoughts of Samantha, an image of her laying naked beside him, just wouldn't leave his mind.

Two hours later Samantha heard someone coming up the stairs. It was probably Cord. Maybe he had some news about Clarissa. She slipped from her bed, moved quietly to her door and opened it.

The only light in the bar was the moonlight flowing through the downstairs windows.

A man approached the landing, his dark silhouette looking large and ominous.

Samantha clutched the doorjamb.

"It's taken care of," Cord said. "You'll know every move she makes, starting in the morning."

She breathed a sigh of relief at recognizing Cord's voice. "Thank you," she whispered.

He paused before her and, reaching up, tucked her chin with his bent forefinger. "You're welcome," he said softly, and dropped a kiss to her forehead. "Now get some sleep and stop worrying."

Cord turned toward his own room, where Suzette was waiting for him, and Samantha closed her door and walked back to her own bed. But she knew sleep wasn't going to come to her yet. She had been sure the sound of someone coming up the stairs had been Cord, and she'd been right, but she couldn't deny that a part of her had been disappointed, because a part of her had been hoping to be wrong, hoping to see Reid at her door. She moved to stand by the window and looked out at the other buildings of Under-the-Hill, at the river beyond them, and at the low, flat horizon of Louisiana in the distance.

Behind the flat, jutting shelf of land that was Natchez—Under-the-Hill, with its crowded mass of cheap, clapboard buildings, the bluffs rose over two hundred feet from the river, crowned by a profusion of wild grapevines, graceful magnolias, and massive live oak trees, their ancient, gnarled and twisting limbs heavily laden with Spanish moss. And there were the mansions, each different, each beautiful in its own way.

On the opposite bank, the landscape was quite different. The alluvial lowlands of northern Louisiana sprawled lazily, all lush and green like a sweeping emerald lawn.

Samantha glanced down at the spot across the street where Reid Sinclaire had stood that first night and looked up at her window. He wasn't there now, and she felt again a sense of disappointment.

"Reid!" Rhonda pounded on his door. "Reid, wake up." She turned away, exasperated. He must be gone. But where would he go at this time of morning? He'd never been an early riser. She knew he wasn't with Clarissa Beaumont, but she couldn't think of where else he would be. She played her fingers together nervously. He had to be in his room. Most likely he'd had too much to drink last night and was still sleeping. She glanced furtively up and down the hall to make certain no one was watching, then pulled a pin from her hat. Moving close to the door so that the folds of her black and white skirt hid what she was doing, she stuck the pin in the lock and began moving it around. Within minutes the tumblers fell into place and Rhonda, with a satisfied smile, pushed the door open.

She stepped inside, then stopped. He wasn't in the bed fast alseep, as she'd assumed. "Damn, damn, and double damn," she muttered, and began to pace. "I'm going to kill him myself."

"You'll probably have to wait in line," Reid said, suddenly appearing at the door she'd absently left standing open.

Rhonda whirled around. As she did, her skirt brushed against the fireplace utensils and sent them crashing to the hearth. "Reid!" She rushed to him. "Oh, thank heavens you're here. You're not going to . . ."

He shrugged out of his jacket and threw a piece of paper onto the table near the settee.

Rhonda caught the words Natchez Telegraph at the top of the paper and instantly lost her train of thought. "What's that?" she asked.

Reid glanced back at the crumbled piece of paper. "I sent a telegram."

"I assumed that from the letterhead," Rhonda said. "But to who? About what?"

Reid sighed deeply and dropped to the settee, suddenly more tired than he had been in days. Things weren't going as he'd planned. Revenge. That had been his primary reason for coming to Natchez. That and the one million dollars. Now there were so many other things involved he felt as if his plan was unraveling at the seams. Samantha. Lillian. Clarissa. And as always of course, Rhonda. He sighed again. How had his life, his plans, become so complicated? Actually he'd sent two telegrams, but he hadn't gotten an answer from his solicitor about his anonymous offer to buy Riversrun, and he didn't want to get Rhonda's hopes up on that one. "To England," he said, wariness clear in his tone.

"Checking up on Lillian?"

"No, the bounty on my head, as well as the status of my so-called marriage."

"Whatever for?" Rhonda asked, perplexed now. "Why don't you just find a judge and tell him you want to dissolve the marriage."

He looked at her sharply. "Knowing Lillian, I'm certain she wouldn't have wanted to stay Mrs. Reid Sinclaire after having a bounty placed on my head, so my guess is I'm not even married anymore. But I'd like proof, and I don't want Lillian to know just yet, which is why I'm not going straight to a judge here. And if I asked Lillian, she just might lie."

Rhonda's brows dived into a frown. "Why do you need proof now?"

"Rhonda, think about it," Reid said, his tone harsher than he'd meant. "If I should want to marry again, I don't need another problem on my hands. Like bigamy," he added, when he saw that she still hadn't grasped what he meant.

"Oh."

"Anyway, Lillian claims we're still married and wants half the money if I win the one million dollars. That's her price for keeping quiet about the fact that I'm married to her. Otherwise she'll tell everyone I'm not only married, but a professional gambler and wanted for murder."

"What?" Rhonda's mouth dropped open.

Reid smiled. "Right. And you know how well that would go over with these people Top-the-Hill. So, now do you see why I sent the telegram?"

"That woman really is a witch."

"Touché."

"She's made friends with Clarissa Beaumont, you know."

Reid frowned. His sister sometimes changed subjects so fast he was at a loss to keep up. "Who made friends with . . ." Suddenly he knew exactly who Rhonda had been referring to, and his heart nearly dropped to his knees. "Lillian is friends with Clarissa?"

Rhonda nodded. "I saw them together downtown shopping, just a little while ago. They were laughing and talking and acting like the best of friends."

"Son of a . . ." Reid bolted up from the settee, began to pace, then slammed his hand into the wall. "This is Cord's fault. Ever since that night, everything in my life's gone wrong. Every damned . . ."

"Reid."

He whirled around, fury turning his eyes dark. "What?"

Rhonda hated it when he got like this, when he remembered Bethany and what had happened to her. Reid had never seemed able to get past that night, to forget and put it behind him, or to forgive his friend. She sighed. "What . . . what are you going to do?"

"I can't do anything," Reid said. "It's just like all the other times. Everything's blowing up in . . ." He stopped, and a sly smile curved his lips as he looked back at her. "I can't do anything, but you can."

"Me?" she squeaked, suddenly not liking the look she saw in his eyes.

"Yes. Listen, it'll be easy. All you have to do is become friends with Clarissa. That way you can keep an eye on Lillian."

"Oh, terrific. Just who I wanted to spend my time with. The woman who makes Satan look like an angel, and another who you describe as a real twit. Wonderful." Her eyes narrowed. "Are you sure there's no other way?"

"Short of shanghaiing our precious Lady Moreleigh,

transporting her down to New Orleans, and selling her to a white slaver? No.''

"Fine." Mischief played about the edges of Rhonda's smile. "But I'd still like to keep that option open. I'm sure we could get a very decent price for her."

Chapter Sixteen

"Got a pretty full house tonight," Cord said, as Samantha exited her office and stepped into the saloon. "Several boats pulled into the landings about an hour ago."

"Umm. Anyone look like trouble?" Samantha asked, looking over the newcomers. All of the tables were full. Cards flashed. Greenbacks sat in piles before the players, or in the center of the tables, and the wheel of fortune was on a rapid spin.

"Nope. Couple of roustabouts started pounding on one another a while ago out front, but Jake broke it up and they wondered on down to Jubilee's."

"Good."

Jake approached just then.

"I hear you've already been in battle tonight," Samantha said, chuckling softly. "Got any more scars?"

He stared down at her in puzzlement. "Scars?"

"Blossom, remember?" Samantha said, smiling and

pressing a finger to his chest, just about where the cat had scratched him.

"Oh, that," Jake mumbled, looking embarrassed.

Samantha glanced toward the eighteen players still participating in her challenge. They were seated at three tables in the rear of the saloon, and cordoned off from the rest of the patrons and tables by a length of rope stretched between them.

Suzette had been assigned to see to their drinks and make certain no one who didn't belong wandered into the area.

At that moment Reid looked up from the cards in his hand he'd been studying, and caught her eyes on him.

Samantha felt her cheeks flame instantly and tried to look away, but she couldn't, because just then, her gaze was caught by the shimmering of white silk next to him. Her eyes moved up its length, and a knot of emotion, like strangling jealousy, caught in her throat.

"Who . . ." She was forced to clear her throat. "Who's the woman standing next to Sinclaire?"

Cord turned and threw them an absent glance. "His wife."

Samantha's knees suddenly went weak. She reached out and grasped the bar behind her. The woman was the most beautiful creature Sam had ever seen. Her dark hair shimmered like rich sable beneath the glow of the chandeliers overhead, her skin resembled the purest of ivory, and the black gown she wore, sprinkled with black rhinestones and drippling black Valenciennes lace, set off both her body and her dark eyes to perfection.

Most women wore black only when in mourning, and on most women the color would have had a look of starkness. On Reid's wife is was not only striking, but exotic.

"Are you certain you don't want me to wait in your room

for you tonight, darling?" Lillian cooed softly into Reid's ear.

"I'm sure," he said, keeping his eyes on his cards.

She ran her hand up the length of his arm. "Reid," she said softly, drawing his name out on a long, whispery breath. "You know we were always so good together, and we could be again."

"Lillian." There was a warning note to his tone.

At one of the other tables, Valic glanced toward Lillian and smiled.

"But, darling . . . I've been so lonesome since you left London."

"What'd you want me to do, stay and get hanged?"

"You know I wouldn't have let that happened," she said with a sulk. "I was just angry with you."

"Remind me never to make you furious," Reid said, his tone dripping with sarcasm.

As Samantha watched Reid and the woman Cord said was his wife, she felt the floor under her feet move, felt her grip on the bar slip. The room seemed suddenly blurred, spinning. She snapped her eyes shut, stiffened her shoulders, and willed herself to remain calm.

"Sam, are you all right?" Jake asked, and touched her shoulder.

She opened her eyes and looked back at Reid. How dared he bring her here. Fury boiled within her breast, and scalded the breath in her throat. "What is she doing back there?" Samantha asked, her tone a cold, sharp whisper. "Behind the rope?"

"She came in a few minutes ago," Cord said. "She wanted to speak to him."

"No one is allowed behind the rope but Suzette and the dealers," Samantha said, turning a glaring eye on Cord. "No one."

"She's his wife, Sam," Cord said, his own tone calm but stern.

"No one!" Sam snapped again. She moved toward Reid's table, lifting the skirts of her midnight blue moiré silk gown in order to gracefully weave her way past the closely situated tables.

"Samantha," Reid said, the word sounding like a purr on his lips. He rose as she paused beside his table.

She looked at the woman standing beside him, aching to slap the arrogant smile off her face. "No one but the players, dealers, and our barmaid are allowed behind the rope during the games," Samantha said coolly, her gaze boring into the other woman's. "You'll have to leave."

Lillian's haughty gaze moved brazenly up and down Samantha in blatant assessment. "Obviously she doesn't think you can win without a little help from me, darling," Lillian said, putting a hand on Reid's arm. She raised her chin defiantly. "I'm his wife."

Samantha's smile was icy. "You have my sympathies, Mrs. Sinclaire, but as I said, you're not allowed back here. However, if you'd like to gamble"—a silken thread of warning edged her tone—"you are more than welcome to do so at any of the tables on the other side of the rope."

It was an insult, and Lillian knew it. Inviting a woman to gamble. She tossed back her head and slammed her dainty hands upon her hips. "Why you insolent little—"

"Lillian." Reid grabbed her arm. "That's enough." He walked her toward the rope, lifted it, and deposited her on the other side. "We'll talk later," he said coldly.

"Count on it," Lillian said.

"Go back to the hotel."

"Humph." She jerked her arm away from him and looked at Samantha. "Sorry, darling, but your little saloon"—she looked around the room, her face screwed into a frown of distaste—"just isn't quite up to the standard of places I'm used to patronizing." With that, she grabbed her shawl and marched toward the door.

"And good riddance," Sam muttered under her breath. Seething with a mixture of rage and jealousy, she glared at Lillian's retreating back, wishing she had something to throw at her.

"Amen," Reid said, drawing Samantha's surprised gaze. He looked at her. "We'll talk later, too."

Her eyes narrowed, and her anger returned. "I don't think so," she said, and walked back to the bar.

For the rest of the evening Reid struggled with the cards. His concentration had been shattered, nearly destroyed, by the encounter between Lillian and Samantha. He wanted to drag Samantha into his arms and damn her for haunting his every thought and making him want her until it drove him mad. And he wanted to wrap his hands around Lillian's throat and squeeze until her eyes popped out and she had no more breath of life left in her.

And, of course, he could do neither, which left him more than frustrated. It left him feeling as if he were teetering on the verge of insanity.

Chapter Seventeen

"She spent the day with Valic Gerard," Cord said, as he dropped into one of the chairs before Samantha's desk.

Sam looked up, dismay etched clearly on her features, distress in her eyes. "Gerard?" It was a surprise. She had thought he was going to tell her Clarissa was spending her time with her new beau, and a small part of Samantha still feared he could be Reid Sinclaire.

Cord nodded. "My man followed them. They went for a buggy ride and had a picnic out near Monmouth. I did find out who this other man she's been seeing is, however."

"You did?" She sat up anxiously. "Who?"

He shrugged. "Jonathan Reid."

Jonathan Reid. Reid Sinclaire. It was close, but not the same. "Who is he?"

Cord shook his head. "I'm not sure. I've got queries out to Boston, which is where he's supposedly from. My information is that he's some kind of textile importer, but so far I haven't come up with anything else."

She nodded. "Okay."

"I figure it's tomorrow night, Sam. The next at the latest."

She looked back up, frowning in puzzlement. "What's tomorrow night?"

"Your game. We lost five players last night. It's getting vicious. I figure tonight or tomorrow night will be it. Two more were on the verge of going under last night just before they quit."

She nodded again.

"How involved are you with Sinclaire?"

Her head shot up and her surprised gaze locked with his. How had he known she was involved with him at all? "I'm . . . I'm not," she said.

He looked at her long and hard. "He's poison, Sam. Just like Dante was. Believe me, I know. Sinclaire and I go back a long way."

She smiled, and seeing the sadness that touched her lips and filled her eyes, he knew he was right. It was already too late.

"I'm fine," she said softly, "but I think I'll skip making an appearance in the saloon tonight. If it's almost time for me to play, maybe I should just get some rest. Maybe even get in some quiet practicing."

"Fine." He rose, but stood looking down at her instead of leaving. "You're my daughter, Sam," he said softly.

She looked up, tears suddenly filling her eyes.

"You know I'd do anything for you."

She reached across the desk, and he took her hand. "Thank you."

He sighed. "When I left your mother, I thought it was for the best. Her father would never have let her marry me, and I couldn't ask her to go away with me. I was a gambler, my parents were farmers up north, I had nothing to offer her, nowhere to take her but to the river, and a riverboat is no home for a lady. She deserved better than me. It was the hardest thing I'd ever done, Sam, but I left her because I loved her.''

"I know.''

"If I'd known she was already carrying you . . .'' His words died away and a look of pain came into his eyes. "I don't know.'' He shook his head.

"It doesn't matter,'' Samantha said, rising and walking around the desk to him. They'd had this conversation before, but she'd never seen him quite so emotional. "We found each other. That's what's important.''

He wrapped her in his arms and hugged her to him. "I don't want you hurt, honey. Not again, and that's all Reid Sinclaire can offer you.''

"I know,'' she said again against his shoulder. "I know.''

Samantha paced her room. She'd sent a note to Dellie, telling her not to worry, that things were "being taken care of'' and she would see her in a few days.

Why was Clarissa still seeing Valic Gerard? She couldn't possible harbor any serious feelings for him. And who was this Jonathan Reid? If he was a respectable suitor, why didn't Clarissa want Dellie to meet him? And why didn't he insist on meeting Clarissa's family?

Or was it Valic her sister had been talking about marrying? The very thought sent a shudder of revulsion coursing through Samantha. No, she wouldn't let that happen. Even if she had to take her gun and shoot the man between the eyes, she would not allow him to use her sister like that, to destroy her life. And Samantha knew that's exactly what Valic Gerard would do if Clarissa was foolish enough to want to marry him.

She paused beside her dressing table, and she looked at the moon beyond the lace panels hanging in front of the window. What a mess things had become. She picked up her brush and began running it through the long tangles of her hair. Finally, after counting two hundred strokes, she set the brush down and began to release the buttons of her dress. What was Clarissa thinking?

But, of course, that was one of the problems: Clarissa usually didn't think. She merely acted.

Sam removed the top jacket of her gown and tossed it on a nearby chair.

How could her sister abide the company of the man who'd killed her father and taken Riversrun from them?

She loosened the ties of her skirt and let it and her petticoats and hoopskirt fall to the floor.

Who was Jonathan Reid?

Her fingers slipped between the silken knot of ribbon that lay between her breasts and held her camisole secure. She pulled it loose.

Was Reid with his wife now? Making love to her? Telling her how much he needed her?

Samantha let the straps of her camisole slide off of her shoulders, then grabbed it before it fell to the floor, and tossed it, too, onto the chair.

How could he have deceived her like that? Made love to her, when all the time he had a wife? She stepped from her pantaloons, stretched wide, then grabbed the nightgown of sheer batiste that hung on a hook beside her dressing table.

How could she have been such a fool to let her heart fall for another gambler?

She raised the gown above her head and let it float down over her arms, her head, her body.

* * *

Reid watched Samantha, the ache of desire burning inside of him almost unbearable. Each movment she made brought him a new onslaught of passion, a need to hold her, love her, make her his. His entire body ached with that need; his insides burned. God, what had she done to him? He'd never needed anyone in his life, and now he needed her more than he needed to breathe.

He fought for control, fought the urge to charge across the street, break down the locked door of the saloon, run up to her room, and drag her into his arms. She'd gotten under his skin. He'd thought making .love to her once would be it. That it would be enough to satisfy the gnawing, aching hunger she'd stirred in him. And he'd been wrong. Damn, how he'd been wrong. He raised the cheroot to his lips, noticing with disgust that his hand was trembling. He inhaled deeply on the apricot-soaked tobacco.

Its burning tip flared bright against the night's darkness.

Why in hell's name hadn't he told Cord that he'd slept with her? Wasn't that why he'd done it? Why he'd set out to seduce her? Cord had taken Bethany away from Reid, and he had planned on taking Samantha away from Cord. An eye for an eye. Except that Cord had gotten Bethany killed, too. Reid had had no intention of things going that far. Instead his plan had been to merely steal Cord's mistress, then bankrupt the man who'd once been like a father to him.

So why didn't he tell him? And why did his quest for revenge seem not so important lately?

He knew the moment she stepped away from the window.

Reid threw the cheroot down, stepped from the board-walk, and headed up Silver Street toward the Durante. Samantha. Lillian. Clarissa. Rhonda. What did he do to deserve this mess? Samantha haunted his every thought and desire. Clarissa offered him an opportunity he might never again get, to marry into real respectability, and be harangued for the rest of his life. Lillian wanted him back in her bed, wanted his money, and threatened to destroy his world . . . again.

And his sister . . . Rhonda was the most headstrong, impulsive, and determinted woman he'd ever met, and he wanted the best for her, which meant he had to keep an eye on her, too. If he married Clarissa, Rhonda would naturally be immediately accepted by the gentry in Natchez, and she would undoubtedly have more than ample opportunity to make a good marriage of her own.

But if he didn't, if he stayed on the river, making his way through life as a gambler, what would there be for Rhonda? Would she have any chance at all at a decent life?

Reid started up the steep incline toward Top-the-Hill, and swore softly. His mind and body were having one hell of a war, and he didn't like it. He had to forget about everyone else and their problems. He'd go after what Reid Sinclaire wanted out of the world, and to hell with everything else.

"Don't double-cross me, Lillian," Valic said, the menace of his tone clearly sparkling from his eyes as well.

She smiled coldly. "Is that a threat, darling?"

He turned, stalking back across the clearing where they'd been meeting. When he stopped, there was barely any room left between them. "Take it any way you want to, *darling,*" he retorted, sneering the endearment. "You owe me, Lillian, which is why I expect you to make certain you remain on my side in this thing."

Lillian suddenly felt a shiver of unease ripple through

her body. Valic was a devastatingly handsome man, but he also had a cruel streak. He'd never turned it on her, but she had seen him vent it on others, and she didn't want to be its next victim. Rather, she preferred to merely outsmart him. She laughed softly. "Valic, precious, you know I came down here to this horrid little river town solely to help you. Why would I do anything now to jeopardize the generous offer you've made me?"

His eyes narrowed. "Because someone, say your husband maybe, made you a better offer?"

She laughed again. "Reid?" She stepped away from him and waved her hand in a dismissing gesture. "Don't be absurd. First of all, he doesn't have anything to offer me, and second, even if he did, I wouldn't want it." She turned back and smiled. "He murdered poor Sir Percival remember, and then ran off and left me nearly penniless. What I do want is to see him destroyed. Once and for all."

"Fine. Then make certain you stay in his way. Make him want you, Lillian. Fill his mind with you. Take his concentration off the damned cards."

"Of course." She turned back to the buggy.

"And Lillian."

She looked over her shoulder at him.

"Watch what you say to Clarissa Beaumont. I plan to ask her to marry me."

The surprise that swept through her was almost more than she could hide, but she struggled to keep it from showing on her face. "Marry you?" she echoed, not certain she'd actually heard him correctly.

"Yes, marry me."

"And you expect her to accept?"

Valic grinned, and Lillian shuddered, suddenly pitying the young girl Valic had set his sights on.

"Yes," he said softly, "I do."

* * *

Samantha was laboring over her ledgers when Jake walked into her office. "You got another note," he said, and dropped it onto the ledger in front of her.

She looked at it, then up at him. "This was delivered today?" She couldn't believe Dellie would send Annie to Under-the-Hill again, and in broad daylight.

"Few minutes ago. Same little thing of a woman, too, all decked out in that cloak." He shook his head. "Hotter than a snake on a rock in July out there, and she's traipsing around draped head to foot in a cloak."

Poor Annie, Samantha thought. A moment later, as she stared at Dellie's hastily scrawled words, all sympathy and thought for Annie fled from her mind. Samantha felt a wild surge of panic. She couldn't let Clarissa marry Valic Gerard. She'd send her to the convent. She'd send her to their cousin in Paris. Anything, but she couldn't let Clarissa throw her life away on a man like Valic. Sam stood so abruptly her skirts knocked over her chair and sent it crashing to the floor.

Jake stared at her, his eyes wide with surprise. "Sam? You okay?"

"No. No, I'm not," she said, and started to brush past him toward the door. She stopped and turned back to face him. "Jake, tell Cord I had to go out, and I don't know when I'll be back."

"Sam . . ."

"Take care of things here, please. Tell Cord I'll . . ." She shook her head. Tell him what? "Tell him I'll be back later. Oh, and would you get my horse, Jake. Have him saddled and tied out back?" Without waiting for him to answer, she turned and ran through the saloon and up the stairs to her room. Throwing open her armoire, she looked hurriedly at the gowns hanging there. Something plain. Unnoticeable. She grabbed a blue riding habit that was so dark it was nearly black, then shoved it back into the closet. If she wore that in the middle of the day, a hot day, people would wonder, and notice, which was exactly what she wanted to avoid. She grabbed another habit: lightweight, cream, with dark blue trim. Within minutes she'd changed. But she couldn't wear a cloak, and she couldn't let anyone see her face. She looked at her day hats. All were small, jaunty styles, except for the brown one and the one she'd worn to her father's funeral. She grabbed the old hatbox from the rear of the armoire, jerked off its top, and stared down at the small midnight blue hat she hadn't worn since Staunton Beaumont's funeral. Its brim was wider than her newer hats, and it had a heavy veil that was meant to be drawn over her face, its ends gathered and pinned on the crown in back. She set it on her head, arranged the veil, and studied herself in the mirror. If anyone looked closely they could still identify her, but she had no intention of allowing anyone to get that close.

Samantha hurried out the back door and mounted Rogue. On her way up the steep incline of Silver Street she passed Foxe Brannigan, on his way down. The man barely nodded at her, yet it gave Sam a moment of uneasiness, wondering if he had acknowledged her merely to be polite, or if he'd recognized her.

The streets of Top-the-Hill were busy. Several riverboats had made dock only an hour or so ago and many of their passengers were wandering about downtown, stretching their legs during the layover before returning to the boats for the remainder of the trip downriver to New Orleans. The everyday collage of buggies and drays maneuvered about each other, while men on horseback, children playing, women out for a stroll, and servants on their way to and from the market tried to cross each other's paths.

Sam kept her head low and Rogue's pace steady and quick. She passed Dellie's house, just in case, glanced over her shoulder, to the left and right, went around the corner, then doubled back, rode up the drive of the house next door to Dellie's, and cut through the shrubbery once at the rear of the houses. Tying Rogue to a tree, out of sight of the street, she held the veil down and hurried into the house through the rear door.

"Elyse!" Dellie cried, looking up from several bolts of fabric she'd spread across the kitchen's wide table. "Oh, I am so glad to see you." She threw her arms around Samantha. "You just don't know."

"I got your note," Sam said. She pulled the note from her pocket and looked at her aunt. "I've been having her followed, Auntie, but so far we still don't know who this new mystery man is."

"Oh, Elyse, I'm not worried about him as much as that other one."

Samantha frowned. "Other . . . ?"

"Gerard. That snake. He was here earlier, and he requested my blessing so that he could ask Clarissa to marry him!"

Her heart nearly stopped. "That's not going to happen, Auntie," Samantha said, cold steel in her tone.

"Well, she is going to the Governor's ball tomorrow afternoon with this new beau of hers, or so she said." Dellie looked doubtful. "But I'm sure Gerard will be there, too, and I'm afraid of what might happen." Her eyes suddenly widened as a thought came to her. "Oh, Elyse," Dellie gasped, and grabbed her arm, "you don't think Gerard will challenge this man or anything do you? That they'll duel?"

A tight smile pulled at Samantha's lips. "Maybe that would solve our problem."

"What problem?" Clarissa said, suddenly appearing on the stairs. She looked from her sister to her aunt.

"Nothing," Samantha said, forcing some warmth into the curve of her lips. "Finances, that's all. Nothing for you to worry about."

Clarissa hurried down the stairs. "Elyse, did Dellie tell you I'm going to the Governor's ball?" Her eyes were wide with excitement. "And it's a masquerade! Isn't that just too wonderful?"

"A masquerade?" Samantha echoed. She'd forgotten that the Governor's annual ball was always a masquerade. An idea began to take form in her mind.

"Yes. Oh, it's going to be such a grand affair. I can barely wait."

The women moved into the parlor, where Clarissa sat on one of the settees, making certain to arrange the folds of her blue and white day gown around her gracefully. "My costume isn't finished yet, but it will be the toast of the ball, I just know it."

"And your costume is what?" Samantha asked, still churning over her own idea in her head.

"I'm going as Marie Antoinette," Clarissa said happily.

Sam cocked her head. "That should be elegant," she said, giving Dellie a sideways glance.

"And expensive," Dellie snapped softly.

Samantha looked back at her sister. "Who are you going with?"

"Well, Valic threw an absolute hissy when I told him I couldn't go with him, and Phillip was livid, too, but I did promise to go with Jonathan, so . . ." She shrugged, then giggled. "Isn't it just too delicious, Samantha?" She nearly bounced in delight. "Three of them. Maybe they'll duel over me."

"Clarissa!" Dellie snapped, her eyes wide with disbelief. "You can't mean you'd let them . . . that you'd want them to . . . Oh!'' She threw her hands up in disgust and plopped down in her favorite rocking chair. "I just don't believe this is happening."

"So, what is your escort going as?" Samantha asked. She had no doubt she'd recognize Valic Gerard, no matter what type of costume he tried to hide behind, and she'd know Phillip Lethrothe anywhere, but this other man, Jonathan Reid, was an unknown to her.

"Oh!" A look of utter disappointment came over Clarissa's pert features. "The man in the velvet mask. Can you imagine? I wanted him to do something more gallant and flashy, like . . .'' She shrugged. "Oh, I don't know. Napoleon or King Louis or Julius Caesar. Someone like that."

The man in the velvet mask would be a very convenient costume for someone who didn't want to be recognized, Samantha thought, suddenly thinking of Reid again. That he could be involved with her sister was absolutely ludicrous, but ever since Dellie had described Clarissa's new beau, Sam hadn't been able to completely rid herself of the haunting, yet ridiculous, suspicion.

"So, when am I going to meet this mysterious Jonathan?" Samantha asked. "He sounds very intriguing."

Clarissa smiled. "I don't know. I can't very well send him down to the Goose, now can I?"

"No, you can't," Samantha said, hanging on to her patience, "but what would you say if I attended the masquerade ball, and you introduced me there?"

"The ball?" Clarissa echoed, looking stunned.

Samantha shrugged aside the flash of doubt that attacked her and plunged ahead with her plan. "Yes. I could arrive and you could act shocked to see me. I could say it's a surprise visit."

"Oh, Elyse, that would be wonderful," Clarissa squealed.

The steady *click-clack* of Dellie's knitting needles stopped. "But, what if someone recognizes you as . . .''

"Samantha?" She smiled. "They won't."

"But how can you be sure?" Dellie pressed, looking doubtful.

"Oh, Auntie," Clarissa moaned, "stop being such an old worrywart."

"I'll make sure," Samantha reasured her aunt softly. "Don't worry."

"Oh, Elyse, this will be such fun," Clarissa said, clapping her hands together. "Oh!" She suddenly frowned. "But what will you wear? You don't have a costume, and it's too late to have one made."

"Don't concern yourself. I'll manage to put something together," Samantha said.

As Dellie and Clarissa began bickering over Clarissa's costume, Samantha turned to look out the window.

The bright light of the afternoon sun sprayed down upon the large oak trees surrounding the house, gilding their dark green leaves with an edging of silver, and casting the formal garden in an array of shadows and light. Toward the southern boundary of the property was a small fountain, the water within its pond still and unmoving, its surface turned to a sleek plane of silver in the reflection of the bright light raining down on it. The smell of jasmine, honeysuckle, and roses floated in the air, combining into a heady fragrance as it wafted into the house through the open window.

This was the first time she'd been Top-the-Hill in broad daylight since the day she'd left it, eight years ago.

An open buggy passed the house, and with a start, Samantha recognized one of her old friends. An ache of longing pierced her, but she quickly brushed it aside. She had made herself a good life Under-the-Hill. She had a profitable business, some very dear and loyal friends, and she had Cord.

Sometimes good things do come from bad, she thought to

herself. If Staunton Beaumont hadn't gambled away Riversrun, Elyse Beaumont wouldn't have been forced to
become Samantha and turn a dirty old run-down hotel
Under-the-Hill into the Silver Goose Saloon. And if she
hadn't done that, she would have never met Dante and
nearly lost it all, and Cord Rydelle would never have come
to her rescue, and been forced to tell her that he was her
real father in order to get her to accept his offer of help.

And, of course, there were Molly and Jake and Suzette
and Curly, and . . . Samantha smiled. Yes, she had a good
life. She refused to acknowledge the image of Blackjack
Reid Sinclaire that tried to push its way into her thoughts.
Her life might not be the one she'd pictured for herself
all those years ago when she'd passed her days in Miss
Wilder's School for Girls in Virginia and dreamed of the
future, but it was a good life. Now she had to make certain
that Clarissa didn't throw hers away.

"Elyse, did you hear me?" Dellie said sharply.

Samantha turned from the window. "Oh, I'm sorry,
Auntie. I guess I was daydreaming."

"Clarissa has just informed me she is going for a carriage
ride with Valic Gerard this afternoon, and he's due to
arrive any moment."

Samantha felt the blood in her veins turn cold. Gerard
was one person she didn't need to see. "Then it's time
for me to leave." She turned and strode into the kitchen.

"Elyse," Clarissa said, following in Samantha and Dellie's footsteps, "you really don't need to avoid Valic. I
mean, he really wouldn't tell anyone about you, and he is
a very nice man."

Samantha, in the middle of arranging the veil over her
face, whirled around to glare at her sister. "He's not right
for you, Clarissa. He's a cheat, a liar, and he murdered
your . . . our father."

Clarissa's face went pale, but her lips tightened and her eyes blazed with anger.

"I'm leaving, Auntie," Samantha said to Dellie. "I'll stop by tomorrow before I go to the Governor's ball." She looked at Clarissa. "I'll see you there."

"Oh, goody," Clarissa sneered.

Samantha paced from one end of her office to the other, which took all of about five steps each way.

Cord opened the door, nearly ramming it into her. "Oh, sorry," he mumbled.

She glared at him. Her mood had dived into a black hole at the confrontation with Clarissa over Valic Gerard, and the hours since had proved to make little improvement in it. "What is it?"

Cord frowned, the gesture pulling at his handsome features and bringing an unusual darkness to his eyes. "Are you all right?"

She faced him, hands rammed on her hips. "No, I'm not. My sister is seeing three men at the same time, finds the idea of them fighting a duel over her to be 'just all too delicious,' and Valic Gerard has asked my aunt for her blessing so that he can propose marriage to Clarissa. Phillip Lethrothe is probably through with her, and I still don't know a thing about this Jonathan Reid person."

"Sounds like . . ."

"And to top that off, there are at least two men still playing in the 'challenge' who I would much rather have the pleasure of putting a bullet between their eyes than sit across the table from and play poker."

"Well, I guess that about says it all," Cord mused. He smiled. "And I asked for it. But I'll come visit you in jail before the hanging anyway."

"Thanks." She dropped into the chair behind her desk. "Sorry. I've had a bad day."

Amusement sparked in his eyes, but the concern was not wholly gone. "I can see that. Anything I can do?"

"Yes. Tell me that the man you have following my sister can make Valic Gerard and Jonathan Reid completely disappear. Forever."

"It can be arranged," Cord said.

She jerked around and stared at him upon hearing his serious tone. "Never mind," she said, afraid he would actually have something done to the two men.

He had missed the first nineteen years of her life, but now that they'd found each other, he had become a very protective, if secret, father, and she knew he was willing to do whatever was necessary to make his daughter happy, and keep her safe. At times that meant Samantha had to be very careful of what she said and wished for around him. Like the disappearance of two men.

"The games are about to start," Cord said, interrupting her thoughts. "That's why I came in here, to get you."

She rose. "I'll see to their opening," she said, "but then I'm going upstairs. I have a giant-sized headache and a costume to make."

He paused in the hall and looked at her, clearly puzzled. "A costume."

A mischievous smile brightened her face, and put a sly twinkle in her eyes. "Yes. I am going"—she leaned close and dropped her voice to a whisper—"to the Govenor's annual masquerade ball tomorrow afternoon."

"What?" His response fairly thundered through the small passageway.

"Shush," Samantha said quickly, slapping his arm. "It's a secret."

"Well, damn," Cord said, dropping his voice to a soft drawl, "what are you doing going to that? Someone's certain to recognize you, and I thought that's what you didn't want to ever happen.''

"It's a masquerade ball," Samantha said, her smile turning smug, "and no one is going to recognize me."

Chapter Eighteen

"What's that?" Reid snapped, staring at Rhonda in total disbelief.

She smiled. "I'm Cleopatra." She twirled about, showing him every inch of the Egyptian costume that was so scanty it revealed more than it hid, and left little to the imagination. "Isn't it wonderful?"

"No." Reid's eyes blazed disapproval. "Just where do you think you're going in that?"

She huffed indignantly. "I'm attending the Governor's ball with Phillip Letrothe. I told you."

"No, you didn't."

Her features set determinedly. "Yes, I did."

"Does Clarissa know this?" he demanded.

Rhonda smiled smugly and Reid felt his heart sink. "Of course. She arranged it."

"And Letrothe was agreeable?" He was having a hard time accepting this new turn of events.

"Quite," Rhonda said.

A groan strangled its way out of his throat. He spun on his heel and walked to the window. It was worse than he'd thought.

Rhonda followed him. "What's the matter? I thought you'd be pleased. He's respectable, good-looking, charming, and he's rich."

Reid turned and looked at her. "He's also Clarissa's ex-fiancé and still in love with her. She's playing games, Rhonnie."

"Maybe," Rhonda said, drawing the word out knowingly, "but we both know I'm much better at playing games than anyone." She laughed softly, which sent Reid's annoyance gauge up another notch. "And anyway, Phillip maybe her ex-fiancé, but I am definitely not of the opinion that he's still in love with her."

"You'll mess up everything I'm trying to do."

Rhonda's eyes narrowed in sudden anger, and she posed defiantly. "Seems to me, brother dear, you're doing a good enough job of messing yourself up, without worrying about me doing it for you."

"You can't go."

Her eyes widened. "What?"

"You can't go."

"I heard you the first time, but . . ."

"You can't go."

She sputtered, bristling with indignation. "And just why shouldn't I go?"

"You're Blackjack Reid Sinclaire's sister."

"So?"

"I'm supposed to be Jonathan Reid."

"And everyone Top-the-Hill knows me as Rhonda Reid. So what?"

"Lillian knows. If she . . ."

"If she hasn't said anything so far, what makes you think she would now? Anyway, she'd ruin her own reputation

Top-the-Hill if she said anything, and I doubt she wants
to do that. At least not yet."

Reid's frustration was growing by the second. To say
nothing of his anger. "Someone else might recognize
you."

"Who?"

"I don't know." He was being unreasonable and he
knew it, but this whole thing about going to the ball was
giving him an uneasy feeling, and he didn't even know
why.

"Fine. That same unknown someone might recognize
you!" she shot back.

"Rhonda . . ."

She tossed her head, sending curls flying about her
shoulders, and her eyes flashed defiance. "Remember,
dear brother, I'm not the *famous* riverboat gambler, Blackjack Reid Sinclaire. I'm not gambling in a million dollar
poker game Under-the-Hill and bedding the saloon
madam while living Top-the-Hill under a different name
and courting one of the genteel's little ladies . . ."

"Rhonda," Reid snapped menacingly.

"I'm not a married man on the run from my wife,"
she continued, ignoring his warning tone. "And I'm not
wanted for murder!"

Lord, but he hated it when she was right, and her
haughty tone and the devilish twinkle in her eyes only
incensed him all the more. "All right. Why should you
listen to me anyway? You never have"—storming past her,
he grabbed the red velvet hood of his costume from the
bureau—"so why start now?" With that, and a billowing
flourish of the long, black cape that hung from his shoulders, its red satin lining a startling slash of color that swirled
around him whenever he moved, Reid slammed out of the
room.

He stalked down the hallway toward the stairs. Why were

beautiful women always so obstinate? And why did they always find their way into his life? Subdued. Shy. Amiable. Gentle. Accommodating. That's the kind of woman he needed in his life. A quiet, caressing stroke of warm sunlight—not a fiery, obstinate, seething firestorm.

Thoughts of Samantha invaded his mind, and he pushed them away.

He turned his mind backward, through time. Bethany had been quiet and gentle. A quiet, caressing stroke of warm sunlight.

And eventually you would have become bored, a voice at the back of his mind reminded him.

He'd loved her, Reid silently argued.

You had already been thinking of breaking the engagement when she was killed.

No. He would have married her. He'd loved her. Deeply. But Cord Rydelle had gotten her killed. Reid strode through the hotel's lobby. At the front door he paused and looked back at the grandfather clock that stood to one side of the concierge's desk. One of the clock's large hands moved. Reid pulled out his pocket watch, flipped its lid open, and compared his time with that of the large clock. He did a quick mental calculation of his schedule. He was taking Clarissa to the Governor's annual masquerade ball this afternoon, but he had to be back in town and down at the Silver Goose by eight this evening.

An image of Samantha filled his mind again, her red touched hair glistening beneath the glow of the saloon's chandeliers, her eyes, bluer than the sky, darker than the night.

"Damn," Reid muttered, dragging his thoughts back to business, and cursing their waywardness. He would have to get Clarissa home by seven thirty. If she wanted to dally at the ball past that, she'd just have to find another way to get home. The last thing he intended to do was lose that one million dollars by default because he was late.

And whoever heard of having a ball in the middle of the afternoon anyway? He'd heard it had something to do with its originator not being well enough to stay up late, but Reid would have figured that some sane, reasonable person would have corrected that mistake of timing by now. No one had soirees in the middle of the day.

A movement of his arm, as he snapped the watch closed and dropped it back into his pocket, caused the cape to swirl away from his body slightly. His eye caught sight of the red satin lining and Reid was instantly reminded of Samantha again—the night she'd worn a gown of red, its brilliant color picking up the highlights in her hair, her eyes seeming to catch and reflect the darkness of the black lace and sequin trim, the way the décolletage had plunged enticingly, just enough to tantalize. He felt a surge of desire heat his loins, then curl there like a tight, agonizing knot that threatened to remain forever.

A parade of pithy oaths slipped from his lips as Reid left the hotel.

The carriage he'd arranged for earlier was waiting a few feet from the hotel's door. Every woman he'd ever met who possessed even an ounce of good looks seemed to also possess a stubborn streak a mile wide. Some acted like clinging vines, some were conniving, and some were just too independent for their own good. But they all had one thing in common—trouble. It either followed them, rose up in their wake, surrounded them, or was created by them.

He climbed into the carriage and snapped the reins.

Rhonda. Samantha. Lillian. Clarissa. Their names and images danced through his mind, tormenting him. Trouble times four. Reid groaned. How in blazes had he gotten himself into this situation in the first place? He should have become a monk!

Ten minutes later he pulled the carriage up in front of the Beaumont town house, but instead of climbing down and walking to the door, he just looked at the house expectantly. Clarissa was usually always halfway down the walkway by the time he brought the carriage to a full stop.

He saw the front door open, but instead of Clarissa, a short, heavyset woman stood in the lighted entryway. A smaller woman appeared at her side, then hurried down the walkway to Reid.

"Miss Delphine wants you to come up to the house," Annie said.

He looked down at the tiny black woman. She had the build of a child of ten or twelve and the face of a woman well over fifty. Reid climbed from the buggy and followed her to the house.

"Well," Dellie said, looking at him sharply, "you are Jonathan Reid, I presume."

"Yes, ma'am," Reid said, taking her hand gently in his and bowing.

She sniffed. "Most gentlemen come to the door when calling for a lady, before they're summoned."

"I'm sorry," Reid said, following her into the parlor. "But I fully expected Clarissa to be halfway down the walkway when I arrived, as she usually is."

"Yes, well, never mind. She's not ready yet." Dellie sat on the settee and motioned him toward a chair.

Reid moved to stand beside the fireplace instead.

She looked him up and down. "You're from up north, Mr. Reid."

It wasn't a question, and Reid got the distinct impression it also wasn't a compliment. "Actually, I'm from Virginia, originally."

That seemed to make her eyes soften a little, and even brought a hint of a smile to Dellie's lips.

He remembered her then: she'd been at the back that first time he'd gone there. He had held the door open for her.

"Virginia? Humm. I have a cousin in Virginia. Rachel Simms. Rich as hades. Do you know her?"

Reid smiled. "No, I'm sorry, but I'd love to meet her someday."

"Humph. Bet you would," Dellie said under her breath. "She's eighty." Subtle challenge laced her next words. "Maybe your mama or grandmere knows her."

"My family is dead," Reid said. He saw the look of chagrin that came instantly to the old woman's features. "But it's been quite a while," he added, feeling a need to get them past the suddenly awkward moment.

"What's been quite a while?" Clarissa asked as she walked into the room.

Reid turned, and his mouth dropped open, the utter disbelief, the shock of what he was seeing forming a wedge in his throat that prevented speech.

"Well?" Clarissa smiled, held up her arms, and did twirled. "How do you like my costume?"

She was dressed head to toe in white, her gown a collage of silk ruffles, organdy flounces, and lace drippings. Her décolletage plunged dramatically, in dire contrast to the general idea of the costume, and her sleeves puffed exaggeratedly, then gathered to hug her arms, and ended in a drip of lace that surrounded each wrist. But it was the large feathered wings at her back and the gold halo bouncing over her head that were giving Reid a start.

Clarissa as an angel was the exact antithesis of how he thought of her.

"I . . ." He cleared his throat as the words caught and

refused to come out. "I thought you were going as Marie Antoinette."

Her smile instantly plunged into a defiant pout. "Well, since you wouldn't go as Napoleon or Louis, I changed my mind."

"You certainly did," Reid said, chuckling softly now as his gaze raked over her. One of Satan's imps would have been a more appropriate costume for Clarissa. "Quite fitting, too," he lied, and looked at her aunt. "Wouldn't you agree, Miss Delphine?"

"No," Dellie said, with a mischievous arch of her brow, "but what does an old lady like me know?"

"Auntie," Clarissa said, feigning shock, "you're terrible." She turned her attention to Reid. "We have to change your costume, too."

He felt a flash of annoyance, mixed with more than a spark of alarm.

Clarissa disappeared momentarily into the foyer, then reappeared with a devilish smile pulling at her lips. She crossed the room and paused before Reid. "Instead of that mask," she said, referring to the red velvet one she'd given him earlier, "you'll wear this." She held up a hair comb, and attached to it were a pair of red, satin horns. Clarissa laughed as he stared at them. "See, I'm an angel, and you'll be the devil. Perfect!"

Reid looked toward Clarissa's aunt, hoping but not expecting some help.

She had busied herself with a pile of yarn and a pair of knitting needles.

He looked back at Clarissa. "I don't think so."

"Oh, Jonathan, don't be stubborn," Clarissa said, and reached up to slide the comb into his hair.

He pushed her hand aside. "No, Clarissa."

Her eyes flared with anger and her lips pursed together.

She stomped her foot and threw her fisted hands down. "Then I won't go."

"Fine."

She instantly looked crestfallen, and her eyes widened in surprise. "Oh, Jonathan, we have to go," she wailed. "It's the Governor's annual masquerade ball. Everyone will be there."

He could make valuable contacts, strengthen those he'd already made. This was what he'd always wanted. The kind of life he'd dreamed of. Definite reasons for going. He offered her his arm.

"Don't be late, dear," Dellie said as they started toward the door. "And don't forget about Elyse."

Clarissa paused at the doorway and Dellie threw her a warning glance.

"Elyse?" Reid echoed, puzzled as he looked from one woman to the other. Hadn't that been the name the old man out at the plantation had mentioned when he'd talked about Clarissa and her sister?

"My sister. She'll be at the soiree today," Clarissa said.

"But I thought she lived in France."

"She does," Dellie said quickly, not trusting Clarissa to get their story right. "But she's stopped by on her way up north to, ah, visit her husband's relatives. His mother's ah . . . umm . . . sick."

"Well, she can ride with us," Reid said, glancing curiously toward the stairs.

"No," Clarissa said, a bit sharply.

Reid turned to look at her.

"I mean, she's not here right now. She went out, but she'll be at the soiree later." Clarissa smiled and tugged on his arm. "And we're going to be late if we don't go."

"But . . ." He frowned. "You won't have much time to visit with her."

"Oh, honestly, Jonathan," Clarissa said, and laughed.

"It's not all that important. Elyse will be back in no time. Anyway, the only reason she's even coming to the soiree at all is to meet you and make certain you're suitable to be a member of our illustrious family."

The response he'd been about to utter suddenly lodged in Reid's throat at Clarissa's words. He stared at her. She was beautiful, seductive, lively, intelligent, graceful, and from one of the oldest and most respected families in Natchez. Only the fact that her family had lost their wealth, and her dowry, detracted from her marital eligibility standing in the genteel society. That didn't matter to Reid, and it had obviously not mattered to Phillip Letrothe or Valic Gerard.

But suddenly, as Reid stared down at Clarissa, her words still ringing in his ears, the thought of her as his wife sent a cold chill racing through his body.

"Sam, if you don't hold still," Molly scolded, "I'll never get this done."

Samantha twisted about to get a better view of herself in the tall mirror standing in one corner of her bedchamber. The gown was scandalous. "I don't know, Molly. Do you think this . . ."

"I think it's beautiful," Molly said, cutting off yet another of Samantha's protests. "There." She tied a knot in her thread and snapped off the end. "Now turn around for me and let me see the whole thing."

Samantha turned toward the mirror. Molly had taken one of Sam's older, red satin gowns and done a few alterations to turn it into the costume Samantha had in mind.

"And now," Molly said, turning to retrieve Samantha's headpiece from the dressing table, "the final touches . . ." She wedged a comb in between the curls piled onto Samantha's crown, then handed her the mask.

Samantha held it to her face and modeled the outfit. "Well? Will it work?"

"Fantastic," Molly said, clapping her hands together. "Absolutely fantastic."

"But can you tell it's me?" Samantha persisted.

"I can, but those hoots who live Top-the-Hill won't be able to."

Samantha inhaled deeply, drawing in both breath and courage. "Well, here goes nothing," she said. Grabbing her reticule, she shoved the mask inside, and drew a lightweight cloak about her shoulders to hide the costume until she arrived at her destination. She walked to the door, then looked back. "I'll be back in plenty of time for the games, but just in case . . ."

"Cord and Jake will be here," Molly said, reassuringly. "If you find something interesting up there"—she giggled and shrugged—"I'm sure they can get along without you for a little while."

"I'll be back by seven thirty," Samantha said, throwing Molly a chastising, but mocking glare.

"We won't wait up," Molly teased.

Reid turned the carriage off the main road and onto the long drive that led to Auburn's mansion.

Clarissa let out a shriek of excitement. "Oh, Jonathan, isn't it beautiful?"

Colorful Chinese lanterns had been tied with white ribbon among the boughs of almost every large oak tree that lined the long, curving drive, and the long ends of the ribbons left to float on the afternoon breeze.

As they drew nearer the brick mansion with its elegant white portico and Corinthian pillars came into view. To the left of the house, several huge awnings had been erected upon the sprawling lawns that swept out in every direction from the mansion. Music floated upon the air, and the aromas of a dozen or more culinary delights parried with the sensually heady scent of flowers set in large baskets and vases all around the area.

There was already a crowd of costumed guests milling about beneath the shade providing awnings. Several others were dancing on a makeshift dance floor that had been erected beneath one of the magnificent oak trees that dotted the landscape.

"Everything is just so perfect, except . . ."

Reid glanced at Clarissa just in time to see a pout pull at her lips. Lord, but he was already tired of that look. He tried to shrug off the annoyance her gesture instilled in him. "Except what?" he forced himself to ask, even though he really didn't care.

"Except there's no rhyme or reason to your costume without your horns."

He sighed. "Fine. Give them to me." If that's all it would take to please her and get that infernal sulk off her face, he'd put the insipid things on.

She smiled brightly and handed him the horns. "Oh, Jonathan," she squealed, and clapped her hands together in delight as he wedged the comb into his hair, "you look devastatingly sinister now."

Reid pulled the carriage up beside the house, where several elegantly liveried servants stood waiting to assist in helping them down and parking the carriage elsewhere.

"If you please, sir," one of the men said, motioning for them to follow the rose-petal-strewn path toward where the others had already gathered, as Reid walked around the carriage to join Clarissa. He tucked Clarissa's hand within the groove of his arm.

"Oh, there's Valic," Clarissa said, smiling and waving toward a group of people standing near the dance floor.

"Wonderful," Reid sneered softly.

Clarissa smiled, taking his less than happy comment as a show of jealousy. "But where are Phillip and Rhonda?" She looked around. "I thought they'd be here by now." She hugged his arm. "You know, I just love your sister, Jonathan. She's so much fun. And she's been to so many places."

"Umm," Reid said noncommitally, wondering exactly what "places" Rhonda had told Clarissa about.

"We simply must go . . ."

"Do you see your sister?" he asked, looking about and nodding to several people he'd met at Rubie's luncheon.

"Oh, she won't be here for a while, most likely. I just hope she wears a suitable costume."

He frowned. "And what would you deem an unsuitable costume?" he asked. Clarissa had such an unusual way of thinking sometimes that he was curious.

She shrugged. "Oh, I don't know. But sometimes, well . . ." She turned quickly and looked up at him. "It wouldn't make any difference to you, would it, Jonathan, if she was . . . different?"

"Not unless she has fangs, or arrives on a flying broom." He laughed. "I'd prefer to be prepared for something like that."

Clarissa shook her head. "No fangs or flying broom," she said softly, praying that Elyse didn't show up in one of her barmaid gowns. Or worse. She squealed before they'd taken more than a half dozen more steps. "Oh, look, there's Varina and Caroline." She pointed across the tent toward two women standing near the small orchestra that had been hired for the ocassion.

"How can you tell?" Reid asked. One was dressed as a gypsy, the other as a some kind of Greek goddess, and both wore masks of feathers and jewels.

"They told me what they'd be wearing, silly," Clarissa said and laughed. "Jonathan, do be a darling and get us some punch, won't you?'' Without waiting for his response, Clarissa slipped her arm from his and skipped across the room toward her two friends.

Twenty minutes later Reid was still standing beside the table that held the punch bowl, and was conversing with several men he'd met at Rubie's gathering. Unlike the ladies, it wasn't hard to identify most of the men present at the Governor's ball. Some of them, like Reid, hadn't worn masks, and those who did kept sliding them up to rest on their foreheads as they talked and smoked.

Reid turned toward the punch bowl to refill his cup, and as he did, the hum of conversation in the room seemed to die. He assumed some entertainers had entered the tented area, and after adding a shot of bourbon to his punch from one of the decanters that had been put on the table for the gentlemen, he turned back to see what had drawn everyone's rapt attention. Reid nearly dropped his drink as his gaze, like that of everyone else present, was drawn toward the entry. He stared in astonishment and appreciation, not quite believing the sight before his eyes. He set the cup of punch down carefully on the table, but didn't take his eyes off of her.

A trellis, entwined with Spanish moss and fully blooming red roses, served as an entry to the main tent, and she had paused just beneath it.

The scene was a striking one.

She was alone, with no escort at her side to guide her entry, or hold her hand. If she noticed the hush that had fallen over the area, or the fact that the eyes of every person present had turned to her, she gave no sign. Instead she calmly looked about from behind a red sequined and feathered mask, as if studying each costume, and deciding whose face was behind each disguise.

Like her mask, her gown was of the brightest red satin and as the rich fabric caught the sun's rays that streamed into the awninged area from behind and beside her, it reflected them in seething radiance.

Curving strips of gold silk rose from within the voluminous folds of the gown's skirt, giving the effect of flames rising from the ground and surrounding her. Her arms were covered by long sleeves that ended in a point just beyond her wrists, and a high, stiff collar rose well above the back of her head and curved downward at each side into dramatic points over her shoulders.

A group of women, chatting among themselves, entered the area from the side, and the woman in red turned to glance at them.

As they spotted her, and finally noticed that everyone else was looking from her to them, the group of women paused, and their chatter abruptly stopped.

It was then Reid noticed the small, red satin horns that protruded from the dark curls whose red highlights intensified the brilliant color of the gown as they fell from the woman's crown and draped one bare, creamy shoulder.

Mystery and daring emanated from her, while the aura of devilish mischief and challenge her costume suggested drew the attention of every man in atendance, and the envy of every woman.

Yet there was something else about her that pulled at Reid, a faint sense of familiarity that he knew was ridiculous. He didn't know that many people in Top-the-Hill, Natchez, especially the women, and he would never have forgotten such a lovely one as this. Nevertheless, the feeling that he did know her kept his gaze fastened upon hers even after the others in the area regathered their wits, composed themselves, and resumed conversations.

Reid made to move toward her when he felt Clarissa's hand on his arm.

Chapter Nineteen

"Wouldn't you know it?" Clarissa snapped peevishly, glaring at the woman in red. "She just had to make a grand entrance. And that horrid costume! This is just the absolute utter end!"

He looked at Clarissa then, puzzled as to the depth of her obvious jealousy.

"I should have known better."

"What are you talking about?" he asked, chiding anger sharpening the words more than he'd intended.

"Elyse!" Clarissa snapped. "Her costume is absolutely scandalous."

Reid looked back at the woman in red, who hadn't moved. *"She's* your sister?"

"Unfortunately, yes," Clarissa grumbled softly beneath her breath.

His mind was suddenly drowning in suspicion and speculation as he looked from Clarissa to the woman she claimed was her sister. With calculated assessment his gaze moved over her slowly, inch by inch, his eyes raking in the sight of her lithe curves, the delicately shaped hands, the tantalizing shadow of bodice that peeked from the plunging décolletage of her gown, the sensual curve of her lips, and the hair that looked aflame whenever a shaft of light touched its curling strands.

It couldn't be her, he told himself. It was impossible. A ludicrous thought. Outrageous. The mere idea that the owner of the Silver Goose Saloon, and mistress of gambler Cord Rydelle, would be at the Governor's annual masquerade ball was a ridiculous one.

Yet the sense of familiarity remained with him, just as thoughts of her seemed always to haunt his mind, and desire his body.

"Honestly, how could she?" Clarissa said, yanking Reid from his musings. "Well, come on, I'll introduce you and then maybe she'll leave."

Then the rest of his revelation hit him. They were sisters! The resemblance wasn't so distinct that he'd see it when they were apart, but now, as they stood mere yards from each other, it was unmistakable, and yet they were still so different. Clarissa's hair seemed a shade paler, the red not quite as brilliant or daring as Samantha's. She was shorter in stature, and her features were not quite as acquiline, but more pert.

The woman in red was smiling at someone off to her left. As Reid and Clarissa drew near, she turned toward them, and as her gaze met Reid's, the smile on her sensuously carved lips froze, then disappeared.

"Elyse," Clarissa said, her tone dripping with contempt, "how could you? That costume is disgraceful."

Disgraceful was definitely not the way Reid would have described it.

"Heavens, all the men are ogling you like a pack of hungry hounds."

Reid knew that was true. He was doing it himself.

"I'm sorry you don't approve of my costume, Clarissa," Samantha said coolly, her gaze never leaving Reid's. The fury simmering in her breast, and the urge to fly at him and rip his eyes out was almost more than she could control.

"Oh, talk about scandal! You and Dellie are always so worried about what I'll do, and look at you!" Clarissa threw a hand up, as if in disgust. "But then, scandal is nothing new to you, is it?"

Samantha's hard gaze moved from the man standing beside her sister, to Clarissa, and back again. The shock of seeing him on her sister's arm had turned the blood in her veins cold, but within seconds the volcanic heat of her fury had nearly overtaken her.

He was dressed completely in black, tight-fitting trousers hugging his long, lean legs, a short-waisted jacket, its silk lapels blending with the black shirt and cravat. The only color on his was the red satin that lined the floor-length cape that draped from his shoulders, and, of course, the horns nestled within the waves of his hair.

Just like her own.

The irony of the costumes each of them had chosen to wear was not lost on her.

In spite of the turmoil of emotions roiling through her, she forced a smile to her face and prayed that she could keep her tone civil. "You haven't introduced me to your beau, Clarissa." She turned her gaze to Reid. She wouldn't expose him for what he was just yet, not here, not tonight. Clarissa would be humiliated in front of her friends, and Samantha didn't want that. But tomorrow . . . A new sense of warmth flowed through her and she almost smiled . . . Tomorrow Blackjack Reid Sinclaire would regret the day he'd ever come to Natchez and crossed swords with her. "Jonathan, isn't it?" she said, and extended a hand toward him.

"Yes," Clarissa said, her tone belligerent, "this is Jonathan Reid. Jonathan, this is my sister, Elyse . . ."

Reid took her hand, bowed slightly, and pressed his lips to it. The scent of jasmine surrounded him. He straightened, his eyes jumping to meet hers.

Samantha felt a tingling of warmth rush up her arm and drew her hand from his.

Clarissa laughed softly and looked at Samantha, her eyes wide with innocence and surprise. "Why, Elyse, I've forgotten your last name."

"Rydelle," Samantha said easily, ignoring her sister's gibe.

Rydelle. The name screamed through Reid's mind.

Hate and anguish battled for control within Samantha as she continued to look at him. How could he have done this? How could it have happened? The man Cord had watching Clarissa had described Jonathan Reid, but Samantha had refused to even give her suspicions an ounce of creedence. She'd been a fool yet again.

"Oh, yes," Clarissa said, drawing Samantha's attention from her thoughts. She wrapped an arm around Reid's possessively. "Silly of me to forget your last name, for heaven's sake, but since I never see your husband. . . ." She shrugged, letting the inference hang on the air between them.

There were probably at least a dozen women in Natchez who wore the scent of jasmine, Reid told himself, trying to argue himself out of the conviction that this woman was Samantha. But her giving the name Rydelle was no coincidence. If he'd had any lingering doubts at all, they were banished with one look into her eyes. In spite of the fact that at the moment they were hard, cold, and full of disdain, he knew that they were the same eyes that had been haunting his every thought for days.

He also knew that he had been trapped by his own lies.

There was suddenly a heavy feeling in the pit of his stomach, but he ignored it. After a long pause, he drew in a deep, calming breath, and smiled, though it was about the last thing he felt like doing. "Elyse, it is a sincere pleasure to meet you at last," he drawled slowly. The blood was pounding in his head like a snare drum as he felt her eyes searing into his, damning him. She was furious, outraged, indignant—and he had an overwhelming desire to pull her into his arms, claim her lips with his, and strip the tantalizing red gown from her body.

Samantha's heart thumped against her breast, wild and loud. She clenched her hands into fists at her sides, willing them to remain still, rather than swing out and slap at his face as she so desperately wanted to do. This situation was impossible. It couldn't be. She damned herself for not having realized sooner, for not having the sense to have known what was happening.

"Why thank you, Mr. Reid. My sister and Aunt Dellie have spoken of you in their letters, and I truly am happy to meet you at last."

The overly sweet tone of her voice was in direct contrast to the penetrating coldness that emanated from her dark blue eyes.

"Thank you." He smiled. "And my compliments on your costume, Mrs. Rydelle. I think you have succeeded in dazzling every man present."

He was flirting with her! Samantha's angered deepened. She smiled and waved a hand in front of her face, as if to ward away some of the afternoon's heat. "Is there a punch bowl anywhere around here?" she asked. "I think I am absolutely parched."

"Allow me," Reid said, and turned toward the table holding the punch bowl.

Samantha released a sigh of relief for the momentary respite from his presence. She watched him walk toward the banquet tables, the black cape billowing out behind him, and for just a moment, a millisecond in time, wished that things could be different, that they were at this soiree together; that she really was Elyse again, and he really was Jonathan, and . . .

She slammed a lid on the treacherous thoughts. She was Samantha, and he was Blackjack Reid Sinclaire—a snake in the grass if there ever was one.

"Humph!" Clarissa tossed her head, sending curls flying over her shoulders.

Samantha looked back at her sister.

"Leave it to Caroline Benseau to throw herself at Jackson Tate the moment he comes back to town."

Samantha followed her sister's gaze across the tented area and saw a man costumed as King Louis XIII offering his arm to a young lady dressed as Mary, Queen of Scots. She remembered Jackson Tate. He was three years older than Clarissa. He had come to Riversrun with his father many times. "He's grown into a very handsome young man," she said.

Clarissa whirled around to face her. "Do you always have to do this, Elyse?" Though she whispered, her tone bristled with indignation.

"Do what?" Samantha asked, confused.

"This!" Clarissa's hands flit about dramatically. "That dress. Your costume. Couldn't you have managed to wear something a little more . . . more . . . more sisterly, for heaven's sake?"

"Clarissa, I . . ." Her gaze moved back toward Reid.

"I knew I should never have agreed to your coming here. Jonathan probably thinks you're the most scandalous person, and since you're my sister . . . Humph!" She stomped her foot and huffed. "You always ruin everything for me, Elyse. Every single thing."

"Clarissa, I didn't mean to . . ."

"Clarissa?"

They both turned at the deep male voice.

Jackson Tate stood beside Clarissa. "May I have the honor of being your escort for the grand march?" he asked, sweeping a hand gracefully before him as he bowed.

Clarissa smiled, her face lighting with excitement, and, as she glanced at Mary, Queen of Scots, triumph. She curtsied and placed her hand in his. "I would be delighted," she said, and slipped an arm around his as they moved toward the dancefloor.

A moment later Reid returned and handed Samantha a glass of punch. "I guess I've been jilted," he said softly, though there was a trace of amusement in his tone.

Samantha glared up at him. "You have my sympathy, Mr. Reid."

He smiled. "You know, every man here wishes they had the nerve to ask you to dance so that they might hold you in their arms, if only for a few moments."

"Then I should leave." She set her glass down on a nearby table and started to turn away.

"No," he said softly, and reached out for her. She was Cord's mistress, or wife, he didn't know which, but he didn't seem to care anymore. His feelings were a jumbled mess, each doing battle with the other. He hated her and he desired her. He wanted never to see her again, and never to let her go. Fury, at her, at himself, burned his blood, and the only way to soothe it was to draw her into his arms.

Before she knew what was happening, his arm had slipped around her waist and pulled her back.

She twisted against him. "Let me . . ."

"Ah, we wouldn't want to cause a scene, would we?" he said softly, his voice taunting.

She looked up at him, taken aback by his tone.

Reid guided her toward the line of couples participating in the grand march.

Don't embarrass Clarissa, Samantha told herself. She suddenly saw Valic Gerard directly in front of them and stumbled as her heart nearly stopped.

"Another admirer?" Reid asked. "Or lover?"

The coldness of his words lashed at her, and though she knew they should have no effect, that she shouldn't care what he thought, she found, much to her dismay, that she cared very much.

"Elyse," Valic said, the gravel-like pitch of his voice grating over her and causing her to shudder as much as the spark of arrogance in his eyes did. "It's so good to see you again."

She forced a smile as they passed him. "I wish he'd drop dead," she muttered softly.

Surprised, Reid glanced down at her, then smiled in amusement. The lady never ceased to amaze him.

The music of the march ended, and Samantha tried to turn away from Reid.

He dragged her back, a fluid, effortless motion that gave no hint to the others around them of the tension that fairly bristled the air between them.

"Reid," Samantha said breathlessly, and tried to push away from his chest.

"Samantha," he said softly, pulling her back.

She stiffened.

They moved into the slowly swirling maze of dancers as the strains of a waltz filled the air.

Another couple moved closer, and the older man smiled at Reid. "Your daring is the envy of every man here tonight, my friend." He laughed and winked at Samantha.

She quickly turned away as a cold chill swept through her. She'd seen him in the Silver Goose.

They moved toward the center of the dance floor. "What

are you doing here?'' Reid asked, careful to keep his voice low.

Her blue eyes clawed him like deadly talons. "I came to meet and get to know my sister's new beau," she said, her words curt and cutting.

Sisters. He still couldn't believe it. But that was a matter to discuss at another time. "Oh, I think we know each other very well already, don't you, Samantha?" he drawled easily, his warm breath caressing her temple.

"You can go straight to . . ." The last strains of the waltz died away and Samantha stopped, not wanting anyone nearby to overhear. She pulled away from him, yanking her arm back, then throwing him a beguiling smile when he reached for her again, and she hurried to avoid his hand. "Perhaps later, Mr. Reid," she said, and laughed. "I really wouldn't want to take up all your time."

Several men nearby threw him consoling glances.

Samantha walked directly to where Clarissa stood talking with Jackson Tate and a young woman dressed as a harem girl. "Clarissa," she said, pulling her sister aside. "I'm not feeling well. I think I'll step outside for a few minutes and get some fresh air. Perhaps even go home."

"You're Clarissa's sister," a young woman said, coming up to them.

Samantha turned, and once again felt her blood turn cold.

The woman smiled and waved a fan before her. "I'm Jonathan's sister, Rhonda, and I'm sure you already know Phillip. I've heard so much about you, Elyse. And that costume"—Rhonda laughed—"it is just absolutely fabulous."

Samantha felt like asking from whom she'd heard about her, Reid or Clarissa. Instead, she smiled. "How do you do?" she said, nodding to both of them. "I'd love to chat awhile, but if you'll excuse me, I have a dreadful headache.

I was just on my way to take a walk through the gardens, and get away from the smoke all these gentlemen seem so happy to create with their cheroots.''

Before anyone could object, or suggest they accompany her, Samantha turned and hurried toward the gardens. Clarissa was right. She shouldn't have worn such a daring costume, but she'd been a bit limited in what she could do with the gowns in her wardrobe. In spite of the fact that it was a costume ball, she'd managed to draw every eye to her, and that's what she should have been trying to avoid. Whatever had she been thinking?

"You weren't," she mumbled to herself. "That's the problem.''

She paused beneath a large oak tree, its wide-spreading branches, each heavily laden with draping strands of gray moss, offered a shelter of cool shade. Leaning against the tree's huge, rough trunk, Samantha let her head fall back and closed her eyes. She placed a hand atop her stomach, as if the gesture might calm the raging upheaval within.

He watched her, and briefly considered returning to the soiree. But something wouldn't let him, the same thing that had drawn him to her before, the same thing that had kept her image in his mind since the first night they'd met. "I was afraid you'd left.''

The sound of his voice was the first inkling Samantha had that he'd followed her. Startled, her eyes shot open and she stiffened, pushing away from the tree. Her heart thumped madly as she looked at him. "You bastard.''

Sunlight, filtering down through the boughs of the oak, played a checkerboard of light and shadows upon the ground, and as she took a step toward him, one of those brilliant rays fell around her. She reminded him of an ancient sorceress rising from the flames. Desire shot through Reid's body, hot, fierce, and consuming. It drove out all thought but one—he wanted her. Yesteday, today, and maybe even tomorrow.

Samantha watched his slow approach, his hair glistening gold whenever the sun touched it, his eyes turning to deep pools of midnight whenever shadowed. She hated him, and she wanted him. Desperately. Every instinct she possessed screamed at her to run, but her heart whispered for her to stay. Her feelings frightened and infuriated her, and left her no will of her own.

Reid paused, leaving several feet of distance between them, and his gaze raked over her, blatantly, assessingly.

The shadows and light alternately enveloped him, one second turning him so dark and sinister she shuddered, and the next creating a halo of light that changed the brown of his eyes to rich pools of cinnamon and the curve of his lips to a silver slash that beckoned her and left her struggling for the strength to resist him.

Silence hung between them as they stared at one another, both fighting and wanting to give in to their desires.

"I didn't know she was your sister," Reid said.

Samantha's eyes narrowed. "So that makes it all right? That you live one life down on the river, and another up here on the hill?"

"Isn't that what you've been doing?" he said, closing the distance between them.

"Get out," she said, her breath ragged with her anger. "Leave Natchez, or I'll ... I'll ..."

"What?" Reid asked, his voice once more a soft drawl that wrapped around her in a caressing embrace she wanted to ignore, and couldn't. "What will you do, Samantha?"

Kill you, she thought, but his mouth came down on hers before she could even try to put the thought into words.

His arms dragged her roughly up against him as his

tongue filled her mouth. Passion swept through her, and she moaned, suddenly feeling as if she were drowning in the flames his touch stoked within her.

Somewhere in the distance a bird chirped, the music from the soiree filtered to them, and Samantha's fury broke through the haze of desire his touch had awaken in her. She broke away from him, twisting her body and pushing at his chest until she was free of his embrace. She hurriedly stepped back. "How dare you?" she said, both her tone and eyes spitting fire.

"We both know I dare a lot."

"You seduce me, and then you have the gall to court my sister?" Emotion burned in her breast, stole her ability to breath.

"I told you I didn't know she was your sister."

"Get out of Natchez," Samantha said again, "or I swear, everyone will know who you are."

"Then they'll know who you are, too," Reid said coldly.

Chapter Twenty

Samantha found Clarissa still hugging the arm of Jackson Tate and forcibly pulled her aside. "Clarissa, I'm going to leave."

"All right," Clarissa said absently, her gaze fixed to Jackson.

"Clarissa," Samantha hissed, so angry she could barely contain herself. "Listen to me. I want you to stay away from Jonathan Reid."

Clarissa turned then, and stared at Samantha. "Jonathan?" She laughed softly, and looked back at Jackson. "Isn't he just a dream, Elyse?"

Suddenly one of the carriage drivers burst past the flower-decorated trellis, nearly knocking it over. "Tornado!" he shouted at the top of his lungs.

"Whatever is that man doing?" Clarissa huffed, glaring at the servant.

"Tornado!" he shouted again. He took several frantic steps in one direction, his gaze whipping from one person to another, then turned and frantically retraced his steps. "Tornado's coming. Just got word. Tornado's coming."

Everyone turned to stare at him in disbelief and confusion, and the music died away.

An older man, Samantha thought she recognized him as an old friend of Staunton Beaumont's, grabbed the servant's arm. "What's this?" he demanded. "What is this you're talking about?"

The servant wheeled on him and grabbed his lapels, jerking them. "We gotta get outta here! We gotta get out!" his voice rose to a hysterical pitch. "Ol' Tom just rode past, fast, coming up from Gibson. There's a tornado coming!" His eyes bulged. "A tornado!" Ripping away from the older man then, the servant, still screaming his warning, dashed back outside and ran toward the group of drivers still clustered near the carriages.

For several seconds an eerie silence fell over the people standing beneath the tent, then suddenly, as if they'd all realized what was about to happen at the same moment, pandemonium broke out.

A woman screamed.

Men began shouting orders, some yelling for everyone to get into the house, others commanding people to get to their carriages and head home.

Someone crashed into one of the banquet tables. It turned over, sending the punch bowl crashing to the ground.

"Hurry!" someone yelled.

Samantha looked around, fear clogging her throat. She tore off her mask and reached out for Clarissa, but her sister was gone. Terror seized her. "Clarissa!"

She whipped around, calling her sister again, but her cries were lost within the havoc and screams of the panicked crowd of guests.

People ran in every direction. Women tripped over their

long skirts and fell to their knees as others ran past. More tables were toppled. A man stumbled against one of the awning posts and fell. The post tore away from the ground and the awning began to collapse.

"Clarissa!" Samantha screamed again. She moved through the crowd, trying to catch sight of her sister's white gown.

In the drive, the liveried drivers fought with suddenly panicking horses. People dove into their carriages, and crowded into some that weren't theirs.

A woman shrieked wildly and threw herself to the ground as a horse reared.

Carriages collided and blocked each other's exit. Horses fought for lead and struggled to move as drivers snapped leather tonged whips overhead in an effort to encourage them to push their way through the crushing milieu.

Suddenly someone pushed Samantha, and ran past.

She stumbled.

Strong hands grasped her arms and pulled her toward one side of the half collapsed awning.

She looked up into Reid's face. "Let go of me," she said, and jerked free of him.

"Damn it, Samantha, this is no time to argue. Come on. We have to get out of here." He grabbed her arm again and, holding her so tight she nearly winced in pain, began to fight his way through the crowd.

"No," Samantha yelled. "I have to find Clarissa."

"She's with Jackson," Reid said over his shoulder.

Samantha continued to struggle against him.

Reid stopped and turned back to her, grabbing her shoulders, his fingers bit hard into her tender flesh. "Listen to me. Clarissa's fine, she's with Jackson, but we won't even be alive much longer if we don't get the hell out of here and into the house."

"The house," Samantha repeated. She glanced at

Auburn, its brick walls looking so strong and impenetrata-
ble, and suddenly thought of the town house, then the
Goose, with its old clapboard sides and unshuttered windows. The town house had a cellar, but the Goose . . . If the
tornado came anywhere near Under-the-Hill, it wouldn't
stand a chance. Cold, paralyzing fear erupted within every
cell of her body as she thought of Molly, Jake, and Cord.
The tornado would rip the Goose apart. They'd be killed!
She had to warn them.

Digging her heels into the lawn, Samantha broke free
of Reid's hold on her, then turned and ran down the
sloping lawn. Tears filled her eyes, threatening to blind
her, but she couldn't stop. She had to get to them.

"Samantha!" Reid yelled, running after her.

The air was filled with the screams of the guests as they
ran for the house, the carriages, or simply down the drive.

"Get out of my way," one of the carriage drivers yelled
at another, and raised his whip.

Panicked horses whinnied loudly and scrambled over
one another, their hooves lashing out at anything in their
way, harnesses tangling. Carriages toppled, broke apart,
and collapsed, their occupants caught in the deadly
squeeze, or jumping for safety, their cries of hysteria blending with those of the frightened animals.

Samantha tripped, gathered up her skirts, ran past several more people, broke through a crowd, and kept running.

Reid thought he saw a flash of red and ran toward it.
"Samantha!"

Someone rammed into his back. He stumbled, fought
for balance, collided with another man.

Both fell in a tangle of limbs.

The air in Reid's lungs shot out in a rush and he gasped
as he scrambled to rise. "Get the hell off me," he growled
at the other man.

He stood and looked around. Where was she? Fear gnawed at his insides; panic began to churn in his stomach. He had to find her. Suddenly, nothing else mattered.

The roar of disaster grew louder.

He couldn't lose her now.

He whipped around, looking everywhere, and opened his mouth to yell her name again . . . and that's when he saw her.

Waves of dark, rich auburn hair billowed out about her shoulders as she ran, an elusive flame of red and gold streaking across the lawn like a tongue of fire.

Fear, like he'd never known in his life, seized him. He bolted after her, continually yelling out her name, only to hear his own voice swallowed up by the pounding, ceaseless, thundering noise of the buffeting winds, and the screams of other people and animals on the verge of hysteria.

A carriage careened in front of him.

Reid slid to a stop, but lost his footing.

The carriage toppled.

Reid scrambled back and fell, as the thrashing hooves of the carriage horse sliced the air, and nearly caught his head. He jumped back to his feet, but Samantha was nowhere insight now. He ran toward the gate.

Samantha reached her carriage. She'd left it tied to a hitching post near the entry gates, far from the others so that, if she'd wanted, she could quietly slip away from the party and leave without drawing anyone's attention. She said a prayer of thanks.

Rogue pawed the ground restlessly, his large head lowering and rising in long sweeping movements as the screams that filled the air pushed at his calm. His ears pricked up at Samantha's approach, his brown eyes following her every move. "It's okay," she said, as she scrambled aboard the carriage and gathered up the reins. "It's okay,

Rogue." She snapped the reins, hard, urging him into movement.

Reed saw her just as she snapped the reins on her horses flank. "Samantha, wait!"

Rogue, already half panicked, bolted forth with a lunge that jerked the carriage violently and nearly toppled Samantha from her seat. Bracing herself as they swerved through the gates, Samantha snapped the reins again, and the horse hastened his pace, his long legs flying through the air, hooves pounding the ground in an effortless race.

Reid looked about frantically. A toppled carriage lay beneath a nearby oak tree, the driver working desperately to unhitch the harness and free the frenzied horse.

A woman nearby fainted. The man running beside her scooped her from the ground and, tossing her unceremoniously over his shoulder, dashed back toward the house.

Reid ran toward the toppled carriage. Without a word, he jerked the restraining hitch off of the horse. The animal instantly made to bolt. Reid held tight to the harness and fought the frightened horse. Holding the reins tightly, he grabbed a fistful of mane in each hand, hoisted himself onto the animal's back and nudged his ribs, but the beast needed no encouragement to run.

Samantha sat on the edge of her seat, feet spread wide to keep her balance as the carriage careened through the busy streets of Natchez.

Wind whipped at everything, bending the trees, picking up small objects and hurling them down the street. A howling sound filled the air, and sent a chill racing up Samantha's spine and deepening the fear in her heart. "Come on, Rogue," she yelled, but her voice was carried away by the lashing wind and its echo of sound.

They sped through the business district. People were

running everywhere. Men raced past on horseback, others in carriages, drays, and landaus. She approached the intersection of Pine and Main Streets and pulled the reins hard to the left. They narrowly missed colliding with an overturned dray lying in the middle of the roadway. Its cargo of fresh fruits and vegetables had been squashed beneath the hooves of other passing horses and carriages.

Reid saw the carriage he assumed was Samantha's swerve onto Pine and he bounded down Main, intending to cut her off. A minute later a carriage appeared out of nowhere and cut in front of him, then swerved crazily around another. Several children running across the road were nearly trampled as a heavily loaded dray's horses bolted out of control.

At Canal Street Reid raced toward Under-the-Hill, a jumble of ugly oaths, curses, and prayers tumbling from his lips in a torrent of incoherent snatches as he pressed the horse for more speed.

The sky was beginning to darken. Gray clouds were sweeping up from the southern horizon, drifting in front of the sun and turning the air ashen.

Samantha's hands trembled and she tightened her grip on the reins. The bluffs, and the steep descent of Silver Street, were just ahead.

Rogue suddenly balked at moving into the crowd of people, horses and wagons surging up the hill, in search of shelter in the upper city.

"No, Rogue, go," Samantha yelled, slapping the reins against his flanks. "Go."

With a shake of his head, ears pricked in annoyance and fear, the huge gelding surged into the crowd and they began inching their way downhill.

She could feel the wind growing stronger. Her hair whipped about, its long tendrils slapping at her face, bringing tears to her eyes. She clawed at it, pushing it aside, only for the flying strands to return.

A gust of wind slammed into the awning of the carriage, lifted it, and caused the buggy to sway violently upon its wheels. For several seconds, their hold on the street, on the very ground, seemed perilously close to disappearing.

A woman fell, and the huge bundle of belongings she was carring on her back slammed into the side of the carriage. Miraculously, it was just the leverage needed to keep Samantha and Rogue from plunging over the steep embankment.

A second later they found the roadway in front of them completely blocked. Two drays had collided as one had tried to move uphill, the other down. The front wheel of one was dislodged and when the wagon had toppled, it had rammed into the side of the other. The two drivers were working furiously at tangled harnesses.

Samantha looked past them and saw the horizon growing darker. "Oh, God," she mewed softly, fear clutching at her heart, racing through her veins.

The howl of the approaching tornado could be heard now, filling the air, its roaring fury growing louder with each passing second as it neared, threatening, destroying everything in its path.

She would never get through in the carriage now. It would have to be left. Samantha stood, and as she did, glanced down at the river. The sight that met her eyes brought a stab of panic to her breast. Half a dozen riverboats were tied at the docks, each bouncing and swaying and crashing into each other as they rode the battering crests of waves.

It looked as if the river had come alive, its dark waters raging furiously in every direction, pushed into rampageous upheaval by the blustering winds.

A huge stack of baled cotton had tumbled across the

docks, and several people from the boats were attempting to scramble over it to get away from the river.

She jumped from the carriage.

Someone pushed against her.

A shoulder jabbed into her arm.

She held to the reins and, grabbing the harness brace, struggled past the pushing crowd streaming uphill, until she reached Rogue's head.

The sky seemed suddenly littered with flying debris of every kind.

Samantha fought with the harness. She wouldn't leave Rogue here. Her trembling fingers lost their grip on the leather. Samantha screamed in frustration, resecured her hold on the harness, and yanked again, and again.

Tears blinded her.

Fear, frustration, urgency tinged her heart's every beat.

The harness finally snapped apart.

Grabbing the reins, she turned to pushed her way down the hill.

Rogue whinnied and jerked on the reins.

They pulled from Samantha's grasp. "No," she screamed.

The crowd surged around her, forcing her to either move back up the hill with them, or be trampled.

As he reached the crest of Silver Street, Reid saw her carriage sitting in the middle of the roadway, people, carts, drays, carriages, all swarming frantically around it in an effort to pass.

The river, far below, was a swirling snake of blackness.

He moved to the outer edge of the street and urged his horse down the hill.

People shoved around him, blocking his descent.

"Samantha!"

The wind was whipping at them now, bits of dust and

foliage flying through the air, whipping at everything and everyone.

Samantha grabbed a fence post at the crest of Silver Street and glanced back at the high, sheer bluffs that towered above and framed the eastern side of Under-the-Hill.

Terror gripped her, nearly stopped her heart, stole her breath.

A huge, swirling mass of black, still off in the distance, rose into the sky, raging out of control, its thunderous roar filling the air. It swerved left, skipped to the right, and seemed to grow ever bigger right before her eyes.

Reid raised an arm to shield his face as he urged the horse to keep moving. He yelled for her, but his shouts were lost within the roaring blend of the approaching tornado's howl, and the screams and cries of the fleeing mob.

Another horse and rider suddenly appeared before Reid.

He tried to urge his mount to the side, away from the edge of the bluff, away from the other horse.

They pushed forward to pass.

The earth beneath the other animal's hooves gave way.

The horse thrashed wildly, and his rider screamed in terror.

Reid grabbed for the man.

He clutched at Reid's arms, and both toppled from their saddles.

Reid's fingers tightened around the small trunk of the bush he'd grabbed as he'd slid over the edge of the hill. He crawled upward, ignoring the jagged rocks that cut into his hands. They had only minutes, and then it would be too late. Heaving himself back onto the roadway, he struggled to catch his breath and got to his feet. Samantha's carriage was still sitting in the middle of the road. He looked around wildly, his gaze darting from one person to another.

Black. Yellow. Blue. Green. Pink. White. Every color of cloth imaginable except ... Then he saw it. Red. But it was at the top of the hill, not the bottom. He pushed through the people still running up the hill, until reaching the opposite side of the street. "Samantha!"

He saw her look up.

Still holding to the fence post, tears streaming down her face, exhaustion wracking her body, her gaze traveled over the crowd until she saw him.

For one fleeting moment, his dark eyes fused with hers.

He pushed his way toward her, his hands roughly shoving people from his way.

Yards. Feet. Inches.

He pulled her into his arms and crushed her to his chest. "Thank God," he murmured absently, drawing in a deep breath.

Someone shoved against them.

Reid grabbed her hand. "Come on, we have to get out of here. That thing is going to be here any second."

"No." Samantha pulled back, twisting her arm in an effort to get free of him. "They're down there. Cord. Jake and Molly." Tears fell down her cheeks. "I can't leave them."

"It's too late," Reid yelled, his voice barely audible above the roar of the wind. He pulled her toward the street and forced her to run.

A faint whinny cut through the other noise and, as if in answer to a prayer, Rogue pranced up beside Samantha and nudged her arm.

Reid didn't stop to wonder about the animal's seemingly miraculous appearance. He was there, and they needed him. Grabbing Samantha, he lifted her onto the horse's back, then swung up behind her and jammed his heels into the gelding's ribs.

Rogue bolted into a gallop, and they charged down Wall Street.

A cat ran across the road in front of them.

Samantha suddenly remembered Blossom. She'd been asleep on Samantha's bed when she'd left the Silver Goose to go to the Governor's ball.

Chapter Twenty-One

The howling wind ripped at Reid's back as he hunched over Samantha, and snapped his heels to Rogue's ribs again, urging the horse to more speed.

Outrunning the menace at their back was their only hope now.

Trees shuddered and shook in the approaching tornado's blast. The gnarled, spreading branches of hundred-year-old live oaks slapped about violently, as if their stiff wooden limbs were still as resilient as young saplings, while the smaller, and younger, magnolias, dogwood, and chestnut trees bent grotesquely under the pounding force. Trailing sheets of Spanish moss, torn from the oaks by cyclonic winds, skittered across the ground, flew through the air, and clung, draping, to any upright object in its path.

Carriages stood empty and deserted everywhere, some with the coach horses still hitched to them, the animals left to fend for themselves as their owners fled the streets in search of safety.

Rogue's large hooves pounded thunderously against the ground, but the sound was lost to the wind.

"There!" Samantha shouted, and pointed toward Dellie's town house. "Go there!"

Reid urged the huge gelding toward the town house, past the front, around to the side. He yanked viciously on the horse's main, and Rogue came to a jarring, sliding halt at the rear of the house. Reid instantly jumped from Rogue's back, his feet no sooner touching the ground than he reached up and drew Samantha down. "Get in the house," he yelled, motioning toward the door as his words disappeared within the wind.

Instead, she grabbed for Rogue.

"I'll bring him," he yelled, and motioned again for her to get to the house.

Out of the corner of her eye, Samantha caught a flash of gold movement and instantly changed direction.

Reid hurriedly pulled his jacket off and wrapped it around the horses neck, grabbing both sleeve ends below the animal's neck to use to guide him. He hunched his shoulders against the wind and turned back toward the house. As he neared the porch, he caught sight of Samantha off to one side, bent over, one hand grasping at the wall for support, the other wrapped around some sort of cage. Her long hair was writhing a violent dance around her face as wind ripped through the tendrils. She stumbled and fell to one knee.

Reid reached for her and, clasping her shoulders, pulled her up. "What are you . . . ?" His words disappeared in the wind. He glanced quickly at the filigreed cage. Within its narrow bars a tiny white bird fluttered about in rising panic.

Holding tight to Rogue, and hugging Samantha to his side, Reid pulled them toward the back door of the house, each step a trudging, determined effort.

The house seemed to tremble against the wind's onslaught.

Reid looked up.

An enormous funnel, black and swirling, ripped through the sky.

"Hurry!" he yelled, pushing Samantha.

They stumbled up the back porch. Reid grabbed the knob and as he turned it, the knob ripped from his hand and the door flew open, crashing against the inner wall. Shards of glass burst from the doors windowpanes, scattering across the floor and countertops of the kitchen.

They practically fell into the house.

Rogue stood in the middle of the large kitchen, nervously thrashing a hoof on the tiled floor and shaking his head, sending his long mane flying about.

Reid slammed the door closed, but the wind stormed through the glassless windows. He slid the latch into place and shoved a chair beneath the handle.

"My land, Elyse!" Dellie exclaimed, rushing into the kitchen. She saw Rogue. "Oh!" Her eyes widened. Wringing her hands, she looked from Samantha to Reid, then noticed the cage in Samantha's arm. "Oh, Pretty Boy!" She rushed across the room. "Poor little thing." Dellie grabbed the cage. "I put him outside for a little sun, and then this wind came up, and I had to see to the shutters, and then Clarissa and her friend ran in, and then . . ."

A loud crash sounded from the parlor and a gust of wind slashed through the house.

Dellie fell against a wall. "Land's sake."

Bric-a-brac crashed to the floor.

Linens from the sinktop took flight.

Windows and doors rattled, shaking violently upon their hings, and furniture began to tremble and bounce around the floors.

Clarissa ran into the kitchen. "Aunt Dellie," she screamed, her eyes shimmering with tears of terror. "We're all going to die."

Jackson Tate appeared in the doorway, then grabbed Clarissa and pulled her to him.

"Samantha," Reid yelled, dragging her to him so that she could hear him, "is there a cellar?"

She nodded.

Relief swept through him. "Show me."

Samantha whirled and pointed to a door set into the wall along the far side of the kitchen. "Through there. Through the pantry."

They all ran for it at once.

Reid turned back and darted into the dining room and grabbed several candles.

Samantha clasped Rogue's mane and pulled him toward the cellar.

The horse balked at the dark entry.

Reid pushed Rogue's rump. "Go," he yelled, and shoved a shoulder against him.

The horse stumbled down the rough plank stairs.

Reid scrambled down after him, then turned and slammed the door, throwing down the wooden plank that was meant to secure it from the inside.

The howl of the tornado was muted now.

"Go all the way in," Reid said, "as far as you can."

As the other shuffled about, Reid took a lucifer from his pocket and scraped its tip against the wall. It instantly burst into flame, which he held to the candle's wick.

A pale yellow glow lit the cellar.

Reid held the candle up and looked around. Jars of preserved foods lined the shelves built against one wall, while trunks, crates, and a hodgepodge of discarded and broken furniture was stacked against the others.

Pulling a crate to the center of the room, Reid wedged the thick candle between the slates of wood, then turned and dragged Samantha into his arms, holding her tight against his chest.

He closed his eyes and drew in a deep breath. They were below ground level here, as safe from the tornado as they could be. He felt the silk waves of her hair beneath his cheek. If he had lost her, he didn't know what he would have done.

Dellie plopped down on the stairs and set the birdcage beside her. "Poor little Pretty Boy," she cooed, reaching into the cage and running a comforting finger across the bird's back. "But you're all right now, sweetie pie. Elyse saved you."

Clarissa stood huddled in Jackson Tate's arms, weeping softly and trembling.

Samantha pulled away from Reid.

"Are you all right?" he asked softly, looking down at her.

She nodded, then moved to sit beside her aunt. Hugging her arms around her bent knees, she lay her head down on them. Cord. Jake. Molly. Blossom. Maybe Curly. They were all Under-the-Hill. Had they gotten to safety? Or were they . . . Tears filled her eyes and an ache so intense she felt it like the stab of a knife, pieced her heart.

Reid knelt beside her. "Samantha," he said softly, and placed a hand on her arm.

She sat up and jerked away from him.

Dellie stood and walked away.

Reid slid onto the step next to Samantha. "We need to talk."

She looked at him. "Talk? About what?"

Before he could respond, she went on.

"That you've been courting my sister under an assumed name?" She took refuge from the pain and worry in her anger at him. "That you've been living Top-the-Hill, lying and most likely cheating everyone out of who knows what?"

"No. Let me explain."

A derisive chuckle escaped her lips as one red brow soared. "You can't," she snapped. "But know this, Blackjack Reid Sinclaire: the charade is over. I don't want you anywhere near my sister or . . ."

"I don't want to be anywhere near your sister," Reid said. "I didn't even know . . ."

"You obviously didn't know a lot," she raged in a whispered voice that simmered with fury. "But it doesn't matter. When this"—she motioned toward the ceiling with her hand—"thing, is over, I want you out of here. Out of this house, and out of Natchez."

Clarissa looked at them in confusion, not having the faintest idea what they were talking about. But then, she was in Jackson Tate's arms, and that's all she really cared about anyway.

"And out of your life?" Reid said softly, aching to draw Samantha into his arms, and sensing she would only reject him again.

"Yes, out of my life. You're despicable. How many women do you need, Mr. Sinclaire? You have a wife. You had me in your bed. Why did you have to pick on a seventeen-year-old girl?"

"Samantha," Reid tried again.

She stood abruptly, then whirled to face him. "No," she yelled, glaring down at him. "Stay away from this family. Go back to the river. Go back to your wife. But just stay away from us."

He stood. "I love you, Samantha," he said, only loud enough for her to hear.

Something smashed against the door at the top of the stairs. "Sam? Sam, you down there?"

Samantha recognized Jake's voice. "Jake?" She ran up the stairs and threw aside the plank. "Oh, Jake."

The door instantly flew open and Jake's huge bulk was

silhouetted at the top of the stairs. "Sam, you all right?" he said, grabbing her as she practically fell into his arms.

"I was so worried. What are you doing here? How did you find me?"

"Hell, Sam, I've always known where you went on them midnight rides of yours. Cord made me follow you, to make sure you got here and back in one piece."

"Where's Cord and Suzette? And Molly? And Blossom?" She looked past him. "Are they all right?"

"I don't know. I was upriver. Found out about the twister from the captain of a paddle wheeler who was trying to outrace it when he stopped for fuel. I just got back. Come in from the east and since I was passing here first, figured I'd better stop or you'd have my hide."

She noticed the quiet. The tornado was gone. "We've got to get to the saloon, Jake." She pushed past him, oblivious of the debris scattered about the house. Almost every piece of glassware was broken; windows were shattered, furniture toppled and broken.

But they were alive. That's all that really mattered. The rest could be fixed.

"Samantha, wait," Reid said, following her. "I'll come with you."

She turned, anger flashing from her eyes. "No." Bitterness strained her voice. "Maybe you'd best go see to your wife, Mr. Sinclaire."

"Damn it, Samantha, I ... Oh, my God." His anger suddenly disappeared as he remembered Rhonda. She hadn't arrived at the ball when the warning had been sounded about the tornado, which meant she'd either been on her way, or still at the hotel.

He charged for the door.

Tears stung the back of Samantha's eyes as she watched him run from the house. Turning, she gave Jake a forced smile. "Give me just a minute," she said, and walked to the cellar steps.

Samantha nudged Rogue's ribs, prodding him into movement. They loped away from the house, riding beside Jake. But she hadn't been totally prepared for the sight that met her eyes. The streets were strewn with debris, evidence of exactly where the brunt force of the tornado had swept past. Drays and carriages had been toppled and torn apart, their roofs, doors, and wheels and bodies lying in broken heaps in the street or yards. Fences had been ripped from their anchoring posts. Holes in the earth attested to where shrubs had once been. Trees had been torn from the ground. Some had fallen across the roads, their twisting roots reaching out like curling, gnarled, black snakes, while others had crashed down or been dropped upon houses, smashing roofs, breaking windows, and destroying furniture.

And, of course, there had been fatalities. People. Dogs. Cats. Horses.

Several blocks later they turned a corner and Samantha was surprised to see that this neighborhood appeared as if nothing more than a strong windstorm had occured. Residents were opening shutters, pulling carriages into barns and entry drives, and picking up a few broken tree limbs.

They neared the crest of Silver Street, and Samantha felt a catch in her throat. She was suddenly as afraid as she was anxious. What if . . . ? She forced the thought away before it could even take hold in her mind. They were all right. They had to be. She reminded herself of the neighborhood they'd just passed. Only slightly damaged. Under-the-Hill could be fine.

They paused at the crest. A moan of despair ripped from

Samantha's throat and she slapped a hand to her mouth, as if to stop the agony welling up within her from spilling out.

Ruin and devastation were everywhere. Except for the sawmill at the far end of the flat, slice of land, Under-the-Hill was gone. Every building, every structure, everything that had once stood upright was lying flat and broken upon the ground.

Chapter Twenty-Two

Reid ignored the pain in his chest, the ache in his legs, and kept running. He leapt over a broken tree limb lying in the street, his heel struck it, and he stumbled and ran on. His eyes stung. He gasped for breath, feeling it burn his lungs.

He had to get to the hotel. He had to find Rhonda. Make sure she was all right. He hadn't prayed since he was a child, but he prayed now, for his sister's life.

The clatter of hooves rose up behind him. A second later a carriage sped by, its spinning wheels throwing dirt and debris into the air, and into his face.

Reid felt something hit his cheek, slice the skin. His strength was giving out. He pushed on and rounded the corner. The Durante Hotel came into view.

The sight brought him to a stunned halt. It was gone. Nothing of the hotel was left standing. There was only a mountain of debris where the three-story building had been. Bricks. Wood. Glass. All broken. Splintered.

"Oh, God. Oh, no," Reid moaned, staggering toward
the scene. "Rhonda." Visions of his sister filled his mind.
Facing that horror alone. Frightened. Screaming. Calling
for him. He suddenly began to run, swerving around wreckage, jumping over it, hurling obstacles out of his way. And
all the while he screamed her name like a madman, over
and over and over.

He grabbed the leg of a chair, jerked it free of the bricks
half covering it, and threw it over his shoulder. "Rhonda?"
He kicked at a half broken door. Shoved what had once
been a bureau out of his way, stumbled through the bricks,
picked one up and smashed it down on a huge shard of
glass. "Rhonda?"

His voice was ragged.

He looked down into the face of the desk clerk, pinned
beneath one of the lobby's huge ceiling beams, his lifeless
eyes staring up at Reid. His search turned frantic, savage.
He tore through the debris, his fingers clawing at what
had once been walls, doors, windowpanes, furniture, the
effort tearing off his flesh. But he ignored the pain and
the blood and kept searching, kept digging.

A long curl of dark hair suddenly fell onto his hand.

Reid froze, staring at it, momentarily unable to breath.
He felt a crushing pain in his chest, watched, as if from
somewhere else, as his hand turned about, the curl falling
into his curled, and trembling fingers. He closed his eyes
then, and drew in a deep breath, feeling the shudder that
shivered through him. Looking back down, he reached
out and pushed aside a piece of jagged-edged plaster, then
began to move the bricks from on top off her.

A moment later, he paused, and kneeled beside her.
Except for the surrounding debris, and the dust and sands
of mortar that covered her skin, clouded her hair, and lay
within the folds of her gown, she could have been sleeping.

Reed looked down at his wife and felt an overwhelming

sense of guilt. He had tried, once, long ago, to love her, and had never been able to. Worse, he had never even been able to even like her. And if he hadn't been in Natchez, she wouldn't have followed him, and she wouldn't have been killed.

"Reid?"

Rhonda's voice shot through him like a hot flash of life, sizzling his senses. He bolted to his feet and swung around.

She stood only a foot away, still dressed in the costume she'd planned to wear to the Governor's masquerade ball, but the stage makeup she'd used around her eyes had been smeared by her tears, so that her cheeks were streaked black.

And she was the most beautiful sight he could have wished for at the moment.

Relief, gratitude, joy flowed through Reid like a torrent of rain. Dragging her into his arms, he hugged her tightly and laughed, long and hard and loud. "I thought you were . . ." He looked back at the debris at his feet. "I didn't know what to do. I thought . . ."

"I know, " she said, her hands on his shoulders, "I thought you were, too." Tears glistened in her eyes. "But we aren't," she said, and laughed. "We . . ." Her gaze fell on Lillian as Reid released her and she stepped back. Rhonda's smile broke. "Oh, my God."

Reid grabbed Rhonda's shoulders and turned her away from the sight of his late wife. "She's gone," he said softly.

"No. I . . . I was just talking with her . . . I mean," Rhonda shook her head. "Just before I left the hotel, I . . . she was arguing with someone, a man. She slapped his face, and he slapped hers." She stopped and looked up at Reid. "She ran past me to her room, and I followed her. I don't know why." She glanced back at Lillian. "He was going to pay her to seduce you away from the game, and Clarissa

Beaumont, but Lillian had changed her mind about doing it.''

Reid frowned. "She told you this?"

Rhonda nodded.

"Who was the man?" he demanded.

"I don't know. I mean, I saw him, but I didn't recognize him, and Lillian was crying, not really too coherent. She just said . . ." Her gaze shot up to him and her hand flew to her mouth as she she gasped, her eyes suddenly wide.

"What?" Reid said, alarmed.

"She'd divorced you." Rhonda grabbed his arm. "I forgot. She said she'd divorced you."

Shocked, his brows pulled together in a frown, his eyes narrowed and darkened. More than a little disbelief kept his shoulders rigid, his mind dwelling in disbelief. "Are you sure?"

"Yes. She said she'd divorced you." Rhonda nodded. "Before leaving England. I don't know why she told me. Maybe she would have said more, but Phillip showed up in the hall looking for me, and Lillian ran to her room and slammed the door, so I left."

Reid gathered Rhonda back into his arms and held her to him as his mind filled with thoughts of the past, and his heart tried to deal with the guilt and sorrow. Maybe he had never really known Lillian. Maybe if he'd tried harder . . .

"She didn't love you," Rhonda said, as if reading his thoughts.

Samantha tore her gaze away from the devastation of Under-the-Hill and looked toward the river, needing a momentary respite from the horror of ruin.

Several yards from the docks, two paddle wheelers floated toward the middle of the now calm river, unmoored, unattended, and seemingly undamaged. Others had not been as lucky. One large riverboat had been tossed aground, smashed upon the landing to which it had been tied. One entire side of the boat was caved in, its tall black smokestacks broken in half. The pilot house was completely destroyed, and the huge wooden paddle wheel was a tangled, broken mess of red splinters and twisted metal.

Debris covered the murky waters of the wide Mississippi as well as what little was left of the docks themselves.

"No," Samantha whispered, and shook her head, as if in a daze. "Oh, no, no, no."

"Sam," Jake said, his voice brusque as it broke through her thoughts. "Come on. We gotta get down there."

She turned and stared at him in disbelief. "There's nothing left," she said, her voice as lifeless as she felt inside.

He kicked his horse. "We don't know that," he growled. "Not for sure."

She looked back toward the Goose, nothing now but a pile of rubble. Nothing—no one, could have survived this. The damage was too complete, the tornado's wrath too deadly. There was nothing left. The Goose was gone. Cord, Suzette, Molly, Blossom. Dead. Tears blinded her, and a sob broke from her trembling lips.

Jake stopped and looked back at her. "Sam!"

They were gone.

"Sam!"

She looked up.

"Come on."

They descended the steep incline.

"We've gotta take Cypress Street," Jake yelled over his shoulder. "Silver's blocked up ahead."

Samantha glanced past him and saw that the brick and stone structure that had been Smithson's boardinghouse had collapsed into the street, the rubble of the building piled at least four feet high and spread across the entire width of Silver Street, half blocking it.

A few bedraggled people staggered past, some crying, some wailing, others moving in stunned silence. Here and there men had begun digging into the mounds of toppled buildings, searching for survivors.

Or maybe they were looters, Samantha thought absently, searching for whatever they could find.

They turned down a side street and approached Silver from the opposite direction, and Samantha gasped in shock. She had known it wouldn't be there, and yet she hadn't really been prepared.

Jake jumped from his horse and waded instantly into the devastation. "Molly?" he yelled, his deep, hoarse voice echoing on the now eerily still afternoon air. "Molly?" He grabbed a huge piece of wood and flung it aside easily, then another, and another. "Molly?"

Samantha began to pick her way over the wreckage. A glittering reflection caught her eye and she turned. Part of the gold trimmed wheel of fortune was poking up through the waste, its carved spindles broken, the visible part of the wheel badly smashed. The bar had toppled forward and now lay half hidden beneath the remains of the building's wall and roof, gleaming pieces of the twin mirrors that had hung behind it lying shattered everywhere.

"I can't find any sign of them," Jake said quietly, coming up beside her.

At his words, Samantha's entire body suddenly began to tremble uncontrollably. Her knees felt too weak to hold her up one second longer, a chill swept through her blood. She sank down amid the pile of broken walls and furniture, dropped her head into her hands, and made no effort to stop the wrenching sob that tore from her throat. "They're gone," she said, desolation heavy in her tone and heart.

"They're gone." Tears rained from her eyes and slid down her cheeks, onto her palms, down her arms.

"No," Jake thundered, wheeling around, stubbornly denying what seemed all too real. "They mighta gotten away in time. Cord was here. He'd of known what to do."

She shook her head.

"Others got out. They did, too," he insisted, turning and picking up a broken chair. He threw it with all the force left in him. It sailed through the air and crashed against the wall of the bluff that stood to the rear of the property.

Samantha reached up for his hand. "What are we going to do, Jake?" she asked softly. Her tears shimmered against the afternoon sun. "What are we going to do?"

"We ain't giving up—that's what we're gonna do. We're gonna keep looking. We ain't found no bodies, and as far as I'm concerned, that means they ain't dead." He sat down next to her and smashed a huge fist into a plank of wood. "We ain't giving up."

"But . . ."

"No," Jake said. "They could have gotten Top-the-Hill, Sam, like lotsa other people did. Maybe they're in one of the churches up there or something, waiting to start looking for us. We gotta go see."

Samantha nodded. It was a long shot, she knew. She was a gambler. The odds weren't good, but he was right: they had to play the game out to the end.

"Come on," he said, standing and offering her a huge, burly paw of a hand.

She placed her hand in his and, as she started to push off the pile of wood she'd been sitting on, felt it begin to move beneath her. Samantha jumped up. "Jake." She grabbed his arm and stared down at the debris, not certain whether she expected some kind of monster to leap out of it, or the ground to open up and swallow them.

The pile shook again. Once. Twice. Then quivered violently. Suddenly the entire pile of rubble flew upward and a square piece of floor crashed back and on top of it, sending a cloud of dust and dirt swirling into the air.

Jake grabbed Samantha, wrapping an arm hastily around her shoulders and jerking her back from the yawning cavern.

Both stared, wide-eyed and shocked.

"I hate dark," a voice grumbled up from the black hole toward them. "And damp. No, stay there. I'll go first. We don't know what's up there."

Samantha's heart leapt at hearing the familiar voice.

"I knew it!" Jake bellowed.

Cord Rydelle climbed from the extremely shallow cellar that had been built beneath the Goose years ago. He looked from Sam to Jake. "Well, I'm sure glad to see you two." He hugged Samantha. "You okay, honey?"

She nodded, too choked with happiness to speek.

He looked around. "Damn. Not much left." Releasing Sam, he turned back to the cellar opening and hunkered down. "Come on up, ladies—it's all over." He reached a hand down into the dark cavity, and a second later assisted first Suzette, then Molly, holding Blossom, up the crude stairs.

"Hot damn, thank the saints," Jake roared, and grabbed Molly into his arms, his enthusiastic bear hug causing Molly's face to beam, and Blossom to screech wildly in protest. The cat jumped from Molly's arms and pranced directly toward Samantha.

"Thank heavens you're all all right," Samantha said, picking up the cat and hugging her fiercely. Blossom mewed, then set to purring.

"Well, it was touch and go there for a spell. We were trying to barricade ourselves in, then Cord remembered that cellar. Good thing, too," she muttered, looking at what was left of the Goose. "Looks like barricading wouldn't have done much good."

"But," Samantha frowned and looked at Cord, "how did you know about the cellar? I'd forgotten all about it."

"Curly," he said. "Stashes the good stuff down there."

"What are we going to do?" Suzette said, finally asking the question on everyone's mind.

"Rebuild," Cord said instantly. He turned to Jake. "We'll need to fix up a tent or something to stay in while we're building."

"I can get some food and blankets from my aunt," Samantha offered. She looked at Suzette's skimpy gown, Molly's dirty one, and her own torn costume. "And some clothes."

The sun was going down.

Reid wiped his forehead against the sleeve of his shirt and straightened to look around. They hadn't found any survivors in the last hour. A movement to his right caught his attention and he turned.

Valic's fingers wrapped around the diamond necklace. It was covered with dust and grime. He grinned to himself and yanked it from the woman's neck.

The clasp broke and scrapped her skin.

He looked down into her eyes, wide open, but sightless within the veil of death. She wouldn't be needing the necklace anymore, and since he had given it to her, it was his to take back.

"Hey, what are you doing?" Reid stepped over a pile of bricks and approached Valic.

He sneered. Sinclaire. The bastard.

Reid's gaze shot to Valic's hand.

The diamond necklace, in spite of the dust and grime

that clung to it, picked up the fading light of the day and sparkled a reflection.

Robbing the dead. Reid looked down at the face of the woman at Valic's feet.

Lillian.

Outrage filled Reid's mind. Murder swelled within his heart. "Why, you lousy . . ."

"Reid, that's him," Rhonda yelled. "He was the man I saw with Lillian."

Reid lunged at Valic, his fingers encircling the man's neck and squeezing hard.

Valic's fist rammed into Reid's stomach.

He lost his breath, but his fingers continued to bear down on Valic's throat.

Valic's fist slammed into Reid's jaw.

Reid fell back, then lunged at Valic again. This time with his fists flying.

The two grappled.

Valic staggered and dragged Reid down with him.

Reid's head hit the edge of a brick, and the skin on his left temple tore away. Stunned, the world spun around him. Blood streamed down the side of his face.

Valic rolled away, shoved a hand into his boot, and drew out a derringer.

Reid struggled to his feet.

Valic raised the gun.

Reid stepped back. The heel of his boot caught on something and he tripped. His arms flailed the air.

Valic pulled the trigger and the explosion of shot shattered the otherwise quiet twilight that had fallen over Natchez in the tornado's wake.

Rhonda screamed.

The bullet slammed into Reid's thigh as he fell back.

* * *

"So what are you going to do?" Rhonda looked at Reid. He shook his head. "I don't know."

She turned to Phillip, who had invited her to stay at his parents' plantation since the hotel had been destroyed. He stood at the fireplace of the grand parlor, an elbow propped casually upon the mantle. His gaze caught hers and he moved to her side, slipping an arm around her shoulders. "You can stay here," he said, "until you know what you want to do."

Reid looked up, but his gaze moved to meet his sister's, not Phillip Letrothe's.

"He's asked me to stay," she said softly, and smiled as her hand moved to slip within Phillip's larger one, and their fingers entwined.

Reid saw the love shining from his sister's eyes, and knew he didn't have to worry about her anymore. He shook his head and stood. "Thanks, but I have a few things to do, then I think I'll take a boat down to New Orleans." He took the hand Rhonda held out to him, then leaned forward and brushed his lips across her cheek. "I'll be okay, Rhonnie," he said softly, seeing the concern in her eyes.

"You'll come back," she said, a touch of fear in her tone now, "before you leave town?"

He nodded and walked to the door, favoring the leg Valic's bullet had pierced. Luckily it had only grazed it. There was no reason for him to stay in Natchez now. If Rhonda married Phillip, and the way Reid saw the two of them looking at each other, he felt that was a most definite possibility, she certainly didn't need a brother like him around. What would the polite genteel of Top-the-Hill think of Mrs. Phillip Letrothe having a gambler for a brother? He could just imagine.

Rhonda ran after him, catching up to Reid on the front gallery of the LeTrothe house. "Reid." She grabbed his arm, forcing him to stop. "What about Samantha?"

He looked up at his sister. "What about her?"

"You're in love with her."

A sad smile touched Reid's lips, and he shook his head. "She hates me now, Rhonda. It's no good."

"Talk to her."

He shook his head again. "I'll see you before I leave."

Half an hour later he reined in the horse Phillip had loaned him, and tied his reins to a bush in front of Dellie Beaumont's town house.

"Why, Mr. Reid," Dellie said, opening the door to his knock. "Come in."

"Jonathan," Clarissa said, stepping into the foyer from one of the other rooms, "or should I call you Reid? Or do you go by Blackjack?" The coolness of her tone was nothing compared to the chill he saw gleaming from her eyes.

He approached her. "I just came by to apologize," he said softly, following her as she turned and walked into the parlor. "And explain."

She walked to a window, then turned to face him. Sunlight flowed into the room and created an aura of brightness around her, intensifying the yellow silk of her dress. "There's nothing to explain. What you did was reprehensible, but"—she smiled and shrugged—"it really doesn't matter now."

He frowned. "Doesn't matter?" Fear touched his heart. Had something happened to Samantha? "What do you mean?" he asked anxiously.

"I'm going to marry Jackson Tate." She smiled triumphantly, and not just a little, smugly.

"That was fast," Reid mumbled, momentarily forgetting himself.

"Perhaps," Clarissa said, ignoring his surprise at realizing he'd spoken aloud, "but all the women are after him. After all, since he's come home from doing whatever it was he was doing up north, all the women are after him." She laughed softly. "But I have him."

"Well, then," Reid said, "please accept my congratulations."

"Oh, not quite yet. I mean, he hasn't asked for my hand yet, but he will. I just wish it was my father who was still alive instead of Elyse's. After all, I'm going to be the one having the big wedding Top-the-Hill, not Elyse, but she has a father who can give her away, and I don't. It just really isn't fair."

Reid was confused. "I don't understand, didn't you and your sister have the same father?"

"Clari, I really think you should be upstairs getting ready," Dellie said, interrupting. "Jackson is due to arrive for you any minute."

Reid turned to the older woman. "I'm leaving town," he said. "Next time you see Samantha"—he paused, trying to get past the feeling of emptiness that had suddenly come over him—"please . . . tell her I'm sorry. That I . . ." He left the sentence unfinished and turned to go then.

"Why don't you tell her yourself?" Clarissa said, from where she stood on the base of the stairs.

He looked at her. "I doubt she wants to ever see me again."

"Jonathan . . . I mean"—Clarissa smiled—"Reid, have you ever met Elyse's father?"

Reid shook his head. "No."

"Umm, too bad," she said thoughtfully. "I don't know whether or not to invite him to my wedding. I mean, I know he's a gambler and all, but he is Elyse's father." She looked at Dellie, then laughed and clapped her hands together. "Auntie, I've decided. Add Cord Rydelle's name to my list of wedding invitations. It wouldn't be right not to invite Elyse's father."

Reid's jaw nearly dropped to the floor. He stared at Clarissa, unable to believe what he'd just heard. It had to be a mistake. She hadn't meant what she'd said. "Cord Rydelle," he echoed. "What are you talking about?"

Clarissa looked at him, clearly puzzled by the question. "Inviting Elyse's father to my wedding, of course. Isn't that what we've just been discussing?"

"Cord Rydelle?" Reid said again. "Cord Rydelle is your sister's father? I thought he was . . ."

"What?" Clarissa asked, curious now.

"Her lover."

Clarissa laughed. "Oh, my, that is precious."

Dellie's eyes widened in shock. "Well, I never!" she gasped.

Ten minutes later Reid walked out of the town house, his mind swimming in the details Clarissa had just divulged.

Cord Rydelle was Samantha's father, but her mother's parents hadn't approved of him, and refused to let their daughter marry him.

He was Samantha's father, not her lover.

The rumors had been wrong.

Reid grabbed his horse's reins and mounted.

His newfound excitement suddenly vanished. In the long run though, what did it matter. She hated him, and he couldn't really say he blamed her.

"Mr. Sinclaire?"

He turned to see Dellie standing on the walkway. "Go down there," she said.

He frowned, not understanding.

"Elyse . . ." She shook her head. "Samantha. Go talk to her."

"She hates me, Miss Beaumont."

The old woman smiled knowingly. "There's a real fine line between hate and love, Mr. Sinclaire. A real fine line."

He turned the horse toward the street, while his mind tried to make sense out of everything that had happened in the last few days. He'd come to Natchez for one reason, and one reason only—to get revenge against Cord Rydelle. Instead, he'd fallen in love, the one thing he'd sworn he would never do again.

He hadn't realized where he was heading, until he looked up and saw that he'd brought the horse to a pause at the crest of Silver Street. It had been three days since the tornado had struck, doing the worst of its damage to Under-the-Hill. Reid looked down at the tents that had spurted up upon the flat levy of land. In several places, the frames of buildings had already been erected, debris cleared away.

Maybe the odds were against him, but he was a gambler, and this stake was the most important of his life. He had to play the hand out.

He heard the voices as he rode toward the plot of land where the Silver Goose Saloon had once stood. Several tents had been erected around the area, and part of a new frame for the building had already been constructed. Dismounting, Reid walked toward the tent, and the voices, raised in anger now. He recognized Samantha's instantly, but the other, a man's, he couldn't place.

Stepping around the corner of the tent, Reid saw Valic Gerard, his finger jabbing the air toward Samantha's face as he yelled. "Nothing's changed. We had a deal, and I want that million dollars. Now!"

"Everything's changed," Samantha snapped back, "or haven't you noticed that the Silver Goose, not to mention the entire Under-the-Hill district, is gone?"

Valic grabbed Samantha's arm. "I want my money, missy." His tone was a threatening growl.

Reid saw Samantha wince as she tried to jerk free of Valic's hold on her arm, and he twisted it cruelly. "Let her go, Gerard," Reid said, stepping toward them.

Valic turned to look at Reid. "Stay out of this," he snarled, hatred glowing from his dark eyes, his features ugly with the emotion.

Samantha twisted free and stepped back. She looked from one man to the other, suddenly more afraid than she had been for herself. Valic Gerard was a man with no conscience, and she suspected he was just a little bit insane.

"It's none of your business, Sinclaire," Valic said. "This is between me and her."

"I'm making it my business."

Valic grinned. "Fine." With lightning speed he drew a derringer from an inside pocket of his jacket.

"No!" Samantha screamed, and flung herself in front of Reid, arms outstretched.

Reid's mind reeled. Suddenly, seeing Samantha standing in front of him, shielding him from Valic Gerard's gun, putting her own life in jeopardy for him, time seemed to stand still, then spin backward—to a night years ago. Cord had tried to tell him that Bethany had flung herself in front of him to save him from a bullet from a man who'd lost to Reid at cards and had been bent on getting his money back. But Reid hadn't believed him. In his rage and grief, he'd convinced himself that Cord was a coward, that he'd purposely hidden behind Bethany to avoid being shot.

But now he knew he'd merely been fooling himself, or maybe it was damning himself for not being there when his fiancée and best friend had needed him the most.

"Drop your gun, Gerard," Reid said, his voice cutting through the brightness of the afternoon like a slash of darkness.

Valic laughed. "I don't think so, *mon ami.*"

"He said, drop your gun."

Both men turned abruptly to see Cord standing nearby, his gun already drawn and aimed at Valic.

Jake stood just behind Cord, a rifle resting cradled in his arms, a murderous anger flashing in his usually gentle eyes.

Valic huffed. "You can shoot me, Rydelle," he said mockingly, "but not before I kill your precious little Samantha here." His eyes lit with malice. "Or should I call her by her real name?" he taunted. "Elyse?" He laughed again. "Elyse Beaumont."

Behind Samantha, Reid drew his own gun.

"I think you've done enough talking," Reid said, gently pushing Samantha aside. His hands hung at his sides, but this time the right one was wrapped around the Colt .45 that had been nestled in the holster at his ribs.

Valic looked from one man to the next.

"The odds are against you on this one, Gerard," Cord said.

A gleam of madness sparked in Valic's eyes. "Then I'll have to try for a wild card, hey, gentlemen?" he said, and turned his gun toward Samantha.

Suddenly the air turned to an explosion of sound.

Samantha screamed.

Reid grabbed her, and dragged her back against him.

Valic Gerard, the white front of his shirt turning crimson, looked at Samantha, then the gun in his hand tilted, escaped the grasp of his fingers and fell to the ground . . . only seconds before Valic did.

Cord turned toward Samantha. "Are you all right?"

She pulled away from Reid and nodded. "I'm fine." She glanced down at Valic. "I just wish it hadn't had to end like this." She shuddered as relief and sorrow swept through her.

"Samantha." Reid closed the distance between them and touched her arm.

She turned. "I said goodbye to you once, Mr. Sinclaire," she said, the coldness in her tone startling him, "it should have been enough." Spinning on her heel, she walked to the tent, threw back its flap and entered.

Reid started to follow.

"No," Cord said, grabbing his arm.

Reid looked at the older man, remembering how close they'd once been, and how he'd thrown that away. "I have to talk to her," he said softly.

"She said goodbye," Jake said, positioning himself in front of the tent flap. "I figure that means she don't wanna talk to you no more."

Reid jerked away from Cord and glared at the tall roust-about. "Get out of my way."

Jake grinned and shoved huge, clenched fists on his hips. "Or what?"

If the man wanted to, Reid felt certain, Jake could make mincemeat out of his face, and as badly as he wanted to talk to Samantha, he didn't exactly want to be beaten to a bloody pulp in his effort to get to her. Not unless it was the only way. He turned to Cord.

Cord shrugged. "I've never been able to change her mind once it's made up on something."

Reid walked to the edge of the street, then turned back. "Valic took her home, Riversrun, right? Swindled her father over poker, then claimed everything as gambling debt?"

Cord's eyes narrowed in suspicion. "Yeah, why?"

"Because I own Riversrun now. Valic didn't pay the taxes on it last year. A little oversight on his part. The bank sent out a notice, but I guess it never caught up with him."

"How'd you know about Riversrun?" Cord asked, his suspicions aroused.

Reid grinned, thinking of Rubies. "A friend, Top-the-Hill. His brother-in-law works at the bank. I had made an offer on the place, anonymously, then I was told about the back taxes."

"So?" Reid said. "You want to sell it to Sam."

"No. I'll give it to her, if she'll just talk to me for a few minutes."

Cord looked at him long and hard.

"I'll leave," Reid said quietly. "I'll give her the plantation, free and clear, then I'll leave and none of you will ever have to see me again, if she'll just talk to me for ten minutes first."

Five minutes later Cord threw up the tent flap and stepped back outside. He looked at Reid. "She said no."

Reid started to push past him, intent on getting into the tent, and to Samantha.

Cord grabbed his arm and stopped him. "She wouldn't accept your offer, but she made one of her own."

Reid felt apprehension seize his heart.

"Three hands of Blackjack," Cord said. "She'll put up her share of the new saloon, and give you your ten minutes, against the plantation. Two out of three wins it all."

"But I don't want her saloon," Reid protested. "I only want to talk to her."

Cord shrugged. "That's the only deal she'll make."

"Fine. Who deals?"

Cord grinned. "I do."

Reid shook his head, knowing Cord was too good—he could deal the cards anyway he wanted. "All I want . . ."

"I know what you want, Reid," Cord said, his voice quiet, his gaze locking steadily with Reid's. "I'll deal honest, but I won't wish you any luck."

Reid watched Cord disappear into the tent, and his stomach began to churn with a sudden qualm. What did it really matter? he suddenly mused. He could tell her the truth, or make up a lie, but whatever he said, she wouldn't believe him. He ran his fingers through his hair. It was no good. The best thing he could do for her, and for himself . . . He turned and looked down at the river. He had to make sure she won.

Forcing a determined smile to her lips, Samantha straightened the skirts of her green and black checkered day gown and swept back the flap of the tent. The glare of the sun fell on her face, and she blinked; then her gaze met his.

Longing that she didn't want to feel filled her.

Desire, traitorous and unwelcome, gnawed at her, hot and consuming. She reached out to clutch at one of the tent's support beams, and closed her eyes to blot out the sight of him until she regained some semblance of composure.

When she reopened her eyes a second later, Reid felt the thin thread of hope he'd been clinging to slip from his grasp. Her face was a mask, a beautiful but cold mask, devoid of all expression and feeling, her eyes gleaming with an icy brilliance.

She was beautiful, and he knew she was the only woman he would ever truly love. But he also knew she was lost to him. Because of his own foolishness, his need for revenge, his desire for wealth, he had lost her.

Samantha smiled, a chill curving movement of her lips that held none of the warmth and passion Reid had seen there when he'd held her in his arms. He felt suddenly empty, as if there was nothing left inside of him, no emotion, no life.

"Two out of three hands, Mr. Sinclaire, winner take all.

If I can trust your word of honor," she said, a trace of accusation evident in her tone.

"You can trust my word, Samantha," Reid said, his voice no more than a hoarse whisper as all of the emotions he'd felt so devoid of only a second ago suddenly seemed to clog his throat. He had never wanted so desperately to reach out and drag a woman into his arms, to feel her lips beneath his, the warmth of her body pressed against his own.

She moved to sit at a small table Cord had set up in the center of the saloon's new framing. "Cord?" Samantha said. "You have the cards?"

He nodded and took his own seat.

Samantha looked at her face card, studying it for a long moment before flipping up the corner of the card that lay face down on the table. An ace of hearts up, the nine of diamonds down.

Reid flipped his own face card over, then lifted the corners of both cards. Jack of spades and a three of clubs. He brushed the bottom corners of the cards on the table, and Cord tossed him another card, faceup. Ten of hearts. Twenty three. "Your win," he said, turning the cards over and tossing them to the center of the table.

Cord drew the discarded cards back into his deck and reshuffled several times; then, he dealt them each a new hand.

Samantha showed a deuce of spades up, Reid a king of hearts.

He flipped over his cards before Samantha could request a hit. "My win," he said, showing a black jack.

They were even now.

Samantha fought to maintain her aura of calmness, keeping her gaze cool, her hands steady. But inside she was trembling with every breath she took as her mind screamed at Cord to hurry up and deal again before she completely broke down. She couldn't stand being in Reid's presence much longer. Every ounce of willpower she possessed was fighting to keep her from flinging herself into his arms.

Cord dealt.

Samantha won.

Cord dealt again.

Reid had an ace up to Samantha's four of spades.

She called for a hit, followed by another, then stayed.

Reid, his brows nettled together, stared at his cards, then, with a soft curse, he slid them facedown beneath the deck that Cord had set back upon the table.

He reached into his pocket and pulled out the deed to Riversrun. "I gave my word," he said softly, his gaze catching and holding Samantha's, "and I'll keep it."

She watched him walk away.

Call him back, a voice deep inside of her whispered. *Call him back before it's too late.*

Samantha closed her eyes.

"He let you win, Sam," Cord said softly.

Her eyes shot open and she looked up at her father.

He fanned the deck of cards across the table.

Her gaze went instantly to the two cards that had been on the bottom, the two cards that Reid had slid back under the deck. Fury swept through her, instant and hot. Samantha stood so abruptly her chair toppled. She spun around. "Reid."

He paused and turned around.

Samantha grabbed the deed to Riversrun from the table and stalked after him. She thrust it at his chest. "You cheated."

"Obviously," he drawled, his tone as smooth as smoke, as dark as brandy. "It's what I do best."

He'd had his share of women, had wooed them, bedded them, and enjoyed them. He'd even given his heart to one: Bethany, or so he had thought. Now he knew better. He had cared deeply for Bethany, but he'd never loved her, not the fierce, possessive, all-consuming way he loved Samantha.

She looked up at him, tears brimming in her eyes, shimmering a silver reflection of the afternoon sun.

"You deserve better," he said hoarsely, fighting the urge to drag her into his arms. "You always have."

"You're right," she answered softly. "I do."

She closed the distance between them.

Reid watched her, waiting for her arm to rise, her hand to strike his face.

Instead, she slid her arms over his shoulders and pressed her body to his.

"Samantha," he said, hope knitting its way through his surprise, "I have to explain, you have to know . . ."

"Later," she whispered, standing on tiptoe and brushing her lips across his.

Epilogue

During the next year, Samantha and Reid were married in a quiet ceremony held on the plantation of Mr. and Mrs. Rowland Bigelow.

The Natchez Vigalance Committe put an end to the saloons Under-the-Hill, but not before Samantha split the winning pot between the finalists of the poker game and wished them well, wherever they went.

Blossom had six kittens.

Cord decided to retire; he married Suzette, and the two embarked on a tour of Europe.

Molly and Jake married and headed out west.

Rhonda became engaged to Phillip Letrothe.

Clarissa broke her engagement to Jackson Tate.

And Samantha gave birth to Corianne Sinclaire.

ROMANCE FROM JANELLE TAYLOR

ANYTHING FOR LOVE   (0-8217-4992-7, $5.99)

DESTINY MINE   (0-8217-5185-9, $5.99)

CHASE THE WIND   (0-8217-4740-1, $5.99)

MIDNIGHT SECRETS   (0-8217-5280-4, $5.99)

MOONBEAMS AND MAGIC   (0-8217-0184-4, $5.99)

SWEET SAVAGE HEART   (0-8217-5276-6, $5.99)

ROMANCE FROM FERN MICHAELS

DEAR EMILY   (0-8217-4952-8, $5.99)

WISH LIST   (0-8217-5228-6, $6.99)

AND IN HARDCOVER:

VEGAS RICH   (1-57566-057-1, $25.00)

ROMANCE FROM ROSANNE BITTNER

CARESS   (0-8217-3791-0, $5.99)

FULL CIRCLE   (0-8217-4711-8, $5.99)

SHAMELESS   (0-8217-4056-3, $5.99)

SIOUX SPLENDOR   (0-8217-5157-3, $4.99)

UNFORGETTABLE   (0-8217-4423-2, $5.50)

TEXAS EMBRACE   (0-8217-5625-7, $5.99)

UNTIL TOMORROW   (0-8217-5064-X, $5.99)

Available wherever paperbacks are sold, or order direct from the Publisher. Send cover price plus 50¢ per copy for mailing and handling to Kensington Publishing Corp., Consumer Orders, or call (toll free) 888-345-BOOK, to place your order using Mastercard or Visa. Residents of New York and Tennessee must include sales tax. DO NOT SEND CASH.